W9-BZD-251

FLUFF DRAGON

FLUFF DRAGON

·BOOK TWO OF THE B<u>A</u>D <u>U</u>NICORN TRILOGY·

BY *Platte F. Clark*

ALADDIN
New York   London   Toronto   Sydney   New Delhi

ALADDIN
An imprint of Simon & Schuster Children's Publishing Division
1230 Avenue of the Americas, New York, NY 10020
First Aladdin hardcover edition April 2014
Text copyright © 2014 by Straw Dogs, LLC.
Jacket illustrations copyright © 2014 by John Hendrix
All rights reserved, including the right of reproduction
in whole or in part in any form.
ALADDIN is a trademark of Simon & Schuster, Inc., and related logo is a
registered trademark of Simon & Schuster, Inc.
For information about special discounts for bulk purchases,
please contact Simon & Schuster Special Sales at 1-866-506-1949 or
business@simonandschuster.com.
The Simon & Schuster Speakers Bureau can bring authors to your live
event. For more information or to book an event contact the
Simon & Schuster Speakers Bureau at 1-866-248-3049 or
visit our website at www.simonspeakers.com.
Jacket design by Jessica Handelman
Interior design by Karina Granda
The text of this book was set in Bembo.
Manufactured in the United States of America 0314 FFG
2 4 6 8 10 9 7 5 3 1
Full CIP data is available from the Library of Congress.
ISBN 978-1-4424-5015-8
ISBN 978-1-4424-5017-2 (eBook)

To Mr. Hansen, who planted the first seed
and offered to buy my first book

ACKNOWLEDGMENTS

I'M EXTREMELY GRATEFUL FOR THE MANY TALENTED AND DEDICATED individuals willing to indulge my flights of fancy and find conversations such as "What does a fluffy dragon look like?" to be perfectly reasonable.

At the top of this list is my amazing editor, Fiona Simpson. She is surrounded by a number of wonderful professionals who all had a hand in creating and promoting this book, including Jessica Handelman, Annie Berger, Karina Granda, Sarah Jane Abbott, Paul Crichton, and many others who work in their respective areas of expertise. A special thanks as well to publisher Bethany Buck.

Taking on the task of illustrating a fluff dragon fell to John Hendrix, whose jacket art perfectly captures the spirit of the book. Other amazing individuals include my agent, Deborah Warren, whose thoughtful stewardship and unending enthusiasm keep me heading down the right paths.

To the Story Monkeys writing group (a name that should tell you much regarding their dispositions and love of bananas), comprising E. J. Patten, David Butler, Eric Holmes, and Michael Dalzen, thank you for the thoughtful, challenging, and often hilarious recommendations.

My love and appreciation go out to my children: Kiaya, Platte Christian, Hailey, Kennidy, Hunter, Allie, and Aidan, for putting up with a dad who insists the Three Stooges are a necessary part of one's formal education. And finally, all my love to my wife, Kathy, who tolerates unicorn-based decor in my office while unconditionally encouraging me in everything else that truly matters.

PROLOGUE

LOKI AND MOKI PADDED TOWARD THE TREE OF WOE. LIKE MOST DAYS IN the Turul wastes, it was hot, and that was exactly the way the two fire kittens liked it. Ahead the ancient tree stretched high into the cloudless sky, with sun-bleached bones hanging from its black limbs. When the wind picked up, the various skeletal bits banged into one another like an unholy wind chime. Beneath the clattering bones a skinny human with pale skin and a long white beard tugged at his chains.

"Well, this must be exciting for you," Loki said to Moki as they approached the old man. Loki had swirls of black and white fur and a pink nose, while Moki was black-nosed with a hodgepodge of orange and white fur. Fire kittens were nearly indistinguishable from regular kittens, except for their ability to do things like fling fire-balls from their tails and talk about the weather. "I mean, being fresh out of the academy and all," Loki continued.

"They said there was only one place for a kitten of my talents"—Moki beamed—"and here I am."

Loki knew exactly what *that* meant. Despite what the Quorum of Kitties said publicly, being assigned to the Tree of Woe was the lowest duty handed out to fire kittens—one given to the most challenged academy graduates, or in Loki's case, to those branded as trouble-makers and malcontents. "Just do everything I tell you, exactly as I tell you, and you'll be fine."

"Because you're the boss?" Moki asked. Loki thought that was obvious, but he supposed one could never over-emphasize the basics.

"Yes . . . because I'm the boss." Moki pointed to a small mailbox resting at an angle in the cracked ground. "Now go and retrieve our orders."

Moki nodded and bounded to the box (with a little too much enthusiasm for Loki's liking), returning with a sealed envelope.

"Looks like we have another prisoner from Thannis," Loki said, studying the wax seal before breaking it open.

It took a special kind of wax to withstand the heat in Turul, harvested from the gooey-eared bog mice of Mephis. Loki made a mental note to wash his paws when he returned to camp. "We get a lot of criminals from the capital these days."

"I'm no criminal!" the human protested. Like all the prisoners delivered to the Tree of Woe, the old man was dressed in a simple loincloth. "I'll have you know I'm a druid of the seventh order, and I've had a vision!"

"Uh-huh," Loki replied, unimpressed. He continued to read from the official papers. "According to this, you've been charged with the use of unauthorized magic—"

"Bah! The Tower knows nothing! I've seen *him* through the mists of the umbraverse. And I know what he brings!"

"Yep," Loki continued. "Then you defaced the king's property."

"I merely wrote *his* name on the city wall so all could see. But the guards stopped me. Fools!"

"And finally—and this is where you really crossed the line—it says you double-parked your horse."

"I can't be bothered with *parking*!" the old man yelped. "He's here! And the blood of the World Sunderer flows through his veins!"

Loki handed the writ to Moki. "No more need for this—I think we know what kind of troublemaker we have here." Moki happily took the paper and tucked it away. "As for you, human," Loki continued in his official-sounding voice, "you've been sentenced to three days' punishment on the Tree of Woe. Here you will be licked by specially trained fire kittens—that's us—as you consider your offenses and reflect on just what a terrible person you are."

"Don't you see?" the human said, tugging at his chains. "The Seven Kingdoms are nothing to the might of the *boy who can read the book!*"

"Can we start at the ankles?" Moki asked. "I like starting at the ankles. You start low like that and you get to work your way up. It's like you see that calf just sitting there, begging for it."

The old man blinked a couple of times as he considered the small kitten's enthusiasm for leg licking. Everyone in the Magrus knew that fire kittens had hot tongues. Regular cat licking was repulsive enough, but fire kittens took it to a whole new level.

"Did you hear that, *magician?*" Loki said, emphasizing the insult with just the right amount of contempt—spell casters hated the term. "My friend here wants to start at your ankles. Do you know what it's like to be licked by a fire kitten?"

The old man shivered despite himself. "Those little tongues of yours are just so . . . gross . . . like sandpaper. But then again, I don't suppose anyone's *died* from it, have they?" The question caught Loki off guard. As far as he knew there had been no reported deaths from fire kitten licks. Such a record was obviously not good for their reputation. "Just as I thought," the druid continued, looking rather pleased with himself. "Your tongues might be icky, but they're not going to kill me."

Loki didn't like where this was going. "So you wanna do it the hard way, is that it?" he asked, moving closer and glaring at the prisoner. "Then maybe we skip the ankle and go right to that little spot just behind the knee. Very sensitive, that spot. I've broken more than a few orcs licking that particular spot." Loki grinned as a flame lit on the end of his tail. Suddenly the human didn't look so confident.

"Whatever you do to me doesn't matter. I've been called to deliver a great message. Even the Wizard's Tower is ignorant! Rezormoor Dreadbringer searches in vain, but only *I* know the location of what he seeks!" The human started to laugh in the way only a half-mad druid tied to a tree can.

Loki considered the ramifications of what he'd just heard. Getting in good with the Wizard's Tower was a promising idea on many levels. The Tower had influence across all of the Seven Kingdoms, and for an enterprising fire kitten that could mean real opportunity.

"You say nobody knows but *you?*" Loki asked, waiting for the human to settle down. Moki circled his paw around his head in the this-guy's-crazy sign. The gesture gave Loki a moment of pause. "You're not having any *other* kinds of strange visions, are you? Perhaps with unicorns or dragons?"

"Oh, oh, I had a dream about a unicorn once!" Moki exclaimed, jumping up and down and waiving his paw in the air. "It was running around trying to stick me with its evil horn! But then a squirrel stepped out and—"

"I was talking to the *prisoner!*" Loki yelled, stamping his paw and causing the flame on his tail to burn brighter. Moki seemed unfazed by the rebuke, however, and simply nodded and grinned some more.

"What I saw came from a spirit of the forest," the old

man continued. "This is not some 'strange vision,' as you call it. Nature does not lie." He looked up at the Tree of Woe as the desert wind moved through its branches. The Tree swayed as a result, giving the druid the distinct impression it had just shrugged him off.

"So, this *boy who can read the book*, do you know where he is?" Loki continued.

The druid looked at the two fire kittens and then set his jaw—he wasn't going to tell them anything more. The old spell caster could smell opportunists a mile away. He turned his head to watch a small scorpion scuttle across the dry earth.

"Oh, so suddenly you're not so talkative, huh?" Loki asked. He whipped his flaming tail at the scorpion, turning it into a black smudge. "Three days is a *long* time," Loki said, walking up and rubbing against the human's ankles, his tail curling dangerously close to the druid's leg. "A very, very long time, in fact."

"You're not a very nice kitty," the human noted.

Moki looked back and forth between the human and Loki. This was much more fun than he'd imagined.

Loki circled back around and sat, giving the prisoner a hard look. "This can really be so very simple. Tell me where I can find this boy, and I promise: not a single lick to your very thin skin."

The old druid looked away.

"Of course, my job can extend beyond the letter of the law," Loki added. "There's no reason I can't take some . . . creative license." He motioned to a fire pit.

"What's in there?" the druid said, squinting. "Are those bones?"

"I bet it's a marshmallow pit!" Moki guessed, bouncing up and down. He liked guessing games, especially if marshmallows were involved.

Loki shook his head. "So what's it going to be, human? You can't very well deliver your message if you never leave this place. And let's just say no one ever complains if a prisoner doesn't make it back. Cuts down on paperwork."

The druid mulled the situation over in his mind. His job was to prepare the Magrus—the magical realm—for the coming of the *boy who could read the book*. He couldn't let a couple of fire kittens stop him. "Fine," he sighed after a few moments. "The boy of prophecy is in Thoran, near Shyr'el. And with some orcs, if you really must know."

Loki grinned. Thoran was composed of the nonhuman

nations of dwarfs, unicorns, and elves—a human boy would stand out there. "And nobody knows this but you?"

"Not yet," the old man replied. "But I'll tell all the Magrus as soon as I'm off this wretched tree." More bones clattered above the druid, and this time he was certain the tree had just told him to shove off.

"Yeah, good luck with that," Loki said, turning and beginning to walk away, his tail flame disappearing with a puff of smoke. "But do mind the *crows*. They stay away when we're around, but when we're not . . . well, you know how birds like to peck at things."

Suddenly the druid understood—the fire kittens were going to leave him! "What?" he shouted. "But we had a deal!"

"I said I wouldn't *lick* you, and I won't. But if you want to make a deal with the crows, you'll have to take it up with them directly."

The druid looked up at the black shapes sitting high in the branches. The wind picked up again, knocking the bones together with an eerie *clank*. "You'll pay for this!" the human shouted as the two fire kittens padded away. He looked around for signs of life—druids drew their magic from the living world, and he thought he might be able to whip up a spell. But he was in the middle of a vast and empty nothing, save for the Tree of Woe itself. And he had the distinct impression the tree didn't like him very much.

"So, uh, we're *not* licking him?" Moki asked as he and Loki headed back to their camp.

"No, my young apprentice," Loki replied. "We're going on a trip."

"We are? That's great! I like going places."

Loki nodded in agreement, but his thoughts were elsewhere. It was time to find his fortune, even if it meant walking away from a steady job with reasonable hours. But deep inside, Loki had always known he was meant for something more—something that included fame and riches and power! It would be a long walk across the wastes to Onig, the goblin city and capital of Turul. But there he'd find the Guild of Indiscriminate Teleportation, which was his best shot at getting closer to the so-called *boy who could read the book*. Thoran happened to be about as far away from the Turul Wastes as anywhere in the Magrus, and ship captains didn't care for fire-flinging kittens aboard their wooden ships. But the boy—whomever he was—was too valuable to pass up. It was enough to know that the Tower wanted him—and the Tower had plenty of gold to pay for what it wanted. "Go and pack," he commanded Moki. "We have a date with destiny."

"Oh, good," Moki said. "I hope she's nice."

CHAPTER ONE

OUT OF THE FRYING PAN

IT WAS EVENING, AND THE CITIZENS OF THE MAGRUS SAT AROUND THEIR various tables and ate their various dinners. And if their talk drifted to that of dragons and wizards, none would consider it particularly odd. This was due to the fact that dragons and wizards could be found in great abundance across the whole of the Seven Kingdoms. And if the rumors were to be believed, it was the ancient and powerful Wizard's Tower itself that was behind the revival of the dragon hunts. There was gold to be made for those adventurers who could take down the great beasts and harvest their scales. And whether delivered to the barbarian king of Kuste or sold through the shadowy guilds of the underworld, dragon scale was in high demand.

Not all the cooking fires across the Magrus were

enjoying such talk, however. At one, a certain ogre camp located deep in the Shyr'el woods, there were other concerns. Specifically, about the three humans and lone dwarf who dropped out of the sky. Of course the orc cook had no idea that these travelers had just been flung through time and space after battling robots in a futuristic world. Nor did she know that the chubbiest of them was called Max Spencer, the last living descendent of the greatest arch-sorcerer who had ever lived: Maximilian Sporazo. And because Sporazo's blood flowed through the boy's veins, Max Spencer was the only soul alive who could read from the most powerful spell book in existence: the *Codex of Infinite Knowability*. And it was inconceivable that the orc cook could have even imagined that Max and his friends had been sent back in time at the hands of Obsikar, the legendary dragon king, on a promise to save the dragons and defeat the one behind their demise: Rezormoor Dreadbringer, regent of the Wizard's Tower.

What concerned the orc cook most, in fact, was if this Max Spencer was a tailor (she desperately needed mittens) and if humans were better served with onions or turnips. Either way, she had plans for him and his friends.

"I am most certainly *not* a sheep!" the creature in the orc's tent announced to Max. And in its defense, it did have a longer neck and more angular head than the sheep Max had seen at the petting zoo. Also, it talked better too. Max had bigger problems to solve, however. Problems involving a very large orc and the fact that his friends were hanging upside down like hams in a butcher's shop.

"I used to *eat* sheep," the creature continued. It was collared and chained to the center tent pole, where they both sat. Animal skins littered the floor, and at Max's feet were the *Codex of Infinite Knowability*, a pair of knitting needles, and finally a ball of fluffy-looking yarn. Max looked at the yarn and back to the creature.

"I don't want to talk about it." The sheep-looking thing scowled. Max decided not to press the issue and turned his attention back to the *Codex*. In addition to being the most powerful spell book in the three realms, which only he could read, it had a mind of its own. When Max tried to pick it up, it actually shocked him—him, the last descendant of the arch-sorcerer who had written it! Not that shocking would-be readers was something new to the magical tome; it had systematically zapped every other person who had ever touched it. But now

Max got the same stinging *SNAP!* that he used to find funny when it happened to his best friend, Dirk.

"If you really must know, I'm a dragon," the creature stated, raising its head and striking its best dragon pose. "Entire armies would cower at the sight of me flying overhead."

"Sure," Max replied absentmindedly. He really didn't have time to deal with the delusional animal at the moment. He had to figure out what was wrong with the *Codex*, because he desperately needed a knitting pattern for orc mittens. This might seem an unusual thing for a twelve-year-old boy, but Max needed the mittens to trade for his friends Sarah, Dirk, and Dwight the Dwarf. They had all managed to escape from a horrible future world only to end up in an orc camp. Thanks to years of gaming, Max knew exactly what an orc was. But he wasn't prepared for the smell. His neighbor had a dog that stayed out in the rain and ate spoiled Spam from the garbage, and it smelled considerably better.

The orc turned as if reading Max's thoughts, and eyed him suspiciously through the open tent flap. Max could see that the hot-tub-sized cauldron had started to boil, and that didn't seem like a particularly good sign. The orc gave him a hard scowl and returned to scraping an oversized cleaver against a leather strap. "You *sure* you make mittens?" the orc grunted. She was considerably bigger than Max and had a carved stump instead of a left foot. But even one-footed, the orc was probably faster than he was. And since Max had spent most of his free time reading comics and playing online games, most of his running (and fighting, for that matter) amounted to hitting keys on a keyboard and clicking a mouse. *Actual* running and fighting had turned out to be a lot harder.

"Sure, no problem," Max called out, hoping that it was true. He'd seen the orc burn her hands on the hot, human-sized pot when he first arrived. "I just need to find the, uh . . . instructions." From his earlier readings, Max knew the *Codex* did in fact have a pattern for orc mittens inside. Why such a pattern happened to be in the combination spell book, encyclopedia, and travel guide was a mystery. But the *Codex* had a habit of being either extremely helpful or particularly *un*helpful. And at the moment it was stuck on the latter.

Max tentatively touched the cover of the book again and breathed a sigh of relief when it didn't shock him. He carefully picked it up and turned to a random page.

It opened to an illustration of an orc—just like the one outside—with green leathery skin, sideways-pointed ears, and a broad, curved nose. The caption below read, *Orcs—Good Warriors but Notoriously Bad Tippers*. But instead of the sprawling, handwritten text that Max was used to, the words in the *Codex* were blurred and vibrating as if it were all they could do to hold themselves together. Max flipped the page and read on:

> A special note to travelers in the Magrus. Anything green and smaller than you is probably harmless (except for the Berserking Grasshoppers of Schil). Goblins and gremlins are generally runtish in size, followed by hoblins, hobgoblins, orcs, and ogres. Both orcs and ogres are known to eat unwary bystanders, so avoid them when possible. And never try to make an ogre laugh, as chronicled in the infamous "an ogre, an orc, and a rabbi walk into a bar" joke told by Manu the Horribly Mangled.

Suddenly the words on the page fell apart, sliding down the paper like black drops of wet ink. Then the book shuddered, slipping from Max's hands and landing on the ground with a thud.

"That's a magic book," the self-proclaimed dragon

said. "I know about such things, and you're far too young to have something like that. Where'd you steal it?"

"I didn't steal it!" Max exclaimed, his frustration getting the better of him.

"I suppose that's true. . . . You're too pudgy to be a thief."

Max fumed. "Well, you're too *fluffy* to be a dragon."

"Ha!" the creature said. "Don't you know anything? That's exactly what I am—a fluff dragon."

Max took a second look at the creature and realized it did have a certain dragon quality about it, if you shrank it down, squished it together, and then covered it in fluffy fur instead of scales.

"Obviously you're not from around these parts," the fluff dragon continued, "so let me fill you in. Dragons and unicorns are the most powerful creatures in the Magrus."

"I already know that," Max said, sounding a bit defensive. "But I've never seen a dragon that looked like a giant Q-tip."

The fluff dragon frowned. "It's not like we're born this way. So you know how dragons and unicorns are the only creatures that can go back and forth between human and animal forms?"

"I guess."

"So dragons have scales, and scales are soft on the inside and hard on the outside because that just sort of makes sense when you think about it. Understand so far?"

"It's not that complicated."

"Good," the fluff dragon continued. "So scales are basically armor, except dragons have a special scale right over our hearts called the serpent's escutcheon. *That* scale is impervious to lance and sword and reflects magic. So as a dragon changes from human to dragon form, we're getting back into our armor. Think of it like slipping into a shirt. I mean, it's obviously more complicated than that, but I'm trying to use words you'll understand."

Max was growing impatient. "I'm sorry, but is there a point to all this?"

"A point? Oh yes, there's a point. You ever wake up first thing in the morning, grab a shirt, and accidentally put it on inside out?"

"Of course," Max replied, remembering the unpleasant day at school when he'd worn his shirt *and* pants inside out.

"Well, there you go," the fluff dragon announced.

"Simple mistake, right? Only when a dragon puts his scales on backward, the serpent's escutcheon reflects all the magic back—and since we're magical creatures, this isn't such a good thing. We grow smaller, lose our spells, and our skin becomes hard on the inside and soft on the outside. Soft and fluffy, and we're stuck that way for the rest of our lives."

"So why are you telling me this?" Max asked, wanting to get back to the *Codex*.

"Why . . . ? Why do you think? Just look at me, chained to a tent pole and used by my captors as a pillow—a *pillow*! Do you know how humiliating that is?"

Suddenly Max felt sorry for the fluff dragon. "Look, I'm sorry I didn't believe you at first," he apologized. "Let's start over. I'm Max Spencer, and I really need to figure out a way to save my friends."

"And I'm Puff," the fluff dragon replied.

"Wait, your name is Puff? Puff the *fluff* dragon?"

Puff frowned. "I assure you nobody thought twice about my name when I was swooping down and scorching castles."

"You there!" the orc bellowed from outside. "You talking to pillow or making mittens?"

"Just getting the, uh, right pattern," Max called back, retrieving the *Codex* and doing his best to look like he wasn't panicking. Thankfully the book didn't shock him again, so he began flipping through its pages.

The last time he'd seen the strange pattern was some time ago, which happened to be in the future when he was preparing to fight a robot army. Now, however, the *Codex* wasn't cooperating. All the pages were filled with strange symbols and shapes, none of which Max could read. He shut the book, his mind scrambling to come up with a solution. Clutching the *Codex* in both hands he concentrated on the ancient tome, commanding it to obey him. He'd had some success connecting with the book before, but this time it didn't feel like anything was even out there.

"Are you really sure you want mittens? Maybe there's something else we could trade?" Max called out.

The orc spat in response. "Need orc husband—but they no want wife that can't cook. Need mittens to cook good. So make now or friends go in stew."

"Okay, okay," Max pleaded. "Just don't cook anybody."

The orc harrumphed in response. "Better hope ogres

hunt good," she added, hopping around on her peg leg and grabbing a rotten head of cabbage from a sack. "If not, you go in pot for sure."

"Hey, Max, listen," Puff said after the orc had turned her back. "Get me out of these chains and we can make a run for it. Come on, just you and me."

"I can't," Max replied, opening the *Codex* again. "I'm not leaving without my friends." Puff's expression fell as Max worked on finding a way out. What he needed was a spell—he'd gotten pretty good with some of the lower-level spells, fireballs mostly. He ran his finger down the side of the ancient page and watched as the symbols suddenly shifted and became legible again: *Attack squirrels favor more traditional military formations, such as the classic L-shaped ambush, rather than a mad scampering toward the enemy . . .* But then the text shimmered and turned back into the pulsating mishmash of unreadable characters. Max slammed the book shut.

"When the ogres come back—and believe me, they will—it doesn't matter if you make mittens or not," Puff said. "They're going to eat all of you."

Max put the *Codex* down and reached for his backpack. Inside he could see Glenn, his magical dagger. The fact that the orc hadn't bothered to take it said a lot about how much of a threat she thought he was. And that was without knowing that Glenn was probably the most useless magical dagger ever created. Max set the pack between his legs and tried to think. Time was running out, and he didn't have a clue what to do to save his friends.

CHAPTER TWO

A HAIRY SITUATION

IT WASN'T REZORMOOR DREADBRINGER'S HABIT TO BE *SUMMONED*. If somebody wanted to talk to the regent of the Wizard's Tower, they came and added their name to a very long list. And if that name was deemed important, it might, at some point, warrant a screening by some low-level wizard who would then determine future appointment worthiness. But to be summoned by a guild? Unheard-of. Not the Assassins', Thieves', or Mercenaries' guilds would dare risk the sorcerer's wrath by commanding his presence. Not any guild, that is, save for one—the guild whose very name was whispered by the most powerful throughout the Seven Kingdoms: the Guild of Toupee Makers.

Most citizens of the Magrus understood that to rise

in power requires time—time to strategize, to influence, to strengthen, to overthrow. Rulers, usurpers, despots, high wizards—such have all paid their dues to become who they are. And the unfortunate consequence of a lifetime cultivating and building such power? Male-pattern baldness. And so it was that the Guild of Toupee Makers served a very particular clientele. A clientele, in fact, who did not become figures of menace and fear just to be called "chrome dome" or "baldy."

It was with such thoughts that Rezormoor Dreadbringer rode in the back of his black coach as it traveled along Aardyre's Guild Row. The zombie duck was harnessed in front as usual, and did the work of an entire team of horses. No citizen with even a modicum of self-preservation would hang around when the flapping sound of webbed feet echoed across the cobblestones. Zombie ducks were notoriously evil.

When the carriage stopped, Rezormoor stepped down to the empty street. It had long passed midnight, and he walked to a nondescript gray building and read the sign above the doorway: THE FRATERNAL BROTHERHOOD OF MIMES. Rezormoor, like most intelligent beings, couldn't understand why someone would want to be a mime. But he'd been told to come here, so here he was.

The sorcerer knocked three times, and in response a narrow slat slid open and a pair of eyes regarded him.

"Why did the miner have a bad temper?" the voice asked through the door.

"Because he had a short fuse," the wizard answered, delivering the code words—painful as they were—exactly as he'd been told. The slat closed, followed by the sounds of several bolts opening and locks unlatching. Finally the door swung inward.

A nonmime human of the old and mostly toothless variety poked his head out from behind the door. "Follow me," he said. He led Rezormoor through various rooms and twisting hallways before opening a door to a utility closet. He motioned for Rezormoor to enter.

"You want me to go in *there*?" the sorcerer asked.

"It's perfectly safe."

Rezormoor grunted and stepped in, doing his best to keep his black robes from touching the dirty mops hanging nearby. As the door shut, the far wall slid away, revealing a long set of stone steps. Rezormoor pushed his long black hair—hair that was straight and shiny and according to the Tower's staff, made him look ten years younger—over his shoulders. It was proper wizard's hair, provided by the master artisans from the very guild he was now visiting. He descended the steps, muttering a spell and lighting the passageway. At the bottom he found another door, which he pushed open and walked past.

The room beyond was oval shaped, somewhat like the top of a human head. Seated on a raised dais in high-backed chairs were seven figures looking down at him. Hooded robes shadowed their faces.

"Come before us in our secret chamber," the one in the center commanded. His voice was old and raspy, and as Rezormoor walked to the center of the room, it reminded him of when, as a student, he was taken before his instructors to pass various magical exams. "You know of the *list*," the man said, and the others echoed the last word:

"The list, the list, the list . . ."

"And *your* name is written upon it," the man said.

The list—the *client* list. All the names of the most powerful members of the Seven Kingdoms who hid their baldness from the world were on that list.

"I am aware," Rezormoor answered. He had to fight the urge to flick his hair back.

"So tell us, sorcerer, how do you like your hairpiece? Does it fit? Is it itch free? Can you take it swimming? Does it not *grow*?"

"Yes," Rezormoor replied. "It is all that was promised and more."

The hooded figures nodded, apparently happy with the answer. They did, after all, have a certain pride of craftsmanship.

"Then you must understand our concern," the center figure continued. "The dragons . . ."

Yes, the dragons, Rezormoor thought. He'd been hunting them, but not officially. The king had begun his own eradication campaign, but word moved through the black markets of the various cities around the Seven Kingdoms that the Tower was paying gold for dragon scale, and in particular, that most singular of scales called the serpent's escutcheon.

"I don't see how that should concern the guild."

"Tell us, sorcerer, do you hunt *all* dragons? What of those that have . . . transformed?"

"Into their human form?" Rezormoor offered. "They always turn eventually. It's the scales, you see. I need them for my research."

"What of *fluff* dragons?"

Suddenly Rezormoor understood. The construction of the guild's hairpieces was a closely held secret. Most assumed it involved some complex combination of magic and rare materials, but now he realized it was something simpler—something more natural.

"The toupees," Rezormoor said, looking up at them. "You fashion them from the fluff of fluff dragons, don't you?"

"Yes!" came the thundering admission, and the word echoed around the small chamber. "Now you understand. If all the dragons are destroyed, the fluff dragons will follow, for the one springs from the other. And without fluff, there can be no more hair!"

It was a stunning admission. Without toupees, the powerful were at risk of being scoffed at. And it took only a little scoffing before *other* ideas began to form in people's heads, and then you had uprisings and rebellions to deal with.

"What do you propose?" Rezormoor asked. "What has been set in motion cannot be undone."

"If only King Kronac were a client, this could be dealt with easily, but those northern barbarians have great heads of hair! So instead we demand that the fluff dragons be rounded up and taken to a place where they'll be protected."

"And sheared."

"Well, of course. But fluff dragons can't be bred, and with the dragons gone, they'll eventually die off. But their fluff, in theory, could be *duplicated*."

It is possible, Rezormoor thought. But harnessing the kind of magic to duplicate something organic wasn't like lighting a candle. He would need the only spell book capable of such a thing: the *Codex of Infinite Knowability*. Fortunately the search for the book was already under way. More importantly, such an arrangement could solve another problem he'd been trying to work out—one that dealt with acquiring a vast amount of gold.

"What you ask is not easy," Rezormoor admitted. "Not easy at all."

"But not impossible?"

"No. Not impossible."

"Good. Then it shall be done."

"Of course," Rezormoor replied, bowing slightly. When he rose, however, his countenance was as hard as steel. "But there are . . . terms."

"Terms?" came the shocked reply. "Did we not already impress upon you the fact that your name is written upon the list? Do you know what would happen to your reputation if your baldness was exposed to the world?"

"Oh yes," the sorcerer answered. He remembered the peasant children painting his face on smooth chicken eggs. They were painful memories. "But at the risk of our mutual demise, I must insist on compensation."

"Compensation? All of this is because *you* had to go off and hunt dragons in the first place!"

"Be that as it may, we must come to terms. If not, I shall endure being disgraced and you will endure the demise of your guild."

"You seem to leave us with little choice," the voice hissed at him. Rezormoor smiled—who'd have thought he'd have the powerful Guild of Toupee Makers under his thumb?

"Then this is what I require," Rezormoor continued. And when he was done, he had forged a deal that would make him rich enough to fuel his ultimate desire.

Rezormoor returned to the Wizard's Tower. He exited the carriage but did not go inside. Instead, he dismissed the zombie duck and walked across the moonlit grounds to the place where he knew the thing was waiting for him. The creature had carved a path of destruction through the very heart of the city until it found itself at the Tower's gate, drawn to it like a moth to a flame. It was, in truth, like nothing the sorcerer had encountered before. It wasn't a demon, or anything born of the Shadrus. And while it did have a certain taint about it, its origins remained a mystery.

The old well had gone dry decades ago, but it made a convenient hiding place for a creature over seven feet tall. Rezormoor found the well and squatted next to the opening.

"Do you know how long I've been stuck down here?" the creature asked. It sounded much more boyish than Rezormoor had first expected.

"It's called *hiding*," Rezormoor replied. "And considering the mess you made, this is the safest place you can be."

"Well, it totally bites." It had a strange vocabulary as well.

"Can you hunt something?" Rezormoor called down.

"I can do anything I want."

"I see. Well, I'd like you to hunt something for me. And if you serve me well, I will find you better accommodations."

"What do you want me to kill?"

Rezormoor smiled; the creature seemed to have the right attitude, at least. "They're called fluff dragons. But I don't want them dead. Not just yet."

"Fluff dragons? That's, like, the stupidest name ever."

"Yes, well, it does describe them," Rezormoor replied.

"Sounds like a hassle."

"You could always refuse and just sit there in the dark."

"Fine," the voice called back. "You don't have to be a dweeb about it."

"Fair enough," Rezormoor sighed. He was growing tired of talking to the thing, but it was an important errand he required it to accomplish. "By the way, what should I call you?"

"You can call me the Kraken, because I like crackin' the bones of my enemies."

"Then seek out the barbarian camps to the north, Kraken," Rezormoor said as he stood. "I believe you'll have luck there." He walked back to the Tower, taking note of something strange in the air, like the whole of the Magrus had been turned on its axis. Rezormoor would have to ponder that—he didn't like questions for which he didn't have the answers.

CHAPTER THREE

LEARNING TO FLY

THE SEEMINGLY ENDLESS PINK SANDS OF THE TURUL WASTES GENERALLY didn't thump. But that's exactly what they were doing, reverberating in a rhythmic subsonic pattern that sent grains of sand vibrating around Loki's and Moki's paws.

"Neat!" Moki exclaimed when it happened again.

Loki didn't share his associate's enthusiasm. In fact, Loki couldn't remember a time when large thumping sounds ever meant something *good* was about to happen. Usually it meant quite the opposite.

They had spent the night in the desert, and now they could see the mountains that rose in the east—mountains that housed Onig, the goblin city. There they could rest and buy passage from the Guild of Indiscriminate Teleportation, making a quick jump somewhere (hopefully) closer to the boy who could read the book. What kind of book it was and why nobody else could read it, Loki didn't know. But he'd figure it all out eventually, and if all went according to plan, he'd be handsomely rewarded for doing so. His thoughts were interrupted, however, as Moki suddenly jumped up and pointed at the horizon.

"Can you see it?" he exclaimed.

Loki turned to see a rainbow on the horizon.

"It's so beautiful!" Moki continued.

And it was, he supposed, if you were into that sort of thing. It was just that you didn't see rainbows in the desert like that. Not ever. There was something else odd about it too. Something that Loki just couldn't put his paws on.

"Does it seem like a *normal* rainbow to you?" Loki asked, squinting and trying to get a better look at it.

"There's no such thing as a *normal* rainbow, silly," Moki announced. "Each one is special."

Loki sighed—it was going to be a long trip.

"Hey, I think it's getting bigger!" Moki exclaimed after a time. Loki realized something else was going on. The rainbow wasn't just growing bigger; it was actually moving.

And not just moving, Loki decided, it was *walking.* In fact, the rainbow was close enough now that they could see each ribbonlike leg lift itself and take a giant step forward, crashing back to the ground in an explosion of sand.

"I didn't know they could do *that*," Moki said, his voice suggesting the world was full of lots of things that surprised the fire kitten. But on this particular point, Loki would have to agree.

"What should we do?" Moki asked.

"The only thing we can do—wait and see what happens."

"Oh, good," Moki said with a grin. "I like waiting."

The rainbow reared to a stop just ahead of the two fire kittens. Reared because now that it was hovering above them Loki could see a unicorn and a guy in a bathrobe standing on top of it. He watched as the unicorn suddenly changed from a white-and-pink horse-looking creature into a blond-haired teenage girl. She shouted something and the rainbow leaned down and gently deposited them on the ground.

They walked toward the pair of fire kittens as if nothing extraordinary were going on. The rainbow righted itself and stood perfectly still, as rainbows were supposed to.

"Hi!" Moki shouted as they approached. Loki grimaced—
he had wanted to speak first.

"Greetings," the human male responded. He was
close enough now that they could see he wasn't wearing a
bathrobe but the moon-and-star robes of a Tower-trained
wizard. Loki would have preferred it if the human *had*
been wearing a bathrobe, because wizards only made
things complicated.

The fire kitten opened his mouth to speak when
Moki exclaimed, "That's an awesome rainbow!"

There was a rumbling sound around them.

"What do you think you're doing?!" the girl scolded.
"*Never* call it a rainbow. I suggest you apologize before it
decides to squash you."

"Oh, I'm sorry," the mostly orange-and-white fire
kitten called out. "You just look so very much like a—"

Loki slapped his paw in front of his associate's face.
No more using the *r* word if whatever it was happened to
be a kitten smasher.

"That's a rain*bro*," the girl said.

The rainbro bent down and regarded the two fire kittens. And now that it was close, Loki could make out the

faint lines that made up the creature's eyes and mouth. The rainbro glared for a moment before it straightened itself.

"Well, now," the girl continued, "I suggest you don't make that mistake again."

"Yeah, no kidding," Loki offered. "I'm Loki, by the way, and this is my assistant, Moki."

"I'm Princess," the girl replied. "And this is my wizard, Magar, but I can't imagine you'll have any need to talk to him."

"It's my pleasure to simply exist," Magar said.

"Just ignore him," Princess said.

"Fellow travelers, then?" Loki offered. "It's uncommon to find someone traveling across the wastes—especially coming from the north. I might guess that you've been walking the long path from the Mesoshire." The Mesoshire was the city between the realms, created when Maximilian Sporazo had attempted to tear magic from the world. It sat between the Magrus and the Techrus, and was theoretically possible to get to. But the journey wasn't easy and required guidance from the monks of the Tree of Attenuation. In all his years spent in the Turul wastes, Loki had only met one other traveler trying to get to the Mesoshire. He'd never met anyone coming *back*.

The wizard and Princess shared a look, and Loki worried that he was pressing for too much information. The last thing he needed was a unicorn and a wizard mad at him. The fire kitten suddenly had a very bad feeling about the two travelers.

"Not that it matters," Loki hurried to add. "As for us, we're on our way to Onig."

"A detestable place," Princess said.

"Yep. We're visiting the top ten detestable places in the Magrus. So I guess we'll just be off, then," Loki said. He looked at Moki, who stared back at him. Loki cleared his throat. "*Off*, as in leaving." But Moki just stood there, nodding and looking perfectly content. Loki sighed then gave his companion a push to get him moving. "That means grab our things so we can *leave*."

"Oh, right!" Moki replied, scurrying around their small camp and stuffing various camping implements into an oversized pack.

"You know, it wouldn't be right of me not to leave you with a passing gift," Princess said, tapping her unicorn wand on her head. "It's tradition."

"Oh no, don't worry about that," Loki replied, help-ing Moki tie the pack down and then strap it on his shoul-ders. "No room in the pack anyway, see? All set."

"Of course," Princess said coolly. "Funny thing is, if I weren't allergic to cat I'd just roast you both over the fire. Unless fire kittens come preheated? I guess I hadn't thought about that."

"Ha, that's a good one," Loki said, forcing a laugh. He gave Moki a shove to get him moving. "Well, good luck and safe travels and all that." He turned and began scam-pering away at a pace that suggested hurried excitement instead of panicked fleeing.

Suddenly the wind began to pick up around them. Loki chanced a look over his shoulder and saw Princess waving her wand in the air. He decided the time for decorum was over and started running as fast as he could.

"Is this a race?" Moki shouted after him, running as best he could with the pack on his back. "I like races! Where we racing to?" Loki could hear Princess laughing as the wind began to build and roar around him.

"Now, just a little push to help you along!" Princess shouted. The two fire kittens suddenly found themselves in the middle of a sandstorm. Loki had been through a number of them before, but this was something else. The world closed in around them in only a matter of seconds, and they instinctively shut their eyes and flattened their ears. Then the wind increased, actually lifting them off their paws. The two fire kittens scrambled to find the ground, their legs frantically pedaling in the air, but the blast sent them soaring upward. All around them the harsh sand whipped about, stinging with every grain, and sending them tumbling head over tail. Then, with a feeling not dissimilar to being kicked in the backside, the two fire kittens went flying forward.

The goblin tax collector noticed them first: two screeching dots that seemed to be falling out of the blue sky. But the wastes were home to all sorts of strange creatures, so he didn't pay them much mind. The king required his taxes, and what the king liked best was to be paid in coin, but some could only offer a share of their crops. This was the case with the farmer, so he stood by and watched as the farmer's two sons loaded turnips into the back of the tax collector's carriage.

"You know the king's taxing us to death," the goblin farmer complained.

"Don't you be worrying about that," the tax collector grunted. "Pay your dues and you'll be protected by the crown."

"Protected? Protected from what? Bands of roaming *turnip* thieves? Not likely we'll be seeing any of those."

The tax collector shrugged; it wasn't his problem.

"If I were part of a marauding band, I don't think I'd be going after turnips," the farmer persisted. "Probably storm a castle or something."

The tax collector scowled. "You get what you deserve, peasant. No use complaining about it." And that's when the two fire kittens, each mewing in a high-pitched wail, fell from the sky and into the nearby water trough. The resulting splash—which would be described in great detail for years to come by the turnip farmer and his two sons—rose in a single wave and crashed down on the tax collector's head.

Loki and Moki scrambled out of the water and began shaking themselves vigorously, sending even more drops the tax collector's way.

"STOP!" the goblin screamed.

Both Loki and Moki stopped midshake.

"How dare you! You're both under arrest!"

Two armored goblins stepped from behind the tax collector's carriage, lowering their swords and eyeing the wet kittens.

"Of course we are." Loki sighed, putting his paws in the air.

ON THE ART OF BERSERKING

⚜

SOONER OR LATER A GROUP OF SOL-diers within any given army will decide that marching around in neat and ordered rows is way less fun than it first appeared. And slowly marching toward an enemy is definitely a downer. To this end, a new tactic called "berserking" arose that included more running around and yelling and considerably less marching.

Berserking was first utilized by the orc raider Vograk Gru, who within the space of twenty minutes broke his favorite dagger, lost his wallet during a skirmish, and received notice his taxes were being audited.

Filled with an unstoppable rage, Vograk broke

ranks with his fellow orcs, screamed at the top of his lungs, and ran headlong into the enemy. Although the attack was considered highly successful, a resulting arrowhead lodged in Vograk's shoulder was considered a "gift" and was duly taxed at his audit.

‡

CHAPTER FOUR

DINNER WITH OGRES

IT WAS DUSK AT THE ORC CAMP AND THE SMELL OF BOILING ONIONS AND turnips filled the cool evening air. Max waited until the orc had turned her back to snatch Glenn, his magical dagger, from his backpack.

"Good thinking," the fluff dragon said quietly. "You can use that to pry my chains off."

The dagger's handle was made of ivory and fashioned into the head and torso of a man with his arms folded. Upon hearing Puff, the small head turned in the fluff dragon's direction and spoke: "Hello there! I'm Glenn, the Legendary Dagger of Motivation."

Puff blinked. "You have a talking dagger?"

"I was forged in the everlasting flame by the great Dagda," Glenn continued. "I've pierced through the toughest armor, slipped past the mightiest shields, deflected the most powerful strikes . . . and the last time I was used was to butter toast."

Max grunted. "I told you that if I *had* a butter knife I would have used it."

"Even so, it was a fine buttering," Glenn added. "You should feel good about it."

"I don't have time for this." Max sighed. "I need to plan a rescue, but I can't read the *Codex*."

"Outside of the Elephant Pigs of Zerhem, reading is my favorite thing to do," Glenn said. "But *inside* it's way too dark to see anything."

"Maybe you should put the dagger back," Puff suggested.

Max slipped Glenn into his belt. Through the tent flap he could see the glow of the cooking coals burning against the rapidly darkening sky. Suddenly there was a crash.

"Well, it's been nice knowing you," Puff said, "but now the ogres have come back." Max heard something heavy moving through the woods, pushing through the trees, and entering the camp. He swallowed—whatever it was, it sounded *big*.

"Don't worry, Max," Glenn chimed. "At times like this it's best to keep your chin up. Unless something's trying to hit you."

"So you're going to get cooked and I'm going to be stuck listening to *that*," Puff said unhappily.

When Max saw the ogres, his heart sank. They were huge—three heads or so taller than the orc cook. And they were big. The ogres had folds of thick green skin that covered their massive necks, hulking arms, and huge bellies. Their heads looked small by comparison, and they had the same pointed ears as the orc cook. But unlike the cook, the ogres had two large teeth that erupted from the bottom of their scowling, oversized mouths.

"We're doomed," Max said.

"Yeah, welcome to my world," Puff replied. "But at least you'll get a quick and relatively painless death. Try being drooled on night after night—then you'd just *wish* you were dead."

"Me hungry!" bellowed one of the ogres as it moved to where Sarah, Dirk, and Dwight were hanging. Sarah screamed, and the terror in her voice was maybe the single worst sound Max had ever heard. His friends were awake, but he couldn't decide if that was a good thing or not.

The ogre turned from Sarah to Dirk, giving him a nudge so that he swung back and forth. Dirk had been Max's best friend since grade school, and seeing him hanging upside down like that made Max start to feel something other than fear. It made him *angry*.

"This one stringy," the ogre announced, looking Dirk up and down.

"Cool," Dirk said, squinting up at the giant looming over him. "You're totally an ogre, aren't you? What's your intelligence, like six or something? Man, that's pretty low. Like, insect low." Dirk also happened to see the world as one giant role-playing game, put together for his personal amusement.

"Shut up, Dirk," Dwight yelled, struggling with his ropes. "We're nothing to them but dinner." Dwight was older than Max and his friends, and was the proprietor of the Dragon's Den, the coolest (and only) game shop in his hometown of Madison. Max had always just thought of Dwight as a little person. It wasn't until they got mixed up in this adventure that he'd learned he was a real dwarf, like in the movies. Maybe if he'd had a longer beard it would have been more obvious.

"That's messed up," Dirk said. "The rule is you never

eat anything that can talk or catch a Frisbee. Everyone knows that."

"Bah!" the ogre answered, spittle flying from his mouth.

"I hope I give you gas," Dwight spat, eyeing the ogre. The beast smiled in response, an act that accentuated his vicious-looking lower teeth.

"Maybe dwarf need to be tenderized," the ogre growled, stepping over to Dwight and raising a huge fist.

"Stop playing with food," the orc yelled as she threw a handful of herbs into the bubbling pot. "Or you can cook!"

The ogre dropped his fist, looking unhappy.

"Ha-ha!" the second ogre shouted, pointing at the first. "You got yelled at!"

"At least I'm not as ugly as you," the second ogre responded.

"Ha! Yes, you are—we're twins!"

As the two ogres continued their bickering, Max reached out to the *Codex* one last time. It had worked before, when a world of machines had thrown him and his friends into an epic battle for survival. And the power he unleashed was almost too overwhelming to comprehend.

He needed that power now more than ever. Max took a deep breath and cleared his mind, willing himself to find the book like he'd done before. But again there was only silence. Exasperated, he kicked at the tent floor. "That's it, the *Codex* isn't going to work!"

"Did you read the instructions?" Puff asked as he picked at his lock with a long nail. "That's the thing I've noticed about humans: You never bother to read the instructions. I remember once when Sir Gallisten the Impatient purchased a siege engine kit, but instead of taking just five minutes to read the instructions—"

Max cut the story short with an audible sigh. "Look, there're no instructions, okay? And even if there were, I couldn't read them—not now, anyway."

"Well, whatever you're going to do, you'd better do it now," Puff announced, motioning outside. Max turned to see the second ogre draw a large knife from his belt and hand it to the cook. The orc tested the edge with her thumb and nodded, pointing at Sarah. "Her first," she grunted. It was obvious there wasn't going to be any trading for orc mittens.

"Max?" Sarah called out. She was looking around for him, her auburn hair brushing against the ground as she swung back and forth. Max hadn't really known Sarah. He knew she was smart and played in the middle school band, but when a misunderstanding led them all to detention they formed a kind of bond. She tagged along when Max and Dirk made for the Dragon's Den after school. But then Max had accidentally cast a spell from the *Codex*, and the four of them went tumbling into a strange and horrible future.

Max was out of time, and he'd run out of options. "If I do something crazy like throw you, can you help?" he asked Glenn.

"Of course!" the dagger exclaimed.

Max straightened. "Then we're going to attack. I'm going to throw you at the biggest one."

"And what good is that going to do?" Puff asked. "That's only one, and you'll probably just make him mad."

"Maybe they won't know where it came from," Max said, trying to convince himself. "It might scare them off."

"Ogres don't scare."

"I could get them to chase me into the woods," Max said.

"Maybe," Puff replied.

"Then maybe I could double back to camp."

"Maybe . . ."

"And free the others and escape," Max said. "Maybe ... *if* I'm lucky."

"There are an awful lot of maybes in that plan of yours," Puff announced.

"Yeah, but that's all I got." He stood and drew Glenn behind his ear just like he'd seen the knife thrower at the circus do. He knew it wasn't the best of plans—it might even be the worst rescue plan in the history of rescue plans. At least he'd go out fighting. Or maybe whimpering. But at least it would be on his terms.

"Last chance," Puff said, watching Max intently. "We can still save ourselves."

Max shook his head. He let out a deep breath and threw the magical dagger for all it was worth.

The blade tumbled end over end and smacked into a large tree some ten feet from where the creatures were standing. It wasn't even close, and Max's heart fell.

Glenn bounced against the tree with a pronounced *twang* and tumbled wildly in the air. But the magical dagger managed to swing back toward the ogres and the orc.

Despite his own overwhelming sense of optimism, Glenn was actually surprised when he found a target. Not as surprised as the orc, however, who grunted loudly when the dagger struck her squarely in the backside.

The orc cook screamed and struck out with her fist as a matter of reflex, smashing it into the face of the ogre standing next to her. The ogre's eyes rolled back as it crumpled to the ground like a sack of potatoes.

The second ogre gave a surprised grunt and made for a knife, all while the orc began hopping in circles, reaching for Glenn. But she lost her balance and crashed into the ogre, who had more important things on his mind than a spinning orc with a dagger stuck in her backside. The collision sent the ogre flailing backward into the large boiling cauldron.

But not exactly *in*.

His ponderous bulk fit snugly around the iron pot's rim. It took only a moment for the beast to realize he was stuck in a boiling pot! The ogre leapt forward, moving faster than Max would have thought possible, and bellowed at the top of his lungs. He completely bowled over the still spinning orc cook with a bone-crunching crash before careening headlong into a nearby tree. The ogre stood there for a moment, the boiling cauldron still attached, then slumped to the ground next to his unconscious twin.

Max stood there hardly believing his eyes—his single throw had incapacitated all three of them!

"Holy cow!" Dirk shouted. "That was awesome!"

Max moved into action at once. He and his friends weren't out of danger; if anything, he'd only managed to buy them some time. He sprang from the tent and hurried to the makeshift kitchen.

The small fluff dragon moved as far as his chains would allow him, peering through the tent flap as Max ran. "I may have underestimated that one," he said to himself. "Or he's the luckiest being who ever lived."

CHAPTER FIVE

LITTLE GIANTS

LOKI WAS NOT HAPPY. SOMEWHERE THERE WAS A BLACKSMITH WHO specialized in forging tiny kitten shackles, and one day that blacksmith was going to watch as his workshop burned to the ground. It was the only bright thought Loki could summon as he hung on the wall in the custom-built kitten cuffs. Behind him his tail had been secured through a hole in the wall and dunked in water. Apparently the dungeons of Onig were prepared for any type of prisoner, including fire kittens. Even more upsetting was the fact nobody had bothered to ask them to explain themselves: no judge inquired as to their guilt, no constable took down written statements, no lawyer asked them to enter a plea. They'd simply been escorted through the streets of Onig and led to the large square building that served as the city's prison.

"I've never been in a jail before," Moki said, looking around. "People talk about them, but you don't really get the *experience* until you've been chained inside."

"I'm glad you're having such a good time." Loki sighed. Suddenly the largest human Loki had ever seen sat up. He blinked his eyes, rubbing at them with fists the size of hams, and let out a long yawn.

"Maybe we're going to meet a new friend!" Moki exclaimed.

"Yes, I'm sure the prisons of Onig are filled with all kinds of nice people," Loki replied. Then the fire kitten turned to the large man. "You there. We don't want any trouble. You stay on your side of the cell, and we'll stay on ours. Deal?"

"Ha! That's a good one!" Moki exclaimed as he started to chuckle. "Stay on *our* side . . . we're chained to the wall!"

Loki didn't think being chained next to a potentially dangerous prisoner was anything to be laughing about. He knew prisons were full of dangerous people, and you needed to sound tough in order to send the right kind of message. Having a giggling kitten next to him was definitely ruining things.

The great beast of a man blinked several times, and his eyes brightened at the sight of Moki. He shifted in his chains, sending huge muscles rippling across his arms and chest.

"That's a funny kitty," the prisoner said in a deep voice.

Loki was about to reply when he realized the man was talking to him in *fire kitten*. Which was impossible, since only fire kittens could speak it. Well, them and—

"Giants . . . ," Loki said aloud.

Moki stopped giggling at once. "Did you say 'giant'?" The fire kitten looked more closely at the other figure. The great mound of muscles *was* a giant, although the *smallest* giant he'd ever seen. Even so, he was much bigger than the average human.

"The goblins call me Tiny. I like that name because it's funny."

"Because you're not tiny at all." Moki giggled. "I get it."

"Greetings," Loki said, trying to tune out the giggling kitten. "I'm Loki, and this is my companion, Moki."

"I can't believe I've seen a unicorn, a wizard, a rain-bro, *and* a giant today!" Moki exclaimed.

"And now you're chained to a wall, like me," Tiny observed.

"A minor setback," Loki insisted. "A misunderstanding with a certain tax collector. I'm sure he'll be coming for us once he cools down."

"Never come between a king and his taxes," Tiny observed. He motioned toward a skeleton chained to a nearby wall. "Just ask George there. He made the tax collector mad too."

Loki swallowed. "I see." Things weren't looking good. And he was technically a deserter, so there'd be no help from the Quorum of Kitties. He looked at the skeleton against the far wall and was struck with a thought. "Uh, Tiny, just how long have you been here?"

The giant shrugged. "Well, I met George before my nap. And now look at him."

They turned in time to see a spider crawl from out of George's bleached skull.

"That's quite a nap," Moki said.

"Giants take long naps," Tiny said, licking his lips. "I always wake up thirsty, though."

"What landed you in here?" Loki said. "If you don't mind me asking?"

"I'd grown tired of the mountains and come to see the city. But I found myself without silver, so the choice was to steal or to starve. Apparently I'm not a very good thief. What about you?"

"Oh, we're on a grand adventure!" Moki said.

"Yes, uh . . . a vacation of sorts," Loki said. "Traveling south to see the sights and all that."

"We're headed to Shyr'el," Moki added.

Loki glared at his companion—the last thing he wanted was a stranger knowing their destination. *The boy who could read the book* was their little secret.

"Shyr'el is many horizons from here," Tiny said. "I have always wanted to travel to the Thoran kingdom and see the five nations."

"Me too!" Moki exclaimed. "The dwarfs, ashen elves, wood elves, faerie, and unicorn."

"But there's nothing we can do imprisoned as we are," Loki said. "I should have known better—fate has never been kind to me."

"How do you plan on traveling to Thoran?" Tiny asked. "It's a very long walk, and fire kittens aren't allowed on wooden ships."

"It was our intention to book a flight at the Guild of Indiscriminate Teleportation," Loki answered. "The Onig terminal is quite famous."

"Of course! Why didn't I think of that?" Tiny exclaimed, his voice ringing throughout the small cell. There came a hard knock at the iron door in response.

"Keep it down!" a guard yelled at them.

They sat in silence for several minutes before Tiny thought it safe enough to whisper. "If I can get us free, will you take me with you to Thoran?"

Could the giant actually bust them out of their cell? Loki considered his options: wait for who knows how long to get before a magistrate (which might be a very long time if skeleton George was any indication), or try to take matters into their own paws. In the end it was an easy choice. "Okay, Tiny, you have a deal. Get us out of here and we'll take you with us."

"This is going to be fun!" Moki exclaimed before casting a nervous glance at the door. He continued in a low voice: "I've never traveled with a giant. Or a small giant for that matter."

"Giants are renowned for their strength. Can you bust these chains?" Loki asked. Tiny shook his head.

"Yours I could, if I could reach them, but mine are too thick."

"Then how are we supposed to escape?" Loki asked.

Tiny smiled. "Don't worry." And then he began to squeak. Loki was convinced that the giant had lost his mind. But then there was more squeaking, this time coming from a rather plump rat that had appeared near the corner of the room.

"May I present to you Oacher the rat, Duke of the Third Sewer. And he says he does not like kittens very much," Tiny reported. "I think he's waiting for an apology."

"An apology? For what?" Loki smirked. Apologizing to a rodent didn't seem like a very good precedent to be setting.

"For feline crimes in general," Tiny said. "Like last year a cat ate his third cousin."

"Fine." Loki sighed. "I apologize for all cats everywhere and especially for their eating your cousin."

Tiny and the rat continued their discussion.

"Oacher says he's not sure you really had your heart in it," Tiny announced after a bit. "But he says it's okay if you'll promise you'll never harm a rat again."

"Seriously?" Loki asked. "Okay, fine, I promise never to harm another rat so long as I live. May a dog use me as a chew toy if I'm lying."

There was more squeaking.

"Oacher, Duke of the Third Sewer," Tiny translated, "will now hold the title of Fire Kitten Vanquisher. And since he's currently single, he's going to be quite the eligible bachelor with a name like that."

"Yeah, I'm sure he's quite the catch," Loki muttered. *If you like fishing in sewers*, he didn't say aloud. "So about our escape?"

"They're on it," Tiny replied. He watched as Oacher scurried away, disappearing into a hole in the wall. "The rats know this place inside and out. They know exactly where your tails are behind the wall and can chew through the ropes. When you get your tails free and nice and dry . . ."

"We can use them to produce flame," Loki answered, catching on. "A flame hot enough to burn through iron, in fact."

"Can we do the *blue* one?" Moki asked, bouncing up and down with enthusiasm. "I love the blue one."

"Indeed we can," Loki said. "That's the hottest one of all."

"Then you can free me from these shackles and I'll bust us the rest of the way out of here," Tiny proclaimed.

"And what about all the guards?" Loki asked.

"No problem," Tiny said, scratching at his chin and thinking it over. "A good old berserking will do the trick."

"I didn't know giants could berserk," Moki said, liking everything he was hearing about bachelor rats, blue flames, and escaping.

Soon Loki felt something scurrying around his tail on the other side of the wall. It was an unnerving sensation, but it meant his new rat allies were doing their jobs. And if all went well, he'd soon be free of Onig's prison and back to his quest.

As it turned out, the berserking had been surprisingly effective. Loki and Moki had hung tightly to Tiny as he'd bashed down doors, knocked out guards, and made a fairly impressive leap across the moat surrounding the prison. Oacher the rat probably claimed he'd run them all off, which was fine by Loki. He just wanted out of the Onig dungeon. Now they found themselves creeping toward the Guild of Indiscriminate Teleportation.

The three escapees moved through Onig's back streets and side alleys, Tiny doing his best not to knock things over or to scare the locals. Loki had been to the city on several occasions, but navigating this way was difficult. After a few wrong turns they caught sight of the guild's massive sandstone structure rising in the distance.

The Guild of Indiscriminate Teleportation looked like an elongated pyramid. It rose skyward, stretching taller than the Egyptian pyramids found on the Techrus. Near the top, each of the building's corners morphed into a pair of hands, each pair holding a massive stone head. The hands were positioned over the large eyes to give the impression that each head (human, goblin, dwarf, and elf) was looking diligently over the horizon. Given the guild's reputation for accuracy, however, it might have been better if the stone carvers had covered the eyes instead. But that was the risk of traveling with the guild—there was no guarantee you'd end up where you wanted.

"That's where we enter," Loki announced as they approached a set of brass double doors at the building's base. They had just hurried across the street and to the entrance when a guard stepped out in front of them. She was an ashen elf, tall and pale under the cloudless Turul sky, and she wore the guild's robes marked by a large question mark and compass.

"Can I help you?" the elf asked with all the enthusiasm of someone making an appointment with the dentist.

Loki felt exposed standing out in the open. "Look, lady, we need to book a flight, and we're in a hurry."

The elf frowned, casting a hard look at Tiny. "This one is too big."

Tiny's face fell and he drew a deep breath. "I should have figured."

"Are you sure?" Moki asked. "Since we're small and he's big, doesn't it even out?"

The elf shook her head. "The proportions of our teleportation chamber are very exacting. Should he touch one of the walls, the explosion would flatten the entire city."

Suddenly a shout rose from the other side of the street. A group of guards had spotted them and were pointing at them with their swords.

"Don't worry, maybe we'll meet again," Tiny said. "And thanks for being my friends." Before the fire kittens could respond, the giant turned and ran into the street, waving his hands.

"Over here, you stupid goblins! What's the matter? Can't catch a little giant?" Tiny turned and ran down the street, propelled by powerful legs the size of tree trunks. The guards took off after him, never noticing the small fire kittens crouched in the guild's doorway.

"Well, that was interesting," the elf said after the commotion had settled down. She turned her attention back to Moki and Loki. "You know, I'm not sure we've ever teleported fire kittens before. If you're willing to help with our research, I can move you to the front of the line."

"If it means leaving quickly, sign us up," Loki replied. The elf nodded and opened the door.

They eventually found themselves standing in a perfectly spherical room. Cogs turned and creaked as a small section of the ceiling began to lower.

"Welcome, travelers," a voice announced. "Thank you for participating in our ongoing research. Are there any questions?"

"Yes," Moki exclaimed, waving his paw in the air. "I've always wanted to know why apartments aren't called 'together-ments' since they're so close together."

There was a pause as Loki rolled his eyes.

"Any question relevant to your teleportation?" the voice corrected itself.

They both shook their heads no.

"Then thank you for choosing the Guild of Indiscriminate Teleportation for your travel needs. Please state your destination."

"Shyr'el," Loki announced. Suddenly glowing dots began to appear around the spherical room. They filled the chamber as the fire kittens felt their fur rise and charge with electricity.

"Please note you may or may not arrive near your desired destination. If you checked luggage, it definitely *won't* end up where you do. In the event of accidental death, please accept our apologies."

"Accidental death?" Loki exclaimed, looking around. There was a brilliant flash of light followed by a belch of purple smoke. When it cleared, the two fire kittens were gone.

CHAPTER SIX

THE GREAT ESCAPE

"MAX, GRAB GLENN!" SARAH SHOUTED.

Max hurried to where the orc lay face down in the dirt. He grimaced as he took hold of the magical dagger, turning his head as he pulled it free.

"Now, that's what I call a hairy situation," Glenn announced. "Seriously, did you see that orc's backside?"

Max ran to his friends and began cutting their ropes.

"What kind of crazy dancing dagger spell did you use?" Dirk exclaimed once he was free.

"It wasn't magic," Max admitted, not sure how to explain what had happened.

"Well, I don't care what it was," Dwight said as he stood, pulling the last of the rope from around his waist. "You did good, but we've got to get out of here."

"Hey, uh, Max . . . ?" Puff called from the tent. "You wouldn't leave me here, would you?" Sarah gave Max an inquisitive look.

"That's Puff," Max replied. "He's been chained up and used as a pillow."

"A what?"

"It's a long story."

Dwight and Dirk followed Max as he ran back to the tent. At the sight of the fluff dragon, Dwight stopped and put his hands on his hips. "You didn't tell me it was one of *them*. Fluff dragons are bad luck; everyone knows that."

"That's no dragon," Dirk said, looking Puff up and down.

"We can't leave him here," Max insisted.

"Yeah, yeah, I know how sentimental you are, and I don't want to argue all day about it," Dwight said. He produced a set of keys and began trying them in the lock. "Found these outside."

Puff gave an audible sigh. "I never really thought you'd actually free me. I mean, don't get me wrong, I'm grateful, but humans and dragons have never really gotten along. And especially not with dwarfs."

"They don't? Why not?" Max asked.

"I can answer that." Dwight grunted. "Ever watch your kin burned alive? Ever seen an entire village leveled flat? Ever had to flee from the mines where you made your living because some monster decided to live there? If you knew dragons like I do, you wouldn't have to ask."

Max didn't know anything about dragons—not the real kind. Puff certainly wasn't what he expected. "Maybe we can talk about this later," he suggested.

"Sure, and I'll regale you with stories of pretty pink faeries, too," Dwight replied as the iron lock popped open. He turned to Puff. "You just stay away from me."

"I don't want any trouble," Puff replied. "Don't worry."

"As for the rest of you, grab your things and let's get out of here," Dwight ordered.

They assembled near the edge of the camp. Dwight was back in his armor with his axe slung across his back; Dirk had found a large orc knife that looked more like a sword in his hands; and Sarah had located her heavy walking stick that doubled as a weapon. They'd found their packs full of the supplies they'd gathered before leaving the frobbit treeshire. That had been in another world and another time, and what had been only hours already felt like a lifetime ago.

"This way," Dwight commanded and they followed the dwarf into the woods. Puff hesitated for a moment before falling in near the rear.

The glow of the campfire was quickly lost as Max and his friends ran deeper into the forest, the night air growing cold. "Keep up and keep moving," Dwight called back. Max gritted his teeth and chased after them, noticing Dirk prancing along like some forest gazelle.

They had pushed through the woods for an hour or so before Dwight slowed to a brisk walk. He stopped to listen for sounds of angry ogres in pursuit. The forest was full of the buzzing insects and the occasional call of wild animals in the distance, but nothing like the lumbering sound of ogres crashing through the trees behind them.

They continued the cycle of walking and listening for several more hours. The canopy above provided occasional glimpses of the star-filled sky, and Max was thankful for any light that made it to the forest floor.

"Dwight, do you know where you're going?" Sarah eventually asked.

"Mostly no," Dwight answered.

"I thought you were navigating by tree bark," Dirk replied. "Like some kind of special dwarf power or something?"

"What I'm doing is putting as much distance between us and the ogres as possible," Dwight answered. "Directions don't matter right now."

"Unless we're going in circles," Sarah said.

"That's it," Max said, coming to a stop. "I need to take a break."

Dwight was sweaty in his armor, while Dirk seemed to draw upon an inexhaustible source of energy and looked as fresh as when they had first set out from the camp.

"Is it safe to stop?" she asked.

"I think if they were after us, we'd know it by now," Dwight answered, sliding his pack from his shoulders. "Chances are the ogres decided to eat the orc."

Dirk scowled. "Gross. *And* it violates the Frisbee-and-talking rule."

"Better her than us, right?" Puff said, trying to work into the conversation.

Sarah leaned down and helped Max remove his backpack. Puff walked over to Max and plopped next to him.

"Here," Puff said to Max. "You can lean against me if you want."

"Okay, thanks," Max said as he settled next to Puff. *No wonder the orcs used him as a pillow*, he thought. The fluff dragon was both soft and warm, and Max's eyes fell shut.

"And don't worry, we haven't been going in circles," Puff said. "I can tell."

"I thought being a pillow was an insult," Dwight said to Puff as he lay his axe against a tree and began to gather pine needles with his foot. He was making a kind of mattress on the forest floor.

"Being *forced* to do anything is an insult," Puff answered. "What I choose to do isn't."

Sarah reached out and put her hand on Puff's head. "Don't mind Dwight, Puff. I'm glad you're looking after Max. I think we forget what a burden it is to be responsible for the *Codex*."

"I can imagine," Puff answered. "Now if you'd please stop petting me, I'd appreciate it."

Sarah paused, looking embarrassed. "Oh, I'm so sorry. It's just that you're so . . ."

"Fluffy?" Puff answered.

"More like *adorable*," Dirk added. "You know, in that stuffed-animal-on-your-bed kind of way. Not that I have any, or use them to keep watch for monsters during the night. I'm just saying."

"An *adorable* dragon," Puff said, dropping his head. "And I thought I couldn't feel worse about myself."

"No sense living in the past," Dirk added. "Any gamer knows you just keep trying until you waste the bad guy and claim the prize. After that, nobody cares how many times you lost."

Sarah retrieved a blanket and laid it over Puff and Max, then wrapped a second around her shoulders. "I wonder how far from home we are now," she said, feeling a kind of sadness at the thought.

"Yeah, I don't remember any ogres in Madison," Dirk said. "Except for the football team."

"Bah," Dwight said. "We're in the Magrus now."

Sarah considered the implications. Because they'd been thrown into the future, getting home had always meant finding the right *time*. But now they were some-place else. Madison was part of the Techrus—the human realm, which had things like TVs, cell phones, and the Internet. If they were in the Magrus, it meant they were in the magical realm—and who knows what they'd have to do to escape that?

"Wait, you're not from this realm?" Puff asked, opening his eyes and looking at them closely.

"Bingo," Dwight answered. "The talking pillow wins the prize for realizing the obvious." And it *was* obvious, in a way. Puff had encountered his share of humans and dwarfs before, but there was something definitely odd about this group.

"How did you get here, exactly?" Puff asked. "Only the strongest of my kind can travel between the realms."

"Man, is *that* a story!" Dirk exclaimed. He settled back and got comfortable. "You see, it all started at Parkside Middle School. I was the misunderstood loner. Teased by the jocks because of my superior intellect, and laughed at by the cheerleaders because they secretly crushed on me—"

"Oh, is that how it was?" Sarah said, laughing despite herself.

Dirk went on to share how they were cast into the future, found the frobbits and snow faeries, and then fought the robots to save the world. Then he told of how they met the dragon king, Obsikar, and made a promise to destroy Rezormoor Dreadbringer in exchange for coming back in time. Sarah had to admit it was interesting hearing it all from Dirk's perspective.

Puff blinked, barely able to take it in.

Meanwhile Dwight climbed into his bed and addressed the group. "So I've been thinking. Now that we've traveled back in time, none of what Dirk just said has happened."

"Wait, what?" Dirk asked, trying to follow Dwight's thinking.

"Look, it's simple. You can't be held to a promise you haven't made yet. So I say we forget about wizards and dragons and focus on getting home. We don't need magic books or spell casters or any of that nonsense. You can walk out of the Magrus, and I should know because I've done it before. It starts at the Tree of Attenuation and then on to the Mesoshire. And from there you can get to just about anywhere, including the Techrus. And that means home."

Dirk scowled. "I *know* I made a promise to Obsikar, because I remember doing it."

"And I remember this dream I had," Dwight replied sourly. "I was dancing around in a tutu and chasing butterflies. But guess what? Just because it's in my head doesn't mean it really happened."

"Dwight does have a point," Sarah admitted. "The future hasn't technically happened."

"So where'd that blanket come from, huh?" Dirk asked, pointing at Sarah's. "Looks pretty real to me."

Sarah frowned—she wasn't used to Dirk making a valid point. Puff, however, was watching in disbelief as the humans talked so casually about the dragon king, time travel, and the *Codex of Infinite Knowability.*

"There's someone I think you should talk to," Puff announced. "He's not far from here, but he's a friend to the dragons and a powerful sorcerer. If anyone can help you it's him."

"Oh sure, let's just get some power-hungry wizard involved, because that sounds like the worst possible idea ever," Dwight said.

"No, not just some wizard," Puff said. "He's called the ancient one, and he's very wise."

"Puff's right," Dirk said. "Every epic quest requires an old wise dude to offer advice and such. And sometimes you even get a magic item or something special."

Dwight shook his head. "Well in the *real* world, when you bother the wrong wizard, they zap you into a pile of ash."

"That's actually a good point," Puff said. "The one I speak of is very old and has removed himself from the world for a reason. When we find him you might want to gag the dwarf."

"I say we go to this wizard and see what he says," Max said with a yawn, his eyes still closed.

"Then that's that," Sarah said to Dwight. "What Max says goes."

"Swell," Dwight grumbled. "But don't say I didn't warn you."

Two kingdoms away, Rezormoor Dreadbringer was led through the large obsidian door that marked the Maelshadow's temple. The place was easy to find—a black cliff that rose at the edge of the mountains just a half day's ride from Aardyre. Stone steps rose along the rock face, marked by the scraping of talons and other nightmarish things. It was definitely not the kind of spot found on Magrus travel brochures.

The black-robed acolytes who shuffled within served the one creature that Rezormoor truly feared: the Maelshadow. The Maelshadow was known by many names: the Lord of Shadows, the Blackness, the Blight, and He Who Pays with Change in the Express Lane. He was also the ruler of the Shadrus, the lower realm marked by demons, nightmarish fiends, and adult contemporary music.

He followed an acolyte into the main chamber, and it was exactly as the sorcerer had remembered it. In the center a great throne carved from the skull of a long-dead giant dominated the space, while a river of black liquid flowed through channels cut into the floor. Along the walls the temple's acolytes kept a silent vigil, their ghost-white hair spilling from their shadowy cowls.

The Tower's regent approached the throne and felt a sudden chill in the air. He sensed more than saw the shadowy form materialize.

"Rezormoor," came the voice of the Maelshadow, filling the columned chamber like a deep sigh. "Have you found what we seek?"

The sorcerer had to be careful here, for not only was he hunting and killing dragons for their magical scale, but he'd sent Princess to the Techrus to find the *Codex*. Rezormoor had enlisted the aid of the Maelshadow for the latter, but he intended to keep the dragon hunts to himself.

"Word was sent to me by the unicorn that she'd found a living descendant who could read the book," Rezormoor said, bowing his head.

"Excellent."

"It appears as if the Gossamer Gimbal is working as planned." That was the name of the compass forged by three magical smiths and designed to find whatever its owner desired. In this case, its owner was the Maelshadow, and what he desired was the *Codex of Infinite Knowability*. Princess had been loaned the Gossamer Gimbal at Rezormoor's request.

"Then why is it *here*?" boomed the Maelshadow, his voice rolling through the small chamber and causing the sorcerer to take a step backward. *Here? What is the Gossamer Gimbal doing here?* Rezormoor's mind scrambled for answers.

"I have felt something . . . off," the sorcerer managed to say. "I did not think it was the Gimbal."

"Nor should you," the Maelshadow continued.

Rezormoor straightened, a bead of sweat breaking out on his forehead. Coming to the Maelshadow was always a dicey affair, and he had to be careful. Did the Lord of Shadows suspect what he was *really* after? If so, his end would come very slowly and with a great deal of screaming.

"The unicorn has returned to the Magrus," the Maelshadow continued, "but she did not teleport between the realms as she was given the power to do."

"Then we must assume something happened to her wand," Rezormoor replied.

"What creature could stand before a unicorn and such power?" the Maelshadow asked. "Princess has returned because that which she hunts has also returned. That is what you feel, sorcerer; the power of the *Codex* in this realm."

"Then soon it will be ours," Rezormoor said. It felt like the right thing to say in front of the Dark Lord.

"We shall see. But do not forget our arrangement," the Maelshadow continued. And suddenly a stinging cold filled the room. It burned the back of the sorcerer's throat and nearly extinguished the torches along the walls. "Once you find the blood descendant of Maximilian Sporazo, you'll deliver the human to ME!" The final word came with such power that it nearly knocked Rezormoor to the ground. Ice began to form along the walls and Rezormoor struggled to draw his breath.

"Know that I have my own hunters as well," the Maelshadow continued. "The undead walk this world in search of the book."

Then I must find it first. Rezormoor bowed a final time and stumbled from the cold. He was gasping by the time he pushed the great door open and felt the sun's kiss on his skin. His chest ached and he took in lungfuls of warm air. The deadly chill was an important reminder that the Lord of Shadows was not to be trifled with.

It was after dusk as he sat in his chambers at the topmost part of the Wizard's Tower. He stared at the fire burning in the large stone hearth. The sorcerer had been unable to get warm, no matter how many logs he added to the flames. The zombie duck looked up from his spot at the foot of Rezormoor's chair, and his hand drifted down to scratch the sandpaper-like skin of the undead fowl's head.

"We are in a race against time, my friend," Rezormoor said. He shifted in his chair and watched the yellow-and-gold flames dance. "I must gather the dragon scale before the Lord of Shadows grows too powerful. And then all hinges on finding the book . . . and the one who can read it."

The zombie duck *gwak*ed, not so much in agreement with the sorcerer but to let him know his hand had stopped scratching.

ON THE HAMMER'S HILT

✜

ONE OF THE GREATEST SIGHTS TO behold in the Magrus is the famed Hammer's Hilt Bridge, which stretches across the Crystal Sea between the kingdoms of Aaredt and Thoran. Most assume that the bridge was so named because of its long and narrow road that ends in an outcropping of rock shaped very much like the head of a hammer.

Despite what some conspiracy theorists and radical historians say, this belief is absolutely correct. Sometimes things are no more or less than what they appear to be. Note: This also holds true for the Elephant Cricket of Turan.

✜

CHAPTER SEVEN

A WIZARD IN THE WOODS

THE NEXT DAY HAD TURNED COLD, SO MAX AND HIS FRIENDS KEPT THEIR blankets around their shoulders as they followed Puff through the woods. The sky was gray and a light snow started to fall, and Dwight had become more and more unhappy about their intended destination.

That evening they made camp by a small gurgling stream. The snow had stopped and the water was fresh and delicious. They drank deeply, filling their water skins when they were done, and ate sparingly from their supplies.

"Isn't there a way to summon us up some food?" Dirk asked as they sat around the fire.

"Like what?" Max replied.

Dirk thought it over. "I don't know . . . you're a magic

user now. How hard could summoning a hot dog be?"

Puff looked confused.

"Look, there's no such thing as a hot dog–summoning spell," Max replied. "And even if there were, it wouldn't work." Max glanced at the *Codex* and sighed. He went on to explain all the difficulties he'd been having with the magical tome.

"Well, that pretty much decides it," Dwight said. "How are we supposed to stop Rezormoor Dreadbringer if the *Codex* isn't working? It's like I told you, we need to find the Mesoshire and get home."

"That's why I think talking to this wizard is a good idea," Max said. "Maybe he can help."

"Or not," Dwight added. "You think far too highly of wizards."

Late the next day as they continued through the woods, Puff suddenly stopped and looked around. The light snow had melted away, but a crisp chill remained in the air.

"We're close," the fluff dragon announced. "I'm beginning to recognize things."

"Every new beginning comes from some other beginning's end," Glenn declared from his spot on Max's belt. "Just something to think about."

"What's that supposed to mean?" Puff asked.

Sarah shook her head. "Best not to think about it."

Puff turned and led the way down a sharp incline. They continued for the better part of an hour, moving through a series of depressions until they came to a small clearing. There, a large, two-story wagon sat unhitched in a field of green grass. The wagon looked a lot like the double-decker buses found in London (Max had seen them on TV), and seemed too big to actually travel through the tree-packed forest. He wondered how it had gotten there. A stovepipe rose from the wagon's side, its white smoke tinted with the smells of something cooking. Max's stomach growled in response.

The door swung open and a figure appeared. He had a long white beard, hair that fell past his shoulders, and thick eyebrows that looked like they'd never been trimmed. He was dressed in a green robe and several butterflies spilled out of the doorway behind him.

"Yep, that's a wizard," Dirk announced after sizing the man up. "And a good one—evil and butterflies can't mix."

The man looked up when he heard Dirk and smiled. Puff approached him with a slight bow. "Please pardon our intrusion. We seek your counsel, great Bellstro."

Dirk elbowed Max. "See? We're about to get some quest stuff."

"Such a motley band of companions," the man said. His voice was rich and not unlike a bow pulled across musical strings. He turned to Max and regarded him closely. "And now the past has caught up with me, it would seem. The very fabric of this world bends around you, young man."

Max swallowed. The only fabric that bent around him was usually attached to sweat pants.

"He saved my life," Puff continued. "I believe this one is good."

"Yes," the man said, still staring at Max. "But he is dangerous, too. A blade can cut both ways—the power to save and the power to destroy are often held in the same hand."

"Oh, I like that one!" Glenn said. "Cuts both ways—I'm going to have to remember that."

"I'm not interested in cutting anything," Max said, feeling somehow guilty under the weight of the wizard's stare. Bellstro grunted, nodding his head.

"Of course you're not," he said, turning to Puff and

smiling. "My friend, please come in. Bring your companions and take shelter as my guests. All that is mine is yours."

"Cool!" Dirk announced, bounding forward before Puff could reply. "I could *really* use a cloak of invisibility. And—oh! Maybe a vorpal blade! Do you have vorpal blades?"

"Dirk!" Max exclaimed as he and the others hurried in after him. "You'll have to forgive my friend here—he doesn't know any better." It was a phrase Max had used often over the course of their lives. "He thinks everything's a game."

"There are worse ways to view the world," Bellstro said with a grin. "Come inside, please. I was about to eat."

Max's stomach loudly accepted the invitation.

It may have been the most comfortable room Max had ever been in. He knew he was still inside Bellstro's wagon, but the space seemed many times larger than what was possible. He was slumped in a large, overstuffed chair, his stomach happily bulging from the six (or was it seven?) bowls of soup he'd eaten. A fire crackled pleasantly in a stone fireplace, and thick rugs were scattered about the floor. An assortment of paintings hung on the walls, showing various views of the Seven Kingdoms.

Sarah had grabbed Dirk by the ear and "volunteered" the pair of them to do the dishes. Meanwhile Dwight had come to the sitting room with Max, standing near a painting of a mountain and studying it closely.

"That's near Vail'ik—I recognize it. I was born not far from there."

"Yes," Bellstro said, rocking in an ornately carved chair while Puff padded around the room and found a spot near the fire. "I have known many from that region over the years. I've counted the dwarfs as my friends for some time."

Dwight seemed to take it in but remained silent. He drifted toward a large sofa and scrambled up to it. "You do make a delicious stew."

"Kind of you to say so. Every few months, the faeries bring me eleven herbs and spices."

"*Eleven* herbs and spices?" Dirk said from the doorway. "Eleven . . . that's interesting. Very, very interesting. I don't suppose you've ever been to Kentucky? Maybe fried up some chicken?"

"Dirk . . . ?" Sarah asked, taking a seat next to Dwight.

Max shook his head. "He has this thing about Kentucky Fried Chicken."

"It's not a *thing*. Take one *e* from the word 'eleven'—just one," Dirk continued. "And you know what you've got then?"

"An idiot with the letter *e*?" Dwight asked.

"No. You've got 'elven'!" Dirk exclaimed. "*Elven* herbs and spices. Don't you see? That makes a lot more sense—it takes elven magic to eat food from a bucket."

"What about popcorn?" Max asked.

"I'm pretty sure I said eleven; didn't I say eleven?" Bellstro asked, looking confused. "I didn't even mention elves."

Dirk had any number of theories, and his belief that Kentucky Fried Chicken was secretly run by elves was just one of them. "Can we talk about something else?" Max pleaded. Dirk nodded and tapped his finger to his forehead, flopping down on the far side of the big sofa.

"Now, do you mind if I see it?" Bellstro asked Max.

"It?"

"Did you think I wouldn't feel its presence?" Bellstro continued. "I knew of it the very moment you arrived in the Magrus. And I felt it draw nearer as you approached. Why do you think I made so much soup?"

"Show him the book," Puff said. "It's okay."

Max was protective of the *Codex*, but Bellstro put him at ease (or maybe it was dinner). Either way, he retrieved it from his backpack.

"It's been a long time since my eyes have gazed upon this," the wizard said, looking at Max. "I can feel the bond between you and it. Strange . . . but perhaps it's because you look so much like him."

"Him?"

"Maximilian Sporazo, your namesake. His blood flows through you, does it not? And yet . . ." Bellstro paused, studying Max.

Suddenly a blue spark shot across the front of the book and zapped Max with an audible *SNAP!* "Ouch!" he cried as he dropped the book and danced around waving his finger in the air.

"Well, now, isn't that interesting?" Bellstro said, looking at the *Codex* on the floor. More blue streaks ran around its surface like lightning.

"Do you know why it's doing that?" Max asked between clenched teeth.

"This book has traveled through the umbraverse. How peculiar."

"So what do we do now?"

"There is only one thing to do," Bellstro continued. "The *Codex* must be taken to the Wizard's Tower—to the very room where it was created. There it will return to its former self."

"That's all well and good," Dwight interjected, "but we don't need the *Codex* anymore. As I've said, we can leave the cursed thing right here and make our way to the Mesoshire. Let's be done with wizards and magic and go home."

"Home?" Bellstro replied. "I did not know dwarfs called the Techrus such."

Dwight scowled, folding his arms. "Not by choice," he admitted.

"We can't go home," Dirk interjected. "Not yet. We made a promise to Obsikar to stop Rezormoor Deaddinger from killing all the dragons."

"*Dreadbringer*," Max corrected.

Bellstro leaned back into his chair, suddenly growing serious. "The dragon king has sent you on an errand to save his family?" He looked down at Puff. "*That* is why the days grow unnaturally cold."

"Dragons' fire is connected to the Magrus," Puff said. "If Rezormoor is killing dragons, the world will grow colder."

"Colder as in 'a nice drink of water'?" Dirk asked. "Or colder as in 'locked in a walk-in freezer that you shouldn't have gone into but you wanted to see what frozen tartar sauce looked like'?"

Bellstro gave Dirk a double take before moving on.

"If Rezormoor succeeds, the Magrus will be destroyed," the wizard announced. He stroked his beard and watched as the last of the lightning played out on the *Codex*'s surface. "You must stop him."

"Epic," Dirk said as a broad smile grew on his face. "Saving the dragons *and* the Magrus. Now we're getting somewhere." But Max felt the full weight of it, and it showed on his face. Bellstro stood and put his arm around him.

"I have used all but the last of my power to prolong my life," the wizard said. "Perhaps it was selfish to do so. I often wondered if I could have done more good by engaging in a great cause in the world instead of simply extending my days upon it. I knew Maximilian Sporazo. He was the only *arch*-sorcerer to have ever lived. He was a good man, despite his demons, and I sense that same strength in you. I know you have your doubts, Max, but you're here for a reason. You have more strength than you can possibly imagine."

"Nice," Dirk proclaimed. "You've just been mentored."

And for a second or two it seemed as if Max might actually believe him. Then a closet door flew open and a skeleton stepped out. Only it wasn't the smiling kind used as Halloween decorations. This one was yellow and brown and draped in a tattered green cloak. Strands of long white hair fell from its skull in dirty clumps, and it oozed a stench like an open grave. "Give us the book," came the otherworldly voice hissing between broken teeth.

"A Shadrus necromancer!" Bellstro called. "Protect yourselves!"

The necromancer advanced, grabbing hold of a large wooden beam as it pulled itself forward. Where the skeletal hand made contact with the frame, the wood turned black and began rotting away. The same happened along the floor where the necromancer walked.

"Who sent you?" Bellstro commanded. The power

of the wizard's voice forced the advancing necromancer to pause, and Max had to take several steps backward or risk being knocked down. Even the walls of the wagon creaked and groaned under the weight of Bellstro's command.

"The Lord of Shadows! The Maelshadow!" The skeleton screeched as it resumed its advance. It raised its head and thousands of tiny shadows erupted from its mouth like a swarm of angry insects. A ringing filled Max's ears, and he threw his hands over his head and dropped to his knees. The swarm of shadows rose like a wave and crashed into the room. It smelled of disease and decay and everything rotten in the world. Max struggled to breathe, and he could hear Sarah and Dirk coughing as the world grew black and cold around them.

CHAPTER EIGHT

CROSSING OVER

MAX HEARD SCUFFLING AND WHAT SOUNDED LIKE THE OLD WIZARD trying to hum a note. It wasn't exactly the sort of thing that seemed a good idea given the suffocating darkness and otherworldly skeleton. Then Bellstro called out, "Listen to me! You must sing, all of you. Sing any song you know, but do it now!"

Max had been told to sing before: during music class, at school assemblies, even at church. But he'd never been commanded to sing by an ancient wizard fighting the undead. Suddenly Dirk's voice broke through the darkness: *"If I was your boyfriend, I'd never let you go—"*

"No!" Bellstro yelled, his voice thundering around the room. "Not *Bieber*! You'll only make it stronger!"

A wheezing laugh sounded out, and Max could

hear the rattling of the skeleton necromancer's steady advance. He frantically cleared his mind and began belting out the first song that came to mind: *"Rudolph the red-nosed reindeer . . ."*

Max heard the skeleton stumble on the wooden floor as if struck.

"Good, good!" Bellstro shouted. "All of you now, keep it up!"

"Here I am," Dirk belted out with all the enthusiasm of a lead singer in a rock band, *"rock you like a hurricane!"* Max wouldn't have been surprised if Dirk was playing air guitar.

And then Sarah jumped in, her voice rising above the others: *"Supercalifragilisticexpialidocious! Even though the sound of it is something quite atrocious . . ."*

"Yes, YES!" Bellstro yelled. He began vigorously humming his own tune. The room filled with the strange mix of melodies and the skeleton shrieked. Max could hear it thrashing about, crashing into furniture in the dark. They pressed on, their voices growing louder.

There was a final cry from the creature before the room exploded. The dark swarm that had enveloped them flew apart like grains of sand in a windstorm. Pieces of the walls, ceiling, and furniture flew outward until the stars were visible above them.

They were standing in the moonlit clearing, wagon debris falling around them. Bellstro stood with his hands held in front of him as small shafts of light collapsed around his fingers. The wizard stumbled a little, as if the light weighed more than he could bear.

"Max!" Sarah called out, running over to him. "Are you okay?" She turned him around by the shoulders and looked him over.

"Yeah, I'm fine," Max said, blushing. *He* should have been running over to see if *she* was okay, not the other way around.

Dwight stepped forward, his battle-axe in his hand. He looked around and frowned. "What in the three realms is going on?"

"There are only two ways to defeat a Shadrus necromancer," Bellstro said, sounding winded. "With magic such as the *Codex* possesses, or through a skeleton key."

"Skeleton key?" Dirk repeated. "Like those magic keys that can open any lock?"

"No," Bellstro replied. "A key as in 'note.' Any

skeleton can be undone if you find the right one."

"That explains the singing," Sarah said.

"I thought we were just making epic battle music," Dirk added, sounding a little unhappy about the new information on skeletons.

Sarah turned to Dwight. "So how come I never heard you sing?"

"Dwarfs can only sing in groups and during meals," Dirk said. "And preferably with a mug in their hands. It's like a rule or something." All eyes turned to Dwight as he shrugged.

"Eh, pretty much."

"No time to dawdle, children," Bellstro announced. "We've damaged the necromancer, but it will return in its shadow form. And I used the last of my magic to protect us from the blast. We must make for the woods." Max grabbed his backpack and shoved the *Codex of Infinite Knowability* inside while the others found their scattered packs. They hurried and ran for the forest, Puff galloping alongside (although it was hard to think of a fuzzy, pillow-like dragon *galloping*).

They flew into the forest, but the wizard tired quickly and they had to slow to a walk. "There isn't much time,

Max," Bellstro exclaimed between breaths. "There was so much more I wanted to tell you."

Max nodded, not knowing what to say. It felt like the wizard was saying good-bye. "Why did that skeleton attack us?"

"It is hunting you."

"But who even knows I'm here?"

Bellstro considered the question for a moment. "Shadrus necromancers were once powerful wizards who bound themselves to the Maelshadow in exchange for power. But after their deaths they remain servants of the Lord of Shadows—or his followers. This does not bode well, I'm afraid."

"The Lord of Shadows?"

"*He*—if he can even be called that—is the Maelshadow, the ruler of the Shadrus. A being of immense power."

"Makes sense," Dirk added. "Typical evil-overlord type bent on world domination. My guess is you're going to have to face him in some kind of final battle of good versus evil. But first you've got to defeat his champion, and that's this Rezormoor Shellshaker dude."

"*Dreadbringer,*" Puff corrected.

Bellstro looked at Dirk. "How do you know Rezormoor is in league with the Maelshadow?"

Dirk shrugged. "Game logic." Bellstro raised an eyebrow but didn't disagree with Dirk's assessment.

"So if singing just hurts the skeleton's body, how do we actually destroy it?" Dwight asked.

"We don't," Bellstro said pointedly. "Maybe when I was young and powerful I might have had a chance, but not now. And we don't have the right weapons."

"If you can't beat your enemy by force, *dazzle* them into submission," Glenn added from his spot on Max's belt. "Never underestimate the power of a good dazzling."

"Uh-huh," Dwight answered. He turned his attention back to Bellstro. "So you're saying there's nothing we can do about this skeleton thing?"

"We can keep fleeing."

"Unless Max can get his spell-casting mojo back," Dirk replied. "That would probably do the trick."

"Not likely," Max answered.

"The *Codex* cannot aid you," Bellstro said, "until you return it to the Wizard's Tower."

"Remember we can always bury the cursed thing and make for the Mesoshire," Dwight reminded them.

"Whatever hunts for the book will hunt for the one who can read it," Bellstro said, his breath labored. "You can't hide from your destiny, Max. Abandon the book and the creatures of the shadows will still seek you out. Your only hope is returning it to the Tower and defeating those who wish to use it to their ends."

Suddenly the groan of a tree sounded as it bent and snapped.

"What was that?" Max exclaimed.

Sarah stepped back and pointed to the ground. "Look!" A black rot was moving through the earth toward them, destroying everything in its path.

"It has found us," Puff said, sounding defeated.

The rot reached a nearby tree, and they watched as the tree shuddered and split in half, peeling away from itself with a loud groan. Max jumped out of the way as it came crashing down where he'd been standing. All around them, more sounds of trees splitting and falling cut into the night air.

"We're surrounded!" Dwight called out, shifting his battle-axe from one hand to the other.

The group moved closer together as the encircling rot advanced. They didn't need to be told what would happen if it reached them—they could see what it did when it touched anything living.

"What do we do?" Max asked, looking at Bellstro.

"I'll try to clear a path," the wizard said. He grabbed a broken branch and began muttering words beneath his breath.

"We're running out of time," Sarah said, stepping closer to the others. The black ring was only a few feet from them.

The ring of shadow closed more. Max and his friends were pressed together as tightly as they could, watching it advance. Bellstro held the stick high in the air as strange white symbols burned along its length.

"Back!" he shouted, and Bellstro thrust the branch into the ground. The shadow immediately drew away from the stick as a light exploded from its base and began cutting a path through the sea of black earth.

"It's working!" Puff shouted, unable to hide his relief.

Now, Max thought to himself. Now was the time to find a spell and burn the necromancer into nothing, despite what Bellstro had said about the Tower. Max gathered his will and pressed his mind into the book, searching for the currents he'd felt before. He held on to it, searching . . . anticipating.

But still there was nothing.

Max groaned in frustration. The others turned to the small path of light that stretched and parted the blight on either side. "Let's go!" Dwight commanded, but Bellstro put his hand on his shoulder and stopped the dwarf before he could start.

"No," Bellstro said. They turned as one and watched as the path began to waver. Then it collapsed and was gone, the shadow pouring into the space like a river down a canal. The blight reached the stick, and the symbols faded as the wood turned to ash.

"No!" Sarah shouted in frustration. She looked at her feet and inched backward, the rot less than an inch from her shoe.

Bellstro collapsed, and Dwight dropped his battle-axe to catch him. Dirk and Sarah grabbed hold and barely managed to keep the wizard from tumbling into the shadow. At their feet, Dwight's battle-axe disappeared into the black.

"Max, if you've got something in your bag of tricks, you better use it!" Dwight grunted, struggling to hold the wizard. But Max had nothing. He braced himself against the hard truth—he had failed, and now they were about to die because of it.

"Dangit!" Dirk exclaimed. "What we really need is silver!" Silver had special properties against spiritual monsters and the undead, and Max supposed it was just about as good of a last wish as any. He turned to Sarah, reading the fear in her eyes. He wanted to say something—to at least apologize. He opened his mouth—

The ground suddenly rumbled around them.

Max's jaw snapped shut as the blight paused its advance. Sarah looked at her feet, the rot millimeters from reaching her. Then the remains of the shattered forest began to explode. All around them patches of shadow sizzled and spewed airborne, collapsing like air escaping from a balloon. The ground erupted like a field full of geysers, and Max caught sight of something where the shadow had been. Silver shimmered in the moonlight. Silver!

All around them the forest was turning to silver, and the advancing blight boiled away at its touch. Even the ground turned to silver, evaporating the shadow in its wake. A great wail of frustration and anger ripped through the air. There was no place for the necromancer to hide, and the creature of shadow shrieked a final time and was gone. Max and his friends found themselves alone, in the midst of a silver forest.

"I've never seen anything so beautiful," Sarah said, looking around her. She helped Dwight lower Bellstro gently to the ground. The ancient wizard's eyes fluttered open, and he looked around him in disbelief. "Oh my," he finally said.

"Is this your doing?" Dwight asked Bellstro. But the wizard shook his head.

"No. Not me."

"And I didn't do it," Max added, anticipating the group's next question.

"Then one of you got into my things, didn't you?" Bellstro asked.

All eyes turned to Dirk.

"I saw them when I was washing the dishes," Dirk confessed. "And technically, you did say *all that is mine is yours*."

"Saw *what* exactly?" Sarah asked.

"A bunch of magic potions in the spice cabinet."

Bellstro frowned. "I never thought anyone would look there."

"It's not like I'm nosey," Dirk said defensively. "Everyone knows you always explore every location you go to. So I saw a stash of potions hidden in the spice cabinet and I figured we'd probably need them at some point. Then I saw this one cool one."

"The dark-blue one?" Bellstro asked.

"Yeah, that's it," Dirk confirmed. "I was going ask you about it, but before I could, the skeleton attacked. So I hurried and drank it."

"I can't believe you did that!" Sarah exclaimed. "You just decided some random liquid in a vial might be a potion and you drank it?"

"Duh," Dirk answered. "Like I said, this is how dungeon crawling works. I'm not stupid—it was in a vial, people. A vial! So yeah, I totally drank it because we needed the buff."

"Buff?" Puff asked.

"Gamer term," Max said. "Like getting extra power or something."

Bellstro grunted disapprovingly. "Not even I'm foolish enough to drink the dark-blue one. I'm amazed you're still alive."

"Yeah, people tell me that all the time," Dirk replied.

"Well, you might not be for long," Bellstro said. "You drank the Ergodic Elixir."

Puff blinked his eyes in surprise and sat with a *thump* (it was actually more of a *thuwoosh*.) "Oh no," he said.

"'Ergodic' means having to do with chance or something, right?" Sarah asked.

"Indeed," Bellstro said with a cough. "The potion was mixed by the Eldritch Circle, an ancient pact of magic users comprised of a druid, a necromancer, a warlock, and a sorcerer. It contained unicorn tears, dragon's blood, shavings from a gracon's horn, and other things lost over time or too unspeakable to mention. It was given to me to safeguard, deemed too dangerous to ever use."

Everyone looked back at Dirk. "It's not my fault," Dirk said with a shrug. "It was next to the paprika."

"What does this potion do?" Dwight asked.

Bellstro motioned to the silver forest around them. "I'd say this, for one," the wizard replied. "And what else? Who's to say? But it's as powerful as it is unpredictable." Bellstro began to cough again, and then the cough turned into a bout of hacking and wheezing. When it passed, the old wizard's hand fell feebly to his side.

"I've used the last of my magic," he muttered. "My

life is slipping away." The old wizard struggled to pull a sheet of weathered parchment from a pocket in his robe.

"Here," he continued, pressing it into Max's hand. "Upon this are the names of the Prime Spells and what they do. Know them and be ready."

Max looked at the paper in his hands.

"To defeat Rezormoor, you'll need more than the *Codex*," Bellstro continued. "You'll need friends—old and new. Now my time is done, children. My next great adventure beckons."

A white light started to rise around Bellstro. Max and the others backed away, watching as the light swarmed around him. Then it moved to form a glimmering archway where an even brighter light poured through from the other side. Bellstro frowned.

"Seriously?" he said. "I didn't know *walking* toward the light was so literal. I'm old and tired—can't you just swoosh me there?"

The group looked at one another and then back to the wizard.

"Fine, fine," Bellstro said. He pulled himself to his feet and walked toward the glowing archway. He paused, turning back. "Mourn me not, young ones. I go to where

I am long overdue . . . and do so in the company of friends. One cannot ask for more. Well, other than not having to *walk*. You'd think they'd have a better system for this by now." Bellstro waved and moved through the glowing arch. "Don't be surprised if I visit you again." Then both the wizard and the archway disappeared.

"He's gone," Sarah said, her voice heavy.

"Not gone," Puff replied. "We must not dishonor him by mourning—it is not the way with one such as him. We came seeking his help and he has told us what we must do."

Max looked at the paper in his hands. He had touched the Prime Spells before, but now he had their names. And names had power.

"What do we do now?" he asked.

"More important, isn't this forest worth, like, a fortune or something?" Dirk asked.

"Yeah, and someday I intend to come back and mine it," Dwight answered. "Might even make this whole misadventure worthwhile. But next we head north. Once we get out of these woods, we'll be in the Dwarven Nation. We'll make for He'ilk." Dwight moved to one of the silver trees and found the end of a very small branch. He snapped it off and held it up for the others to see. "Silver's too hard to mine without a pickaxe, but we can break off enough to buy us whatever we need. If we're going to do this, we'll need supplies."

Max and his friends spent the next few hours gathering as much silver as they could carry before moving to the edge of the forest, where they made camp. That night Max dreamed he was being tossed about on a small boat on a silver sea. And below the waves, watching him with unblinking eyes, a monster bided its time.

ON THE FIFTEEN PRIME SPELLS

⌗

ALL MAGIC IS A REFLECTION OF THE Fifteen Prime Spells. The origin of the Fifteen Primes are unknown, having not so much been created as found. And of all the great sorcerer's, only Maximilian Sporazo had enough understanding of them to capture and utilize them in their raw form. It is further admonished the Fifteen Prime Spells not be used in cooking. You'd think that part would be obvious, but it bears repeating.

The Fifteen Prime Spells, in alphabetical order, include the spells of:

- Captivity
- Density
- Elemenity
- Fixity
- Futurity
- Gallimaufry
- Gravity
- Irony
- Liquidity
- Nimiety
- Panoply
- Parity
- Tutelary
- Unity
- Vacuity

CHAPTER NINE

THAT'S A BIG HEAD

THEY HAD NEVER SEEN A CITY LIKE HE'ILK. THE ENTRANCE WAS CARVED from the skull of some monstrous creature that had died there. Max stood in awe at the great rows of teeth thrust into the ground like the creature was trying to devour the very earth—the white elongated skull the size of a football stadium, the two huge horns rising into the air, and, at their tops, two flags fluttering triumphantly in the wind.

"Tiamus," Puff said reverently. "The last DragonVir— the great ancestor to all dragons."

"What happened to it?" Sarah asked, her mind trying to get around the size of the thing.

"It was caught between the realms during the Great Sundering," Puff continued. "Buried deep in the earth,

Tiamus fought to claw its way out. And it almost made it."

"It's said the great mountains of Thoran were formed from the beast's struggle to push its way to the surface," Dwight added.

Puff nodded. "All dragons hold this place sacred."

"Which is all well and good so long as you remember the dwarfs were here first," Dwight added.

"This is how the enmity between dwarfs and dragons began," Glenn announced from Max's belt. "But as I've always said, it's better to have an enemy ahead of you than a manatee behind you."

"Huh?" Sarah asked. "What are you even talking about?"

"Manatees—don't turn your back on them," Glenn said. "Consider yourself warned."

They were standing on a long road that lead to the city's entrance. It had taken five days to get clear of the forest and then another three to cross the grass plains.

"I'm starving," Dirk announced, voicing exactly what Max was thinking. "Cities have food and we have silver."

"Yeah," Max added. "I don't think I can stomach another forest berry."

"For once we agree. So let's get going," Dwight said

without moving. The group stood for several moments waiting for the dwarf to start, but he seemed content to stand there and stare at the city in the distance. They all knew Dwight had a problem with tight places—it was a huge disgrace for a dwarf to be claustrophobic. And that had something to do with why he'd opened a gaming store in the Techrus.

As they continued to stand there (everyone thought better of bringing up the phobia business) an ornate wagon drove toward them. The driver pulled on the reins of two small horses and brought the vehicle to a stop. She looked down and acknowledged them with a tip of her head. She was thin with brownish skin and large almond-shaped eyes, and her long brown hair was pulled back behind her head. Dirk pointed at her, his face breaking out into a wide grin.

"You're an elf!" Dirk exclaimed. Sarah quickly stepped in front of him.

"Please excuse my friend," she said, lowering Dirk's arm. "That was extremely rude."

The elf offered a good-natured smile. "No offense taken. And if you don't mind my asking, I noticed you've been standing here for some time. Is everything all right?"

"Fine, fine," Dwight said. "Just taking everything in. You don't often see sights like the skull of Tiamus."

"A true wonder, yes," the elf replied. "Perhaps you might be interested in a lift? I'm on my way to pick up a passenger and deliver them to Vail'ik. Many prefer to ride in the comfort of my coach rather than making the journey on foot."

Sarah approached the ornately decorated wagon. It was painted with a complex design of overlapping leaves that seemed to move as she turned her head. "Your wagon is beautiful," she said as she stepped around it.

"Guys, we *totally* have to ride in that!" Dirk exclaimed. He walked over and tried to peer through a glass window, but it was stained with a smoky tint.

"Many of my clients prefer their privacy," the elf said. "Discretion, comfort, and ease of mind—it's all part of what I offer." The whole idea of not being seen appealed to Max. He had no desire to run into another necromancer.

"Peace of mind, you say?" Dwight repeated, taking a closer look at the carriage. He could see various runes inscribed in the highly polished wood.

"Indeed," the elf replied. "This carriage has been

in my family for generations. It was built by the finest craftsmen, then imbued with certain . . . enhancements."

"Magic," Dwight said.

"If you like," the elf replied. "While the elven nations are not home to the wizards' towers, we have our own ways with such things. But as to your question, those who ride within find a certain tranquility and easing of their burdens. It makes for a most pleasant journey."

"Dude, that might totally help you with your claustro—" Dirk started to say, but Max elbowed him in the ribs before he could get it out.

"We have silver that needs to be smelted and traded for coin," the dwarf said. "If you're willing to wait for payment, we could use a ride about town."

"I will take you at your word," the elf said. "Shall we say ten silver? I'm not due to pick up my client until this evening, and you may have my coach until then."

"Done!" Dwight announced, not bothering to ask the others. Max had already decided the coach was a good idea.

"Ten silver?" Puff said. "You could *buy* a wagon and horses for that much."

Dirk was already stepping up to the carriage's door

and opening it. He paused, looking inside. "Oh man, this is awesome!"

"Stay here if you want," Dwight said to Puff. "But we're riding in style."

Puff shrugged—who was he to argue with how they spent their money? He scampered up the steps and made his way into the carriage. Once they were inside, the elf moved her hand and the door shut behind the group. "Make yourself comfortable," she said, turning to speak through a small sliding panel near where she sat. "My name is Sumyl. This carriage was first built for my great-great-great-uncle, who found few joys in life."

"Nothing sadder than an unhappy elf," Dirk said from within the wagon.

"Yes," Sumyl replied. "He had elf-esteem issues."

The inside of the carriage reminded Max of walking into Bellstro's home: the dimensions were far bigger on the inside than should have been possible. In the center was a long curved bench, covered in thick red velvet and stuffed with soft padding. It was shaped like a crescent moon and was thick enough that one could easily stretch out and sleep on it. The bench was recessed into the floor and surrounded by a walkway big enough to stand on and peer out the windows (of which there were many more on the inside than on the outside). Several stuffed chairs were pressed into the far corners, and at the front a small desk was equipped with parchment and ink. The back wall was crammed with shelves full of books.

Most important, opposite the writing desk was a pantry stocked with a variety of fruit, breads, and other delicacies. Dirk had even found a square box that functioned like a refrigerator. A sign above it announced, FOOD AND DRINK TO BE CHARGED IN ADDITION TO TRANSPORT FEE. It was probably going to be the most expensive meal they'd ever eaten, but after going without for so long, nobody thought twice about diving in.

Soon the wagon approached the gaping mouth of Tiamus, and Max and his friends carried handfuls of food to the windows for a better view. Dwarven guards in heavy plate armor watched stoically as they rolled into the city.

"They've all got beards," Dirk noted, turning to Dwight (who had a couple weeks of stubble going but no real beard as such). "How come you don't have a beard? I thought it was, like, a dwarf requirement?"

Dwight harrumphed. "You don't know nothing about nothing."

"I know most dwarfs have beards," Dirk answered.

"Yeah? Well, keep it to yourself," Dwight replied, turning back to the window.

The carriage drove into the busy city square. They could see numerous folk (mostly dwarfs, faeries, elves, and humans, but also a handful of hobgoblins, orcs, and frobbits), and the space was crammed with merchants selling their wares from brightly painted stalls.

"We totally have to buy something," Dirk said, his face pressed against the window.

"Not here," Dwight grumbled.

Suddenly the fluff dragon began pointing excitedly. "Look at that! There's a slaver over there! Trading in dragons!" Puff motioned to a line of tethered fluff dragons led by an orc trader. "That's illegal," Puff continued. "And look, the dwarfs aren't doing anything about it."

"You'll find no love for dragons here," Dwight said. "*You* may see a band of sheeplike creatures, but *dwarfs* see fire-breathing monsters once wrapped in magic and ill intent."

"Maybe a long time ago," Puff admitted with a sigh. "We've . . . evolved. All we want is a more enlightened existence."

"Yeah?" Dwight said. "Well, I'd say you *lightened* up quite a bit, pipsqueak!" Then he started laughing loudly.

The carriage continued forward, rolling past a military barracks, and then on to a large fountain at the edge of the square. Carved into the stone was a statue of a muscular dwarf straining to hold a large block over his head. At his feet was a pool of water fed by two fountains that flowed from each of the statue's armpits.

"Really?" Sarah said. "Is that supposed to be dwarf humor?"

"Don't be squeamish," Dwight said proudly. "That there's the famous Bombark the Moist. His strength was legendary."

Dirk snickered. "In more ways than one."

They rode past the fountain and felt the road begin to turn downward.

"We're going down now?" Sarah asked.

"That's right," Dwight replied. "All dwarf cities build down instead of up." Normally Dwight would have cringed at the very thought of what he'd just said, but the magic surrounding the carriage kept him from worrying about it. Instead he and the others simply watched as the carriage descended deeper into He'ilk.

On either side of the stone road, bright-yellow flames burned along stone troughs, the smoke disappearing into vents above them.

"Tiamus's Flame," Puff said, seeing Max staring at it. "It can never be extinguished. The dwarf builders found it burning below the mountain. Their engineers channeled it throughout the city. Quite impressive, actually."

"A compliment from a pillow," Dwight announced sarcastically. "What's next? Maybe a towel will write me a sonnet?"

The wagon wove through several more streets until it came to a stop. The sliding panel opened and Sumyl peered back at them. "We've arrived at the smelt house."

"Great," Dwight said, grabbing the backpack full of silver. "Stay here and I'll be back with coin."

"No way!" Dirk shouted. "You're not leaving us here. I'm going, and so is Max."

Max had just made his way back to the very comfortable velvet bench and was preparing to lie down. He'd gotten quite full on breads and other goodies and now his body wanted nothing more than to take a nap. "Oh, uh, that's okay. You guys go ahead."

Dirk frowned at his old friend. "Dude, we're in a

Dwarven city. There's no way I'm letting you just sit there. Remember when you slept through the raid of Embul and everyone but you got magical armor? Or the time you watched that Mansquito movie instead of going to the comic convention? Or how about when you refused to look at that weird snake by the lake because you were afraid of getting thistles in your sweat pants? How many regrets can one man live with?"

Max knew Dirk, and he knew he wasn't going to let him take a nap. "Fine," Max said, leaving the soft goodness of the cushioned seat. "I'll go."

Dwight pushed the carriage door open and said, "Come on, then." But the moment the dwarf stepped outside, the sense of ease he'd been enjoying vanished. Instead he felt the crushing weight of being surrounded by stone. He immediately turned around and thrust the bag of silver into Max's hands. "On second thought, you can do it."

"Me?"

"Just take it in there and have it smelted into bars," Dwight said as he took a seat. He breathed deeply before continuing. "Next to the smelt house is the coin vendor. Trade the bars for coin and come back."

Max took the backpack and followed Dirk into the street. As long as he didn't get robbed, swindled, captured, or break some unknown rule of Dwarven etiquette, he'd probably be fine.

"Do you think a dwarf would let me pull on his beard?" Dirk asked. Max figured their odds of survival had just dropped significantly.

ON BEING A FIRST MATE

⸸

THE SEVEN KINGDOMS OF THE MAGRUS are shaped more or less like a mass of potatoes floating in a soup, and as a result many decide to take up a career in shipping. The most dangerous job at sea is that of first mate. As every Magrus captain knows, there are two rules he or she must follow: First, the captain always goes down with the ship. And second (and perhaps more important), a captain may promote the first mate to captain at any time. Thus Magrus maritime disasters often involve the captain running after the first mate with some exciting promotion news.

CHAPTER TEN

FIRE IN THE MOUNTAINS

MAX HAD TO ADMIT HE WAS A LITTLE SURPRISED TO BE PULLING AWAY from He'ilk in one piece. He'd smelted the large bag of silver into weighted bars, traded it for two smaller bags of silver and gold coins, then spent the afternoon shopping. He didn't particularly enjoy shopping, even in a Dwarven city. It might have been because the only shops he could find anything in that fit him had names like The Portly Gentleman, Husky House, and Pandall's Paunchy Pantaloons.

In the end Max didn't like how any of the armor felt, so he decided to go with several sets of comfortable travel clothes. Thankfully Sarah was around to help pick things out. Dirk was thin enough to fit into elf clothing, and ended up looking very much a woodsman in tall boots, leathers, and a long green cloak. He buckled an elvish blade to his side, but only after he promised he wouldn't swing it around while any of the others were standing nearby.

Sarah found a leather jerkin made by pixie tailors that was both incredibly light and strong. It tied up the front and had a fur-lined hood, and even though it was the most expensive item of the lot, nobody was willing to tell her she couldn't have it. She bought a number of other travel clothes, as well as two daggers she attached to a belt around her hips. Max already knew Sarah was tough, but the thought of her with daggers sent a shiver down his spine. She looked . . . dangerous.

Dwight ended up choosing light Dwarven armor, a new axe, and a mysterious bag that he'd obtained at the Guild of Toupee Makers. Everyone thought better than to ask about *that*. They also purchased packs, supplies, and a team of Dwarven ponies—which were like regular ponies but with beards. They were also stockier and more temperamental. Finally they bought a small cart that held both their supplies and Puff, who was thrilled at the idea of getting to drive.

They said good-bye to Sumyl and stayed the night in

a comfortable inn, where they each had a bath and a large supper. They slept with full bellies on soft beds, and after a big breakfast, headed out again. They rode away from the city gate with new equipment and supplies, looking and feeling much better than they had in weeks.

"Now we look like an adventuring party," Dirk announced. Max smiled at his friend's enthusiasm, but his thoughts turned back to the *Codex*. He kept it close, bundled in a shoulder pouch he'd purchased and now wore beneath his coat. Sometimes he could feel the ancient book—a chaotic surging of energy that sent his skin tingling. Max had long since memorized Bellstro's list, moving through the Prime Spells in his head if for no other reason than to break up the long hours of travel.

They journeyed along the winding road from He'ilk, camping along the roadside each night. They enjoyed sleeping in their new tents and eating from their stash of new supplies, and the mood remained light. During Max's watch he saw lights flickering on the mountains. The next day Puff told him it was probably dragon fire.

"They're returning to Tiamus's sacred mountains," Puff said. "Taking refuge against a world out to destroy them." Max wasn't sure how he felt about heading toward a bunch of dragons. Based on what he'd seen with Obsikar, they weren't something to mess around with.

It took four days to reach the foot of the Thoran Mountains. Later, as they made their ascent up the winding trail, they heard a sound that stopped them cold. It came like thunder roaring across the sky and shook the ground. The ponies began to shift nervously as Max and the others looked around, craning their necks to try to get a glimpse of what was causing the commotion. Thinking it might be an approaching storm, they pressed on. Soon, however, other sounds joined the roaring thunder: the clanking of steel and the shouts of combat.

"What do we do?" Max asked. The sounds were coming from off the trail.

"We stay on the path," Dwight answered flatly. "It's not our concern." They continued around a small bend, doing their best to keep their ponies in line, when two travelers scrambling past, fleeing in the opposite direction.

"Dragon!" one of the men exclaimed. "If it slays the knights, we'll be next!"

"Did you hear that?" Puff cried.

"Yes. So we'll wait until the beast is dead so we can

safely pass," Dwight replied. Sarah shot him an angry look.

"We're here to do exactly the opposite," she challenged the dwarf. "Our promise was to help *save* the dragons, remember?"

"Not one at a time," Dwight countered. "And not by stepping between a dragon and some foolish knight."

Dirk slid off his pony, however, and began running toward the din of the battle. "We have to save it," he shouted. "Come on!"

"Dirk, stop!" Max called after him. Dirk had the habit of acting first and thinking later, only this time it could get him killed. But if Dirk heard his cry, he never acknowledged it. His friend kept running, disappearing over the ridge.

"We have to go after him!" Sarah exclaimed. She jumped off her pony and grabbed Max, practically pulling him off of his. "Hurry!"

Dwight shook his head but grabbed his axe and dismounted. "Watch the gear," he called back to Puff.

The three of them scrambled over sharp rocks and a small incline, chasing after Dirk. As they ran, the sounds of the battle grew louder, and with it the smell of smoke and ash filled the air.

Dragons breathe fire! Max's mind shouted at him. He took a deep breath and continued after his friend. He remembered a vision he'd had when he'd first used the *Codex*—a woman burned and suffering in the Wizard's Tower. A woman burned by dragon's fire.

They were breathing hard by the time they reached a large cave. A battle was raging, and Max could see a dozen or so knights lying motionless on the ground. Dirk continued running toward them, not even slowing down.

At the mouth of the cave, three knights in shining armor pressed their attack against the dragon. The beast was about the size of a city bus, its head pulled back and smoke billowing from its nostrils, and it moved much more quickly than something that size should have been able to. The sunlight danced off scales that hinted at the muscle beneath, and its wings flexed open and shut as it reared. Dirk was running straight for the dragon and waving his hands. Fire erupted from the creature's mouth, but at the last second a large knight stepped forward and raised a giant rectangular shield.

Heat crashed over Dirk, nearly knocking him off his feet. But he'd gotten close enough to the shield to avoid getting burned. When the fire stopped, one of the three knights had fallen to the ground, his armor singed and steaming. The larger knight swung his smoking shield aside and made way as the third, dressed in ornate armor, drove forward with a lance.

Max's eyes fixated on the long weapon. He'd grown accustomed to the way magic felt, and he could practically see the waves of power pulsating from the lance's tip. The knight drove the point into the dragon's breast. It was a tremendous blow and the creature reared, bellowing in anger. But the lance didn't penetrate the hard scale. Instead it broke in two as the dragon crashed down, its momentum throwing the smaller knight against a smoldering tree. The knight crumpled to the earth as the other ran to him, calling out in a voice laced with rage. The dragon snatched him, however, holding the knight in its jaw and raising him into the air.

Dirk had seen enough. He charged headlong to where the dragon was biting down, its teeth pressing dents into the hard plate armor. "Stop!" he yelled at the top of his lungs. The dragon turned his attention to the strange elf-dressed boy who was jumping up and down and waving at it.

"Fool!" Dwight spat. "He doesn't even have his sword drawn!"

Max could only think to keep running, watching helplessly as the dragon lowered its head to regard his friend, the knight limply hanging from its mouth.

"Dude, you totally won, so stop!" Dirk yelled. The dragon's nostrils flared, and for a terrible moment Max thought he was about to lose his best friend to a burst of flame. But instead, the dragon sniffed at Dirk. Its eyes grew wide in surprise. The others ran up to where Dirk was standing, unsure what to do now that they were there.

"Impossible," the dragon said as it dropped the knight from its mouth, its voice rolling over them.

"Please, don't hurt him," Sarah said, holding her hands up. Then she turned to Dwight. "Put your axe away."

The dragon regarded the dwarf and then sniffed at him. "You too?" the dragon said as Dwight reluctantly lowered his weapon. "How is this possible?"

"It's okay," Dirk said. "We're here to save you."

The dragon regarded the strange human, measuring the impossibility of what was happening against the off chance that it had taken a blow to the head. After all, humans certainly didn't run *toward* raging dragons, and they didn't declare themselves to be their defenders. But it was the magical scent that puzzled the dragon the most—something ancient, powerful, and tainted with the deepest regions of the Shadrus. "You carry the scent of one you cannot know—one that had you been in his presence would have destroyed you."

"Obsikar," Max said, the dragon king's name falling from his lips. The dragon whirled toward him in response.

"YOU DARE SPEAK HIS NAME?" it roared, forcing Max and the others to step back.

"Don't worry, we're totally buds," Dirk replied. "Obsikar sent us back from the future."

It was too impossible to be true. Or perhaps it was so impossible that it might actually be true? The dragon had to think. "You *spoke* with the dragon king?"

"Yes," Sarah answered.

"And you claim to have done so in another time?" the dragon continued.

"Yeah, that's my fault," Max admitted. "We ended up in the future and Obsikar found us there. Then he sent us back."

The dragon considered that for a moment, then asked, "And why would he do that?"

"To save you guys," Dirk answered. "He knows who's hunting you."

"If Obsikar knew this, he would destroy them," the dragon answered, its voice continuing to rumble around the cave. "The kings of Kuste and Mor Luin have made their decrees, but they are just puppets. Someone is pulling their strings. But regardless, Obsikar would have no need of you to exact his revenge."

"I know this sounds totally weird," Max said, stepping forward, "but Obsikar didn't know any of this *now*. He worked it out later—much later, after it was too late. But he had one more move to make, and that involved us. We were stuck in the future and he needed something done in the past. So we made a deal."

"You are a puzzle," the dragon replied. "You carry the scent of Obsikar, there is no doubt. And I sense a very old power in you—a power that stretches back to the sundering itself. Perhaps power enough to send you through time, as you've said." Nearby the large knight regained consciousness, raising his visor and blinking in disbelief.

"It's like I said, we're all on the same team here," Dirk said to the dragon. "So you don't need to fight anymore."

"They attacked *me*," the dragon countered.

The large knight rose to his feet. "The king's decree is

that all dragons must be slain. Do not converse with this monster—take up your arms and strike it!"

"And you expect *me* to show mercy?" the dragon asked. "There is no goodwill left between humans and dragons."

"That's not true," Max said. "I'm a friend of a dragon—he's a fluff dragon now, but he used to be like you. And he doesn't have all the fire and magic and stuff, but he's still a dragon at heart. And he's a pretty good guy. Half the problems in this world are because people don't see what's on the inside, only what's on the outside. Go to middle school and, believe me, you'll know how that feels. So I think we have to forget about our differences and figure out what makes us the same. Even when some king or somebody tells us not to, or we've done it for so long we don't know anything else. It has to start somewhere. We don't have to kill each other if we don't want to."

The dragon considered Max for a moment. "I am beginning to understand what Obsikar saw in you. You are not what you appear to be, childlings."

"Max," Sarah said, putting her hand on his shoulder, "well said."

Dirk turned to the knight. "Don't worry, dragons

aren't your enemy. I know you got totally wasted here and want revenge. But save it for the guy who really deserves it—Rezormoor Leadfinger."

"Dreadbringer," Dwight corrected.

"Be grateful," the dragon said, leaning down to the knight. "These children have saved your life today."

"Yeah, and I command you to stop hunting dragons," Dirk said. "You know, because you owe us a life debt and such."

The knight shook his head, moving to where the smaller knight was slumped against a tree.

"So the Wizard's Tower seeks our demise—then you must not press farther into the mountains," the dragon announced. "Many of my kin have taken refuge here, and they will likely attack you on sight. Take the path to Jiilk instead. From there you can turn north again to Kuste."

Dwight nodded, but he didn't look pleased about it.

"Now go, in Obsikar's name," the dragon said, turning around and disappearing into the cave. "I must ponder what took place this day—and how I can warn the others."

"Help me," the big knight suddenly called out, and

the group ran over to where he was removing the helmet from the smaller knight's head. Long locks of curly blond hair fell out, and a handsome youth blinked several times in the sunlight. "He may be injured."

"We are victorious?" the blond knight asked as Sarah's face came into focus. "And we rescued a beautiful maiden, too?" Sarah blushed, and Max decided quickly that this golden-haired knight was not somebody to be trusted.

"We saved you, if you really want to know," Max said, sounding more defensive than he intended. The boy looked at the larger knight, who nodded, wearing a pained expression.

"I'm afraid it's a long story, my lord," the knight said. "I am Sir Maron," he announced to the group, "and here before you is Prince Conall, heir to the Mor Luin crown. Check on the other knights and help me tend to his wounds."

Sarah bent down to Conall. "Are you okay? What can I get for you?"

"I am well, thank you. And you have done enough already," the prince said with a smile.

"I haven't done anything at all," Sarah answered, confused.

"Then why do I feel so much better?" the prince said with a laugh. Sarah smiled, blushing again.

Prince Conall, Max thought. He was exactly the kind of complication they didn't need at the moment, and it had nothing to do with the way Sarah kept staring at the golden-haired noble. *Nothing at all.*

CHAPTER ELEVEN

REZORMOOR FLUFF DADDY

THE KRAKEN RAN BENEATH THE LIGHT OF A CRESCENT MOON. TUCKED under each arm was a muzzled and bound fluff dragon, their small legs wiggling in hopes of breaking free from the monster's grip. He had found himself at the edge of a lake some days ago, and for the first time he paused to peer into the water and regard the face that looked back at him.

He was bigger than the average human, by at least half. He had long red hair that looked almost like lava in the moonlight, and beneath his skin ran rivers of red veins that crisscrossed like cracking ice. It seemed in many ways that a stranger was looking back at him, in part because the Kraken had other memories. And what he remembered most were those who had wronged him:

Max Spencer, Sarah Jepson, and Dirk . . . well, just Dirk. He'd known them from somewhere—a school, it seemed. They'd embarrassed him in front of people who mattered, then disappeared without a trace. Everyone had blamed him. But now he wore the amulet: a black skull with three small horns and crimson eyes hanging from a silver chain around his neck. The moment he'd put the amulet on he'd stopped being Ricky Reynolds and become the Kraken. He rose and ran toward the city.

Some time later, Rezormoor heard the rapping at his window. He turned and was surprised to see the Kraken hanging there, one fluff dragon under his massive arm and another in his mouth. The sorcerer waved him in and the Kraken pulled his massive frame inside, breaking several panes of glass in the process. Rezormoor tried not to look too irritated about the glass.

"*I fown wha ewe sempth meh fur,*" the Kraken muttered, then pulled the fluff dragon from his mouth, spitting out a wad of fluff in the process. "I found what you sent me for."

"Ah, excellent," Rezormoor replied, walking over to the two fluff dragons.

"What's this all about, then?" the first fluff dragon

said, shaking himself off like a wet dog (he'd been the one in the Kraken's mouth).

"Yeah, we've done nothing against the Tower," the second fluff dragon chimed in.

"Don't be afraid," Rezormoor said, his voice oily and slick. "You are much safer here than anywhere else."

Just then the zombie duck poked its head out from behind the sorcerer's chair, and the fluff dragons took two involuntary steps backward.

"Uh, I'm not so sure about that," the first one said, eyeing the duck warily.

"Yeah. If it's all the same to you, I'd like to go back to being a tetherball," the second added. Rezormoor looked at the Kraken, who shrugged.

"I found them at a barbarian camp. That one was hanging from a pole."

"You've served me well," Rezormoor replied. "You've kept your part of the bargain."

The Kraken wasn't ready to trust the sorcerer fully, but his best chance of escaping the well probably lay with the Tower regent. And if not, he could always find some castle in the middle of nowhere, kill all the inhabitants, and take it over. Either way, the Kraken had options.

"Don't keep me waiting too long," the Kraken warned, stepping back through the window. "I don't like it when people mess with me." Then he disappeared.

"Wow, that guy's got issues," the first fluff dragon said, waiting long enough for the creature to be out of earshot.

"You know what a guy like that does reflects on your whole organization," said the second fluff dragon. "Might want to keep that in mind."

"Yes," Rezormoor said, offering a forced smile. "In any case, consider yourselves guests of the Tower."

"Guests as in we get a set of keys and food privileges?" the first fluff dragon asked. "Or guests as in if we try and leave you'll squash us?"

"The latter, I'm afraid," Rezormoor said. "But tell me, do you have any dealings with the Guild of Toupee Makers?"

The two fluff dragons looked at each other. "There are rumors that they have an interest in us."

"Oh, more than an interest," Rezormoor said, bending down and putting his hand on the fluff dragon's head. His long hair moved forward, and suddenly the fluff dragon understood.

"Your hair," the fluff dragon said. "That's ours. . . . It comes from us!"

"Yes," Rezormoor replied. "Somewhere the guild harvests your fluff, making the world's most exquisite hairpieces. My fear, however, is that this is done, shall we say, rather harshly."

The sorcerer stood, his black robes billowing around him as he turned, his hands clasped behind his back. "Part of the Tower's obligation to the world is to protect all creatures of magic, and to keep balance. Dragons are such creatures—even in your current state. I am not about to forget your heritage. I think it best if the Tower were to step in and protect fluff dragons. And should you decide to sell your fluff to the guild, the Tower would ensure you are treated fairly."

"We've heard stories of our brothers being captured and taken to the Dwarven cities," the second fluff dragon offered.

Rezormoor considered this. "Given the natural enmity between dwarfs and dragons, I can see how they might look the other way. Yes, that does make sense."

"Wouldn't all this protecting of the fluff dragons and helping us with the Guild of Toupee Makers put the Tower in control of the fluff supply?" the first fluff dragon asked.

"You see, many forget that long before you were captured in your current form you were beings of great intelligence and wisdom," Rezormoor replied.

"I'll take that as a yes," the fluff dragon said.

Rezormoor shrugged. "A mutually beneficial relationship. And in the meantime, as my *guests*, I would like to study you a bit further."

The first fluff dragon sighed—maybe life in the Tower wouldn't be as bad as living with the barbarians. At least they had sewers. "We understand," he said. Rezormoor nodded and summoned two servants to take the dragons to his laboratory.

The sorcerer returned to his chair and considered the day's events. Unlocking the secret of replicating the fluff dragons for the guild would give him tremendous leverage. Controlling the supply of fluff as well would make him wealthy. Money would allow him to fund an army, and with the *Codex of Infinite Knowability*, he could use the Prime Spells to achieve his ultimate goal: break free from the Maelshadow's yoke and take control of the three realms. It was a dangerous game he was playing, but the pieces on the board were moving as he intended.

His thoughts turned to capturing the descendant of Maximilian Sporazo and securing the *Codex of Infinite Knowability*. Everything hinged on that.

CHAPTER TWELVE

KITTENS AND RAINBOWS

LOKI SAT AT A CORNER TABLE AT THE TAVERN OF THE FISH-FACED HUMAN. He and Moki had been lapping up milk all afternoon, watching the entrance carefully. Loki had decided that it was worth a couple of days' time to wait and see if a human boy walked through the door. It seemed to him that the Dwarven capital of Jiilk was the most natural stopping point for someone coming out of the woods above Shyr'el. And for any human entering the city, the first friendly establishment was the Tavern of the Fish-Faced Human. Many Dwarven taverns had a strictly "dwarf-only" policy. But the Fish-Faced Human catered to all kinds of nondwarfs as well.

∽

At the same moment, Princess the Destroyer was galloping away from Issir, a medium-sized city located in the
heart of Aaredt. Behind her Magar held tightly to the
mane of a woefully undersized donkey that galloped as
if its tail was on fire—which was a distinct possibility.
Behind Princess and Magar, black smoke billowed into
the air and the sounds of a battle rang out across the open
plain. Princess lowered her head, sending a lightning bolt
from her horn and igniting a farmer's bale of hay as she
passed. When the farmer began yelling, she did the same
to him.

"Now, *this* is what I miss!" she shouted to Magar, who
looked absolutely ridiculous in his flowing moon-and-
stars robe while clutching the donkey's neck for dear life.

They'd managed to make fairly good time riding the rainbro over the Wallan mountain range and
across the open sea of grass that marked the Aaredt
plain. With the Gossamer Gimbal in hand, Princess
had done her best to lead the rainbro away from pop-
ulated areas. The nasty dispositions of rainbros were
not as well known in the southern kingdoms as they
were in Turul. But the beast had a mind of its own, and

when they came across Issir something had caught the rainbro's attention. Unfortunately for the town, a bored guard watched as they approached and shouted, "Hey look, everyone, a rainbow!" By then the multicolored creature had had enough. Princess and Magar slid off the creature's back as the rainbro turned to the city's outer wall and smashed it.

With the rainbro on the attack, Princess realized there was only one thing to do: join in on the fun! She began firing bolts of lightning from her magical horn, blowing guard towers into bits, igniting rooftops, and sharpshooting various crossbow-wielding guards from behind the battlements.

"Are you sure this is such a good idea?" Magar asked, watching the rainbro kick a cow over the horizon.

"I've passed through two whole kingdoms without so much as lighting a single frobbit on fire," Princess protested as she zapped another guard from off of the wall.

"Issir has a Tower here," Magar said. "The wizards will be assembling."

"Do you really think I'm afraid of a few wizards?" Princess laughed.

"No, I don't," Magar said as a crossbow bolt flew over

his head. "But if they recognize us, they'll be able to get the word out. We need to pass unnoticed if we expect to find Max Spencer."

Princess blew up a trebuchet and then sighed. Magar was always spoiling her fun. "Very well, it's always work with you, isn't it?"

After putting some distance between themselves and the city, Princess and Magar came to a stop and turned to survey the damage behind them. Rays of blue light were shooting from the walls and driving the rainbro back. "The wizards have joined the fray," Magar said.

Princess shifted into her human form and withdrew the Gossamer Gimbal from the folds of her dress. She watched as the three interlocking rings began to spin, taking note of the direction the floating arrow was pointing.

"Sporazo's heir seems to be moving to the east," Princess announced.

Magar considered their relative location. "Hammer's Hilt Bridge is to the east," he said after a moment. "Then the dwarf capital."

"We're closing in on him, Magar," she announced, putting the Gimbal away. She wasn't about to forget the promise made to her by Rezormoor Dreadbringer: an all-you-can-eat human buffet in a place called Texas. She longed for something to devour that wasn't tainted with magic, and the well-marbled Texans sounded delicious.

"I think I'll walk awhile in my human form," Princess said, already forgetting the chaos behind her.

"A prudent move, Your Highness," Magar confirmed as he sent the frightened donkey on its way. "Two travelers fleeing the city will hardly be worth noting. But a unicorn will certainly draw attention."

They turned from the burning city as the rainbro toppled over, walking in silence as Magar considered his situation. While it was true he was trapped into serving Princess as part of a Tower contract, he secretly hoped that Max Spencer might be able to give the unicorn a little payback. But that was a thought he kept buried in the deepest part of his mind.

CHAPTER THIRTEEN

PRINCE OBNOXIOUS

THE FUNERAL PYRE BURNED IN THE DISTANCE.

"Those knights brought honor to their families," Conall announced to the group after several miles of quiet reflection.

"The lance," Max said after a time, the image vivid in his mind. "It was magic, wasn't it?"

"Yes," Conall answered. "Dragons are magical creatures, so our high mage strengthens the lance's barb to help even the odds. But even the most enchanted weapon fails to pierce the dragon's chest."

"Because you strike the serpent's escutcheon," Puff announced. "It's impervious to magic and steel, no matter how many knights try to prove otherwise."

"Even so, in making the attempt they did their duty,"

Conall said. "For their service their families will be given stipends from the crown and have their names added to the great book of Mor Luin heroes."

"Heroes . . . I totally get that," Dirk said. "That's what we're all about."

"A hero is defined by what he or she does," Conall continued. "And more often than not that comes at the expense of the self. It's not an easy thing to obtain."

"Dude, we've already saved the world once," Dirk replied. "And when we defeat Rezormoor Dreadbringer we'll do it again."

"Dread . . . ," Max started to correct before realizing Dirk got it right. "Oh."

"The Tower's regent?" Sir Maron grunted. "Pay them no heed, my lord. These are fools on a fool's errand."

"You'll have to excuse Sir Maron," Conall said. "Like a sword, he sometimes cuts by mistake. But I have to say, this does not sound like a wise quest. The Tower exists peacefully with the Seven Kingdoms. They are practically everywhere . . . and they serve each king honorably. No kingdom is without a high mage, sent from the Tower to serve at the king's pleasure."

"Sorry, but we know the truth," Dirk countered. "It's

Rezormoor who's behind killing the dragons. Not only that, he's been hunting Max here."

Conall looked down at Max with a critical eye. "And what makes you so interesting to the regent of the Wizard's Tower?"

Max never liked talking about himself, and he was pretty sure that he didn't want to start letting the world know who he was or what he was carrying. But when he caught glimpses of Sarah and saw the way she kept looking at Conall, it irritated him. Conall was just like every other jock in middle school who had made his life so miserable. On any other day Max would have shrugged and turned the conversation a different direction, but not today.

"Well, if you really want to know, I'm the last living descendant of Maximilian Sporazo, and that makes me the only person in the world who can cast spells from the *Codex of Infinite Knowability*—maybe you've heard of it? It's only the most powerful magic book ever written. And so the reason this Rezormoor wants me is because I can do stuff he can't. In fact, I can do things *nobody* can."

"As I said," Sir Maron grunted from his horse, "fools."

"He's telling the truth," Sarah said from her pony. "Every word."

Conall regarded Sarah for a moment. "Then I believe every word. And you will not say otherwise, Sir Maron."

"As you wish, my lord," Sir Maron replied with as much enthusiasm as if he'd been ordered to muck out stables.

"How do you know the Tower is behind this?" Conall continued.

"The king of the dragons told us," Dirk replied.

Conall considered this for a moment. "What if this dragon king is using you?"

"A fair point," Dwight added. "None of us really knows what's going on here. We don't know if Obsikar was telling the truth."

"If you kill the dragons, you will plunge this world into an age of ice," Puff added from his spot on the wagon. "That should be enough."

"Stories we were told as babes," Sir Maron announced. "Dragon fire warming the world is nonsense."

Conall turned to Sarah. She shrugged. "That part I don't know. But Puff has no reason to lie to us."

"A charitable outlook," Conall said, flashing Sarah his

perfect smile. Just then the wind picked up, tossing his blond hair over his shoulder. Max cursed the wind and its horrible timing.

"But Puff *is* a dragon, after all. And he does, in fact, have every reason," Conall said, turning to Puff. "Not that I'm accusing you, just making an academic point." Puff frowned but continued to listen.

"As I was saying," the prince said, "both this king of the dragons and your friend here have every reason for you to do what you're doing. They're fighting for their very survival, and they need help. The question really is, in whom do you trust?"

"What do you mean?" Sarah asked.

"Well, let us compare the Tower with the dragons," Conall continued. "The Tower has been in the service of the empire for thousands of years. Moreover, Max here is actually a blood descendant of the Tower—and a magic user at that. You've never sat with Rezormoor Dreadbringer, I assume. You've never heard from his lips what he wants from you—what his side of the story might be?"

"We know Princess the Unicorn works for him," Max objected. "And Princess pretty much destroyed our entire world. Or at least she will . . . in the future. Maybe, if we don't stop her now." Max was getting frustrated with his inability to make a point. "She's a very bad unicorn!" he finally exclaimed.

"I see. So *she* is your enemy," Conall said, "but do you know for a fact that she serves the Tower? Is it possible this bad unicorn ignored what she was hired to do and went off on her own? What if she was simply sent by the Tower to find you and bring you back?"

Max didn't like where this was going. It had been so clear who his friends and enemies were, but now Prince Goldilocks was confusing everything.

"*You* are connected to the Tower by blood," Conall continued. "I am connected to Mor Luin by blood. We each serve because that is who we are in a very literal sense—they are in us. To turn against something that is so much a part of you? That is not an insignificant choice. Perhaps your true quest lies not in defeating the Tower but in joining it?"

"It doesn't change anything," Max replied. "I still have to go to the Wizard's Tower and fix the *Codex*, some-body sent a Shadrus necromancer after us, and Princess is still hunting me."

"Then come with me. You'll find all the allies you need in Mor Luin," Conall offered. "If you truly have the *Codex*, bring it to my father. We'll take it to the Tower together and you'll have an army to protect you."

"Max, that's not a bad idea," Sarah said. "We don't have to do this alone."

"*We* don't have to do anything," Max said. "I'm the one who has to go. And right now I'd rather just do it myself." Max spurred his pony forward and moved ahead of the group.

"I didn't mean to offend him," Conall said to Sarah.

"No, it's okay," Sarah replied. "I think it was important for him to hear what you have to say. Things have been hard for us, that's all."

"You saved me," Conall said, tipping his head. "And for that I will be in your debt forever."

Outside the towering main entrance to Jiilk, Dwight had led the group to a stable, where their mounts were fed and watered. He then excused himself, grabbing a bag and disappearing behind the structure. When he returned he was wearing a long, thick beard. He held up his hand before anyone could say anything.

"I was cast out of the city," Dwight said. "I was forced to shave because of it. If we're to go in and get resupplied, I can't be recognized."

"Dude, you totally look like a dwarf now," Dirk replied.

"Because I *am* a dwarf," Dwight spat. "So get your gawking over with and let's get this done." It had been decided that Conall and Sir Maron would stay with Puff and watch over the mounts and their gear. Conall had complained that the dwarf king would receive a prince of Mor Luin and they would be treated as honored guests, but Max and his friends thought it was better if they kept a low profile. Once Sarah insisted it was a good idea Conall politely agreed.

They walked into the side of a towering mountain, surrounded by huge dwarf statues that marked the entrance to the city.

"The first dwarf kin," Dwight announced, trying to keep his mind off the growing anxiety he felt as the world closed in around him. "We call them the Seven."

"The Seven? Really, dude?" Dirk asked.

Dwight frowned. "What of it?"

"The Seven Dwarfs?" Dirk said, laughing. "Your big dwarf heroes are called the *Seven Dwarfs.*"

"You better watch what you say next," Dwight threatened. But Dirk had found a statue with a stern expression and pointed to it.

"Hey, look, it's Grumpy!" he exclaimed. "And over there, that must be Bashful."

"Nobody mocks the Seven," Dwight yelled, running after Dirk. Dirk took off and they disappeared into the crowd ahead.

"Do you think he'll catch him this time?" Sarah asked.

"Nobody runs as fast as Dirk," Max replied. "If people could catch him, he would have been pulverized years ago."

Sarah nodded as they passed beneath the shadow of the mountain's entrance.

When they found Dirk and Dwight, they were standing outside a tavern with a sign that showed a human knight with a fish head. Dirk was smiling and looking around, while Dwight was bent over and taking deep breaths, his hands on his knees.

"I don't want to talk about it," Dwight said before any of them could ask questions. "We'll go in here— nobody knows me." The dwarf straightened and walked purposefully through the tavern door. Dirk shrugged and the others followed him in.

The first thing Max noticed was that for a dwarf bar, there were practically no dwarfs inside. Dwight motioned for them to take a seat while he went to converse with the tavern's owner about supply options. Dirk, Max, and Sarah found a table near the back of the room.

"This is awesome," Dirk said, looking around. "A real dwarf tavern."

"Without any dwarfs," Sarah added.

From across the room, Loki blinked several times, noticing for the first time the group of humans. He reached over and shook the napping Moki awake. "That's him—it has to be!" he whispered excitedly. He gave himself a vigorous fur licking, cleared his throat, and made his way over to the table with Moki in tow.

"Excuse me, sir," Loki announced, bowing.

"A talking cat!" Sarah exclaimed, unable to help herself. Loki grimaced, trying not to let his irritation show.

"Fire kitten, to be more exact," Loki continued. "I am Loki and this is my companion Moki. We're strangers here, looking for a friendly face. Might we join you?"

Max didn't think it was a good idea, but he could tell Sarah had made up her mind the moment she saw them.

"Of course you can," she said. Moki and Loki jumped up onto an empty chair. Moki then lay flat so Loki could sit on him and reach the table.

"Now, that's just adorable," Sarah said. "But are you sure he doesn't mind you sitting on him like that?"

"It's his life's dream to be so useful," Loki replied before he could get Moki's opinion on the matter. "In any case, what brings such a distinguished group to the Fish-Faced Human? Traveling?"

"We're on our way to the Wizard's Tower," Dirk said. Both Sarah and Max elbowed him at the same time. "It's just a couple of cats. They're probably just curious," Dirk complained. "Besides, who are they going to tell?"

"Certainly not the mice," Moki added from his spot under Loki. "They're the biggest blabbermouths around."

"Now, don't worry, our lips are sealed," Loki said. "It just so happens we're headed in the same direction. By the way, I heard the strangest talk from a druid not long ago. Says he was here to announce the arrival of the *boy who could read the book*—you haven't heard anything about that, have you?" It only took a second for Loki to catch the uncomfortable look that spread across the three humans' faces—and the fact that two of them cast quick glances at the chubby dark-haired boy sitting at the table. Loki had found his prize.

"Uh, never heard that one before," Max said. "A boy who can read a book? Doesn't sound like something you go around bragging about."

Loki grinned and turned the conversation to other things, taking note of their names as they introduced themselves. So the *boy who could read the book* was called Max Spencer. Loki wasn't about to forget *that* name. Dwight soon appeared at the table, dropping into his seat and putting a large mug down with a *thud*. He opened his mouth, about to speak, but then noticed the two fire kittens.

"Uh, there're two fire kittens at our table," Dwight said. "Why are there two fire kittens at our table?"

"Oh, just fellow travelers is all," Loki replied.

Dwight grunted, turning to the others. He looked pale and was sweating, but he was doing a decent job holding himself together. "The innkeeper will take care of our resupplies. I had to give him a bit of a tip, but if he does all the legwork, that will save us time and get us on our way."

"Speaking of which," Loki said, "fire kittens are

highly prized as travel companions in cold weather. We can easily heat an entire tent just by ourselves. Any chance you'd allow us to accompany you north?"

Dwight grimaced at that. "Sorry, but we don't need—"

"Of course you can come with us," Sarah said. And the way she said it left no doubt.

"This is a mistake," Dwight added as he started to rise. Not having worn a long beard for some time, however, Dwight hadn't seen that the end of his beard had fallen over the table. Nor had he seen that his mug had been set right on top of it. When he stood, his beard pulled away from his face and the mug tipped over, crashing to the floor. There were several gasps, and the entire room went silent. The innkeeper pointed at Dwight from across the room.

"You dare shame us with a false beard!" he roared.

"Hey, what's the big deal?" Dirk said, looking around. "I used a magic marker to color in a mustache during seventh grade. Nobody even knew."

"We all knew," Max said.

Two burly dwarf guards pushed their way through the crowd and surrounded Dwight.

"Beard falsification is a serious crime," one of them announced.

"You'll have to answer to the king for that," the second added.

The two guards grabbed Dwight and began dragging him out. "Find my father," Dwight shouted as Max and the others stood. "He runs the Tearful Troll."

"I bet that's another tavern," Dirk said.

"Uh . . . not quite," Loki replied.

Princess passed through Bazel—the city at the foot of Hammer's Hilt Bridge—without incident. Word of the attack had traveled fast, most likely by pyro pigeons sent out from Issir's Tower to every other one across the Seven Kingdoms. She heard the gossip in the streets, but there were no descriptions of a unicorn and a wizard, so it appeared they had gotten away unseen. Mor Luin had posted a very large bounty on her head after her first bout of rampaging, and she'd had to deal with pompous knights on at least one occasion before.

Still in her human form, Princess discreetly checked the Gossamer Gimbal. It pointed almost perfectly east.

"Jiilk, the Dwarven capital," she said with a smile. "That's where they are."

"Do we risk entering the city?" Magar asked. "The dwarfs are not an enemy we want right now. Getting the boy out could be messy."

"It's not the dwarfs so much as their high mage," Princess said, thinking it over. "I met her once, and she's far more capable then she lets on." Magar raised an eyebrow at that—it wasn't often Princess showed anything but disdain for Tower-trained spell casters.

"Then what do you suggest?"

"We'll circle around," Princess said. "We'll go north and set an ambush."

ON THE ERGODIC ELIXIR

✠

ONE MIGHT WONDER HOW IT CAME TO be that representatives from each of the schools of magic (authorized and unauthorized) gathered to create a potion of unspeakable power. So powerful, in fact, that it was well understood that under no circumstances should anyone even attempt to handle it–let alone drink it. Nevertheless, for academic-leaning spell casters, the idea of concocting something so terrifically bad that it shouldn't exist was a worthwhile challenge.

With funding in place from the Kingdom of Turul (who had a grant specifically for the unspeakably dangerous) the band of spell casters began work on the Ergodic Elixir. It required five years to finish (fortunately the spell casters had both a large supply of interns and gratuitous-death and dismemberment release forms.)

Deemed too dangerous to exist upon its successful completion, the Ergodic Elixir was hidden away (and presumably remains so to this day).

CHAPTER FOURTEEN

FROM ZERO TO HERO

THE TEARFUL TROLL WASN'T A TAVERN AT ALL. LOKI, WHO HAD SOME knowledge of the Dwarven city, offered to lead the group to the small, nondescript building. Outside hung a sign. It was adorned with a troll, its head lowered and a single tear glistening near its eye. As they were about to go inside, the door suddenly flew open. A dwarf walked out, blowing his nose into a handkerchief with a resounding *honk*.

"My pa always wanted me to be a miner," he announced to no one in particular. "But in my heart I've always wanted to *dance*." The dwarf blew his nose again. "I'm not made of granite, you know. I'm delicate and full of life, like a beautiful swan that just wants to fly." The dwarf pushed past the group and walked slowly down the street.

"Apparently he likes to dance," Dirk noted.

"Just what kind of place is this?" Max asked.

Loki cleared his throat. "A place you go to talk about your problems."

"You mean like a therapist?" Sarah said.

"Wait just a second," Dirk said. "Dwarfs are tavern owners, blacksmiths, soldiers, and miners. They are definitely *not* therapists."

"Apparently Dwight's dad is," Sarah said, moving to the door. Max hurried and opened it for her.

Inside was a small, sparse office with several diplomas hanging on the wall. Max looked them over.

"They're in English," he said, surprised that he could read them.

"The Techrus is the only place that offers these kinds of things," Loki said.

Max nodded—he supposed that made sense. "Weird," he announced after reading one such diploma. "Dwight's dad has a degree in animal husbandry."

"Ah, that would be for orc marriage counseling," Loki said.

Max read the name on the diploma: Bartholomew Prodding.

"But you can call me Bart," a voice called out. Max turned to find a heavyset dwarf looking up at him and smiling. He was dressed in a blue Techrus-style sweat suit with white sneakers. "Welcome to the Tearful Troll. You've got a problem, I've got a listening ear."

"I got problems," Dirk answered. "All kinds of problems."

"We *really* don't have time for that," Sarah said. "Sir, do you happen to a have a son named Dwight?"

At the mention of the name, Bart's face suddenly fell. "I'm sorry," he said, "did I forget to mention that we close early today? Perhaps you could come back some other time."

"We're friends of his," Sarah pressed on. "But I think he's in trouble."

Bart scratched at his long beard. "There really isn't anything I can do. My son's not even in this realm."

"No, he's here," Dirk said. That seemed to surprise the dwarf, who walked over to a chair and flopped down.

"Here?" Bart asked. "But he'd never come here. Not after being branded an outcast."

"He's here because of me," Max said. "We're all here because of me, and it's really a long story. But now they've

arrested Dwight and charged him with wearing a fake
beard or something—"

"A fake beard?" Bart gasped. "He'll be sentenced to the
mines for sure. This is horrible news. But what can I do?"

"He told us to find you," Max said.

Bart seemed surprised at that. "They'll take him
before the king right away, so we'll need to hurry."

The Hall of Judgment was an enormous cavern. A long,
solitary walkway led to a tall throne, where the dwarf
king sat. On either side of the throne were pillars carved
as giant war hammers, inclined so that they appeared to
be ready to fall on anyone found unworthy. Stone benches
lined the far walls so citizens of Jiilk could watch the
king's justice being dispensed.

Max and the others followed Bart into the viewing
area, where they moved to get a seat as close to the front
as possible. Max could see the king on his throne, dressed
in black-and-gold armor, his long white beard knotted
and running nearly to his knees. His equally white hair
was pulled back tight and tied in a knot, and his eyes were
like two hard diamonds.

Dwight walked in chains down the long walkway,

his fake beard hanging haphazardly from the side of his face. He was still wearing his armor and his axe hung on his back.

"A king who lets you carry a weapon is not the kind of king who's afraid of much," Dirk said.

"I don't think that's a good sign," Sarah added.

"Not every sign says stop," Glenn piped up from Max's belt. "Flip it around and it's just an octagon stuck on a pole."

"Oh nice, Glenn," Max said to his magical dagger. "I forgot you were even here."

"It's fine," Glenn said. "I do all kinds of crazy stuff when you're asleep."

Bart shushed them as Dwight was taken before the king.

"Am I to understand that you are Dwight of House Prodding?"

"I am," Dwight said. Max could see his friend looked pale and was drenched in sweat. It was the claustrophobia, Max was sure, but it made Dwight look awfully guilty.

"And as Dwight of House Prodding, was it not my decree that you were banished from Jiilk?"

"It was," Dwight said.

"And further," the king continued, his voice filling the cavernous room, "you not only disobeyed my command, but you did so by donning a false beard and sneaking back into my city!"

"I did."

"Then by your own admission, and before I pronounce judgment, I want to hear *why*," the king said harshly. "I want to understand why a dwarf could dishonor his people not once, but twice! I want to understand why a dwarf finds his king's commands something to simply disobey on a whim! I want to know why you stand before me now, so I can make an example of you so extreme— not only through my reign but the reign of a thousand of my descendants—that no dwarf would ever even think of doing what you have done!" The dwarf king suddenly stood. "Why? I demand you tell me, WHY?"

"So how do you think it's going so far?" Dirk said, leaning over to Max and Sarah. Max would have swatted him on the back of the head, but not knowing dwarf law, he didn't want to do anything that might get him into trouble. Not with *that* king.

"I don't think we'll be leaving with your friend any time soon," Loki offered. "Fortunately I know the way to the Tower, and will be happy to serve as your guide."

"Loki knows all his directions really good," Moki added, trying to be helpful. "All three of them."

They turned their attention back to Dwight as he cleared his throat.

"I know what I've done feels like I've dishonored you," Dwight said. "But my actions take place in the shadow of the greatest dishonor the dwarfs have ever known—losing the *Codex of Infinite Knowability*." Gasps and murmurs broke out all around the room. "In the beginning the *Codex* was given to us by Maximilian Sporazo, and we were charged with its safekeeping. But we failed in that duty. And still to this very day, no king completely trusts the Dwarven vaults. Our honor and reputation have never recovered."

The king sat back down on his throne, glaring at Dwight. "You had better make a point and make it quick. You are treading on dangerous rock here."

"My point, my liege," Dwight said with a slight bow, "is that I have done small dishonors in order to bring the greatest honor back to us. For I have brought the *Codex of Infinite Knowability* with me, carried by the last descendant of its author and ready to be returned to its place of safekeeping!" Dwight lifted his arm and pointed to Max, and suddenly every eye in the chamber was on him.

"I think he's talking about you," Dirk whispered. Max scrunched down in his seat, wishing he could disappear. It never worked, however.

"Bring them to me," the king commanded, his diamond-like eyes locked on Max.

They had all been taken to the king's private chambers (including Moki and Loki, who had insisted they had nothing to do with any of it), and now they stood before the king and his guards. Dwight was led in, and if there was a hint of him being sorry for what he'd done, he didn't show it.

"Show me," the dwarf king ordered them.

"Do it, Max," Dwight said. "It's for the best."

"How dare you!" Sarah shot back, barely containing her rage. "You sold us out!"

Max reached into his satchel and drew out the *Codex*. He didn't see any other choice.

The king gave it a hard look, leaning forward in his chair. "Is that it?"

An intense-looking dwarf wearing an armored,

rune-covered battle dress stepped forward. Max could feel the aura of magic around her as she approached. Whoever she was, she was powerful.

"Well, high mage, is it the book or isn't it?" the king asked again.

High mage, Max thought to himself. What had he read in the *Codex* about mages? They were different from wizards, although both were trained in magic. Mages were fighters, as likely to swing a sword as cast a spell. And their magic was almost always destructive in nature. It was something they used when they challenged one another for position, and any mage strong enough to serve a king was very dangerous.

"Don't be afraid," she told Max. The mage slowly reached for the book, and Max watched the sparks begin to dance around the cover, moving precariously close to her fingers. The mage hesitated, withdrawing her hand. "It can be none other," she announced.

"Release that dwarf at once!" the king bellowed, motioning to Dwight. "Our honor has been restored!" A sense of excitement began building in the room, but the mage kept her eyes locked on Max.

"What's your name?" she asked.

"I, uh . . . Max Spencer."

"Max Spencer," she repeated, "who holds the book from Maximilian Sporazo. You are his blood." It was a statement, not a question, and Max simply nodded.

"Hey, guys, I don't want to rain on your parade," Dirk announced, "but that book isn't yours."

The king frowned as startled gasps sounded out.

"And besides," Dirk continued, "we're, like, totally in the middle of a quest right now, so we should probably get going."

"I don't remember asking your opinion on the matter," the king rumbled. "I'll have the rest of you escorted from this chamber—and be glad I don't charge you with the book's theft!"

One of the guards stepped forward, throwing his arm over Sarah's neck and putting her into a kind of headlock. But Sarah was fast and well trained. The dwarf guard wasn't tall, but he was wide and heavy in his armor. And heavy was exactly the kind of opponent Sarah liked.

She threw her left arm in front of the dwarf, wrapping it around his leg and stepping behind his foot—thrusting her arm under the guard's knee. Then she moved, pivoting her hips and using her leverage to trip the dwarf over her leg. The guard, surprised and off-balance, let go of Sarah as he tried to keep from toppling over. But Sarah kept twisting, the dwarf's heavy armor and momentum doing most of the work as she lifted his leg high into the air and brought him down.

The dwarf landed on his back with a metallic *smack*, the air blasted from his lungs. Sarah spun away from the startled guard and faced the king. "Please don't treat us like criminals," she said. "And don't threaten to take what isn't yours."

All turned to the king, whose eyes were locked on Sarah. He held her in his hard gaze for a long time, then without warning he began to laugh. It was the bellowing kind of laugh that started deep inside a person before erupting and filling the room with its sound. The king clutched at his side as tears welled up in his eyes.

"One of the king's own dropped by a little girl!" he bellowed. "I haven't seen someone look so shocked in years!" He continued laughing, and the others joined in with him.

"That *was* pretty great," Moki said with a smile. He was having a good time too.

After a minute or so the laughing settled down and the

king regained his senses. He cleared his throat and waved the guards back. "I've obviously underestimated your companions, Dwight. Best we leave them be before they topple my kingdom!" A few more laughs broke out as the red-faced guard got back to his feet. The king reached for a goblet and drank heavily before he spoke again.

"Tell us, girl," he said to Sarah, "where did you learn to fight like that?"

"My parents taught me," Sarah replied. She was still trying to understand what was so funny.

"Sarah is, like, a kung fu master," Dirk said.

"Judo," Sarah corrected.

"And what you did to my guard just now?" the king continued. "That was judo?"

"Just a simple scoop throw—a *sukui nage*."

"Ah . . . ," the dwarf king continued. "So you are a band of fighters on a quest, and you carry the *Codex of Infinite Knowability* with you. What is the nature of this quest?"

Max looked at the mage and then said, "It's not something we can really talk about. I don't mean to be rude; it's just complicated."

"It is, is it?" the king replied. "Then until you convince

me otherwise, I have little choice." The king rose in his seat. "The charge to protect the book has not been lifted from the Dwarven Nation. The World Sunderer himself secured it in our vaults, and that is where it shall go."

The king turned to address Max. "I appreciate your zeal. You and your friends are welcome to stay as our guests. Should you decide to make a plea for why the *Codex* should be returned to you, I'll hear it. But it is our duty and our honor to keep it here."

The king rose motioned at his high mage. "Secure the *Codex of Infinite Knowability* within our deepest vault."

The high mage nodded as two dwarfs wheeled in a heavy black chest. They opened it and stepped aside. "Place the *Codex* within," the high mage said to Max. Max swallowed and looked inside—cut within a thick layer of velvet lining was a spot the exact size of the book.

"It must be this way," Dwight said. His voice wavered, and he looked exhausted. The place was quickly getting the best of him.

Max sighed and gently laid the *Codex* down. There was nothing else he could do, and his gut told him to keep quiet about their mission. His only chance in defeating Rezormoor Dreadbringer was to catch the sorcerer by surprise. He didn't need the high mage knowing what they were up to. Chances were she was connected to the Tower. Max stepped back as the dwarfs closed the lid and wheeled the chest out of sight.

The king moved to Dwight, throwing his arm around him and addressing Bart.

"Your son is a hero—a true hero of the dwarfs! His shame is forgiven and forgotten. His name and likeness will be carved into the stone of this city, and for generations dwarfs will know that it was Dwight who returned the *Codex* after it was lost. It was Dwight who gave us back our honor!"

Loki scrambled to come up with his next move. As far as he knew the Tower needed only the boy, not the book. And if they did need the book, they'd know exactly where to find it. Vaults had doors for a reason—things were not meant to stay in them forever.

"Dwarfs are fun," Moki said, looking around the room.

"I don't suppose you've met anyone you haven't liked?" Loki said with a sigh.

"Not yet."

The king gave Dwight and Bart a last hug, and then

turned his attention to the rest of the group. "You are my guests," the king announced. "Rest, relax, bathe, and then join us for the grand celebration." Max didn't feel like celebrating.

"We need to find Conall," Sarah said to Max. "His father's a king—maybe he can get the dwarfs to give us the *Codex* back?"

"Maybe." Max sighed. But the last thing he wanted was help from *him*.

CHAPTER FIFTEEN

A MATTER OF CHARACTER

"DWIGHT! HOW COULD YOU?" SARAH SHOUTED ONCE THE LARGE DOUBLE doors to their suite had been closed.

"My son, a true hero!" Bart said before Dwight could respond. "And did you hear, a celebration! I have to go and get ready. I want all the world to see my son returned to his home." Bart smiled at Max and his friends and then slipped out the door. "Tonight!" he called out from the other side. As soon as he was gone, Dwight stumbled to a chair and practically fell into it.

"Ah, the ravages of guilt," Dirk announced.

"It's not guilt, you moron, it's being here again," Dwight moaned. "There's no sky—I feel like the walls are closing in on me."

Sarah hesitated, feeling sorry for him, but then pressed

on. "I'm sorry you're sick, but how could you do that to us?"

"I didn't have a choice," Dwight answered. "You saw the king—do you know what he would have done to me? Cast me in the mines for the rest of my life. I can't do it . . . not that. Anything but that."

Sarah wanted to respond about how selfish he was and how he'd jeopardized everything, but she held her tongue. She looked around and saw several doors surrounding the antechamber. "Why don't you find a bed and lie down."

"Yeah, okay," Dwight grumbled, pushing himself out of the chair and to the nearest door. He opened it to find a large bedroom. "Some sleep will do me good," he said as he disappeared into the room, closing the door behind him.

"So now what?" Max asked.

Loki cleared his throat. "You were headed to the Tower, right? We should go there as soon as possible. Find this Rezormoor and tell him he can retrieve his book from the dwarfs."

"Hey, whiskers," Dirk said, "we can't just walk up and talk to Rezormoor RedSinger—"

"*Dreadbringer*," practically everyone said.

"Yeah, him," Dirk continued. "He's the one who sent the evil unicorn after us and is hunting all the dragons."

"If Obsikar was telling us the truth," Sarah said, but her words sounded hollow.

Dirk frowned. "Of course he was telling us the truth."

"And besides," Max said to Loki, "the whole reason for going to the Tower was to get the *Codex* fixed. Without it the Tower's the last place we should be headed."

Loki realized that so long as Max and the *Codex* weren't together, he'd never get him to the Tower. And Loki needed Max to get close enough to put his own plan in motion. "Then I guess we just have to get your book back," he announced.

"I think we should talk to Prince Conall," Sarah said. "What we need here is a diplomatic solution."

"No king is going to get the dwarfs to give up their charge," Loki replied. The last thing he wanted was for royals to get involved.

"I wish Ratticus were here," Dirk said. "He's my seventieth-level online character, and is like this totally awesome thief."

"Unfortunately for us, this is real and not one of your

computer games," Sarah said. Then Max felt it—a wind that seemed to blow right through him, threatening to knock him off his feet. It was a surge of magical power, and it seemed to have come from their very room!

There was a knock at the door.

"Be careful," Max started to say, unsure of what was going on. Sarah opened the door to find a small man in brown leathers and a black hood standing there. He had reinforced pads on his elbows and knees, and when he raised his head, they saw that he had a long black mustache and a patch over his left eye.

"Ratticus . . . ?" Dirk asked, his mouth hanging open in surprise.

"My master!" the small man exclaimed in a heavy French accent, slipping past Sarah and bowing before Dirk. "You have summoned me to your world."

"Uh, Dirk . . . ?" Sarah began as she closed the door.

Max recognized him too. He'd spent long hours playing online with Dirk, and this appeared to be his actual character in the flesh. As impossible as it was, Ratticus the thief was standing before them! It was enough to give Max an instant headache.

"Wait, you can call men from thin air?" Loki asked,

looking around. He wondered if maybe the dwarf king was right—there was more to these humans than what met the eye.

"Transdimensional summoning is pretty neat," Moki added.

"It's that stupid potion Dirk drank," Sarah said. "Turning the forest to silver, and now this."

"Yeah, but I feel different now," Dirk said. "I think it's gone. Probably took a lot of magic to bring my character to life." Magic so big, in fact, that Max could feel it.

"We have a mission, yes?" Ratticus asked, looking eager.

Dirk looked around the group and nodded triumphantly. "Oh yeah, we have a mission—to steal the *Codex of Infinite Knowability* from the Dwarven vaults of Jiilk!"

"Have I played this area before?" Ratticus asked as he rose to his feet. "It feels new."

"We're the first," Dirk replied.

"Even better, then," the thief said with a smile.

"Why does your thief talk with an outrageous French accent?" Sarah asked Dirk. Dirk thought about it for a second.

"I don't know. I think it's the mustache."

"So we send your thief to go and retrieve this book and bring it back to us?" Loki asked. That sounded like just the kind of plan he could support.

"I think it best if my master is with me," Ratticus replied.

"We're not sending just Dirk," Max said. He'd been his best friend long enough to know Dirk needed watching.

"I know the way to the vaults, but let's be clear," Loki said. "These are not simple safes locked behind heavy doors. The Dwarven vaults use a lock so devious that no thief has *ever* been able to best them. I mean no disrespect to Ratticus, but how does a single thief do what's never been done before?"

All eyes turned to Ratticus. The thief shrugged.

"Well, all I know is we have to try," Max finally said. "But I don't think the king is just going to let us wander around the city."

"Ratticus," Dirk said, suddenly remembering something, "do you have your Cloak of Seeing Is Bee-Leaving?"

Ratticus nodded. "Of course."

"Then I know how we can get to the vaults without

anyone knowing it's us," Dirk said. "But I think this is a party quest—we should all go."

"Agreed," Sarah said. "Let's go before the celebration."

"A *celebration*, you say?" the thief asked.

"Yeah," Max answered. "The dwarfs are going to hold a big party because they got the *Codex* back."

"It's a big deal." Loki nodded. "Every dwarf in the city will want to be there. And if they can't get in, I'm sure every tavern will be full as the entire city turns into one big party."

"Then that is when we strike," Ratticus announced. "After too much food and drink lulls wits and makes eyelids heavy."

"I suppose that makes sense," Sarah admitted. "Then I'll take dibs on the first bath. Some soap and water and clean clothes sound really good right now."

Ratticus sniffed the air several times. "Good idea," he agreed. "You rest and prepare yourselves for tonight, and I'll watch the door. Never fear, Ratticus is here!"

"What about Dwight?" Sarah asked Max.

"Good question," Max admitted. It felt like an awfully big secret to keep from him—especially when the whole city was going to celebrate Dwight's returning them to honor. But on the other hand, this was their only chance to get the *Codex* back, and they couldn't risk messing that up. "I think we just let him sleep and do this ourselves."

While the others prepared, Moki and Loki found themselves on a long, comfortable couch, biding their time before they made for the vaults. "We don't have to take a bath, do we?" Moki asked as the two were settling in. They had already scratched the couch legs up while the humans napped and took turns getting clean. Fire kittens, like other felines, believed in a few governing rules that held the universe together. One of which was: The more costly and irreplaceable the furniture, the better it was for sharpening claws.

"Sitting in a tub of tepid water that's filled with your own dirt and filth? Of course we don't have to subject ourselves to that," Loki said, cringing at the very thought of it. "We may be on an adventure where we will be required to do many hard and unpleasant things, but we don't have to sink to *that*."

Moki nodded, liking the answer. "Baths are not great," he purred. "Not at all."

∽

Ratticus had been right—the entire city of Jiilk had decided to join the celebration. Max and his friends had arrived late and left early. They had bathed and were wearing clean clothes, and it was tempting to dive into the various trays of food being circulated throughout the king's hall. But Ratticus had told them to eat light—looking Max up and down when he said it. They needed to be nimble while the rest of the city got good and stuffed.

Dwight had truly been the dwarf of the hour. He channeled his claustrophobic fear into eating and drinking, and by the time he was carried back to their chamber he was out cold and snoring up a storm. The dwarf high mage had been there as well, and her gaze fell on Max more than he liked. So when it was time to excuse themselves, Max was more than happy to go.

In the early hours of the morning, they left their room and made their way to the heart of Jiilk. It was similar to He'ilk in many ways: large streets and high ceilings, with homes and shops expertly carved out of the dense rock. But unlike the bright flames that were channeled throughout He'ilk, Jiilk had an intricate pattern of designs carved into the walls that gave off a warm light. Since it was night, however, the yellow light had been replaced with a cold blue one, and that gave the city an eerie feel.

"Dwarf ants," Loki said, noticing Max looking at the light pattern on the wall. He and Moki were riding in Max's backpack.

"Excuse me?" Max replied.

"The light," Loki answered. "The first dwarfs carved the patterns long ago. Most assume its filled with some kind of glowing stone or magic. But actually there are billions of dwarf ants in there."

"*Dwarf* ants?" Sarah asked.

Loki shrugged. "You know, like regular ants, but shorter, grumpier, and—"

"Let me guess, they have beards," Sarah interrupted.

"The kind that just go under the chin," Loki continued. "Otherwise they get stuck in their mandibles."

"I still don't understand," Max said, picturing a chin-bearded ant in his head.

"Each dwarf ant carries a backpack filled with a fluorescent stone."

"That means it glows," Sarah said, anticipating Max's question.

"Oh."

"Millions and millions of the ants march through the

rock patterns with their backpacks. Then at night they change shifts with the new color."

"Huh," Max said, trying to imagine millions of little ants with glowing backpacks. "In the Techrus, we mostly just step on ants."

"Big mistake here," Loki replied. "The ant unions have one of the more powerful lobbies. And ant lawyers can lift more than fifty times their own body weight in legal papers."

"The streets are surprisingly empty," Ratticus said. "But it won't be long before we'll need my magic cloak."

They continued through the city. Max paid special attention to Ratticus, watching as the thief moved.

"Ratticus," Max whispered. "How do you walk so quietly?"

"Years of training," the thief whispered back. "Plus, I'm wearing powerful magic: Boots of Skittish Scampering, Leg Warmers of the Dandelion, Breeches of the Underfed Ballerina—"

"Okay, I think we get the point," Sarah interrupted.

"Even my mustache is waxed to be more aero-dynamic," Ratticus said.

They continued past the occasional set of guards, all asleep with their hands on their bellies and their helmets pulled over their eyes. Then they rounded a corner and found themselves on an empty street leading to a heavy circular door carved into the stone. Two guards stood as still as statues, obviously not having indulged in the celebration like the others. Ratticus put his hand up and backed the group around the corner. He began unwrapping what looked like a folded blanket from around his waist. He laid it on the street and began unfolding again and again, until it grew in size so that it was big enough to cover all of them.

"The Cloak of Seeing Is Bee-Leaving," Ratticus announced. "It's magic—a prize won when we cleared out the Caves of the Bat Demon." Max remembered playing that particular dungeon. The bat demon bit him and turned him into a bat minion.

"So what does it do?" Sarah asked.

"Whoever hides beneath it will disappear!" Ratticus said, his French accent adding a nice bit of showmanship. "Well, not disappear entirely. We will look like a swarm of bees."

"A swarm of bees?" Max said.

"How is looking like a swarm of bees helpful?" Sarah asked.

"I thought the same thing at first," Ratticus said. "But then I realized that people don't like bees—at least not in swarm form."

"Anything that swarms should be avoided," Dirk agreed. "That's, like, a basic survival rule."

"And bees trapped inside your armor?" Ratticus continued. "Very bad."

"Remember," Glenn suddenly piped up from Max's belt, "if you want the honey, you have to get past the bees. Unless you just buy it in a jar. So yeah, there's that."

"I see you have your own magic," Ratticus said, looking at Glenn.

"Yeah." Max sighed. "Do you want to trade for those ballerina pants?"

Dirk scowled. "We're not trading Glenn, dude. He's been with us since the beginning."

"Plus, he did stab that orc," Sarah reminded him.

"Okay, fine," Max said. "Let's just get going."

Ratticus nodded, and Max and his friends got under the blanket. From the inside, it appeared as if nothing at all had changed. But from the outside, the group had taken on the appearance of a swarm of bees hovering in the air.

"I don't understand why you'd come up with a magic

blanket that makes you look like bees," Sarah said. "Why not just turn everyone invisible or something? Wouldn't that just make things easier?"

"Nobody goes on adventures because they're easy," Dirk said. And with that the group set off across the street. One of the guards noticed the blurry object moving toward him at a distance. He rubbed his eyes, assuming he was just getting tired.

"You see that?" the other guard announced, leaning forward. The first guard rubbed his eyes again, this time hearing a strange buzzing sound.

"You ever been outside?" the first guard said.

"Not if I can help it."

"I did once. Went to pick a flower for my mom and got stung."

"That's why I've always hated flowers," the second said.

"But it wasn't the flower, it was a bee hiding inside of it."

"That's an interesting story and all, and don't take this the wrong way, but who cares?"

"Well, it was just one tiny little bee, and it sounded a whole lot like that black cloud coming toward us. I mean, if you took that one and added a thousand or so more."

They both watched as the cloud of bees drew closer, the buzzing definitely louder in the early-morning quiet.

"Yep," the first guard finally confirmed. "What we got here is a whole cloud of flying, stinging bees."

"So what do we do?" the second guard asked. "I didn't take this job just to get stung by a bunch of bees."

"First we don't get to go to the party. Now we have to stand here and get stung by bees. I'm starting to think this job isn't for me."

"Well, I could have told you that. I've been wanting to go to the tavern all night."

"Good idea," the guard announced. And with that they dropped their axes and walked off.

Max and the others made it to the large door, guard free.

"Bees," Ratticus said with a smile. He turned his attention to the large lock, studying it for a moment before producing several lock picks. He deftly inserted the small metal shafts into the mechanism, using his fingers to feel his way past the various pin tumblers inside. After a moment he nodded, then turned the handle with a satisfying *click*.

"Voilà!" Ratticus announced. He pushed on the door as it swung open on huge, silent hinges.

"Well, that wasn't too hard, was it?" Max said hopefully.

"Oh no, my chubby little friend," Ratticus answered, peering into the room. "We haven't even started."

CHAPTER SIXTEEN

GUESSING GAMES

THEY STOOD IN A SMALL ROOM WITH TWO HEAVY DOORS. ON EITHER SIDE of the doors, the bearded face of a giant dwarf guardian was carved into the wall: one looking down with clenched teeth and a furrowed brow, as if it was about to go into battle, the other with a large smile as if he had just come across a great treasure.

"This is bad," Ratticus said as they shut the main door behind them. "I've heard of these locks before, but I've never seen one."

"Face locks?" Dirk asked.

"No," Ratticus answered as he stroked his mustache. "Dwarven probability locks."

"Probability locks?" Sarah repeated, looking at the two doors.

"Yes," Ratticus continued. "The only lock that can't be picked."

"I don't understand," Max said.

"Let me explain," the thief said. "We have two doors in front of us. If we pick the correct one, we will enter the vaults. If we pick the wrong one, we will die instantly. They are both unlocked."

"It's like a puzzle," Dirk said, looking around for clues. But the only thing in the room besides the large carvings of the dwarf heads were the patterns in the walls giving off the subdued blue light.

"It doesn't seem like a very effective lock," Sarah said. "I mean, you have a fifty-fifty chance of picking the right one."

"Or picking the wrong one," Loki said, poking his head out of Max's backpack.

"And that's just it," Ratticus said. "A lock that is always open—there is no challenge to a thief here. It doesn't matter how many thousands of locks you've picked before. You choose correctly or you die, and those are not the kind of odds a well-trained thief accepts."

"It's simply luck," Sarah said. "Anybody could do it."

"So nobody does," Max said, starting to understand.

"Unless there's a key to it all—a pattern of some kind," Sarah said, slightly annoyed that she might be agreeing with Dirk.

"Exactly!" Dirk exclaimed. "Like counting the number of teeth on the mad dwarf's face and then dividing by two."

"Or following their eyes," Loki added, staring at the carving of the happy dwarf. "Maybe they're looking at the right one?"

"Can you touch them?" Max asked Ratticus. "Maybe one is warm and one is cold?"

Loki scratched at his ear. "Or if you listen closely, you might hear something on the other side."

Ratticus shrugged. "It's all quite possible."

"Oh, oh, I know!" Dirk called out. "It's not either door! They're both fakes, and the real one is triggered by a secret latch or something."

"Here we stand before two unlocked doors," Ratticus said, "and we are no closer to knowing which to open."

Max had read a million fantasy books with puzzles like this, or played them online with Dirk. There was always a key somewhere. And then Glenn spoke up, as if reading his mind. "The key to a locked door is always found in the last place you look," he said. Everyone stopped and turned to the magical dagger.

"Glenn, do you know the answer to this?" Sarah asked. "Do you know where the key is?"

Glenn shrugged his tiny, ivory shoulders. "I've got no idea. I'm just saying the key's in the last place you look because once you find it you stop looking. I mean, who'd keep looking for something after they found it?" They all groaned and returned to studying the room.

"We are going to have to make a choice soon," Ratticus said after they had spent several minutes looking for clues. "Eventually the dwarfs will notice the guards are absent. Somebody is going to have to decide." Everyone looked at Max.

"Why are you guys looking at me?" he said, shrinking under the weight of the attention.

"You're the magic user," Ratticus said. "You have . . . intuition."

"What I have is a stomachache," Max replied.

"You've got magic feelings and stuff," Dirk said to Max. "You have to use those to tell us what door to open."

Max turned to the two doors and stared at them. "So one opens and one wipes us out?"

"If we keep studying the room, we may find the answer," Loki said. "The dwarfs are tricky like that—they love their puzzles."

"Instant death?" Max asked, still not liking what he had heard.

"More or less," Ratticus replied. "The ceiling may drop out and smash us, the room may fill with water, or fire may shoot from the dwarf's mouth—it's hard to say."

Max swallowed. "You know, maybe Sarah was right all along. We could go get Prince Conall and have him tell his father about what's going on."

"Or just abandon this trap and find another way," Loki suggested. Max sighed and stepped forward.

"Okay, I'm just going to pick one," he said. "We can't just stand around here all night." He tried to reach out with his mind like he did when he was able to connect to the *Codex*. But if there were any magical clues, he didn't feel anything, nor could he sense the *Codex* beyond. Max didn't want to get smashed or burned alive, and he certainly didn't want any of his friends to get hurt. But he knew he had to make a choice. He took a deep breath, looked the two identical doors over, and then pointed at the one closest to the smiling dwarf.

"That one," Max said, his voice betraying his uncertainty. But before he could take it back or say he wasn't sure, Ratticus grabbed the handle and pulled the door open. Everyone ducked out of instinct, but instead of instant death they were met with another room, slightly bigger than the one they were in.

"Max, you did it!" Sarah exclaimed, running over and giving him a hug. Suddenly Max felt better about things.

"Yeah, I did," he said.

Loki let out an audible sigh of relief and Ratticus turned, patting Max on the shoulder. "Well done," he said.

The celebration was short-lived.

The next room was nearly identical to the first, but as they entered they found that they were facing *three* doors. The angry and happy dwarf carvings were on either wall as before, but now they were joined by a *crying* dwarf looking down at them from the ceiling. Ratticus closed the door behind them as they stood and took it all in.

"Oh no . . . not again," Loki said. "I don't think I can go through that again."

"Dwarfs and their probability locks," Ratticus said. "You have to hand it to them—our odds have just dropped again."

"One in three," Sarah said, looking at the three doors. "One in three—that's not very good."

"Not at all," Loki agreed.

"But now there's a new face," Dirk said, looking up at the carving of the crying dwarf on the ceiling. "There's a system here if we can just figure it out."

"I didn't use a system," Max said bleakly. "I didn't even have a magical feeling. I just guessed."

"Oh, great," Loki said, putting his paw to his head. He was starting to regret his decision to leave the Tree of Woe.

"I like guessing," Moki added, looking around with a big smile. "Guessing is fun."

"We just need to figure this out," Sarah said, walking around to the various carvings. "There has to be a clue here."

"I still think it has to do with their teeth," Dirk said. "Look, the crying one has a couple of teeth showing."

"There's no way of knowing if it's about teeth or not," Max said, growing frustrated.

"Then why the carvings?" Dirk asked, turning to him. "Decoration? I don't think so. When you've played as many dungeons as I have, you know that things are put places for a reason."

"Dirk is probably right," Loki agreed. "But how long will it take us to figure it out?"

"We're running out of time," Ratticus added.

"I'm working on it," Sarah said as she continued studying the room. "We'll figure it out—we just have to keep working through the possibilities."

"Yep, guessing games are fun," Moki said again.

Loki was ready to chastise his companion when a thought hit him. He looked at the group moving through the various carvings, examining the floor, or watching for patterns in the lights. There were plenty of clues all around, but Loki wondered if that was part of what made the probability locks so successful—people spent hour upon hour looking for something that wasn't there. Overthinking it was exactly the *wrong* thing to do.

"Just pick a door," Loki said, not really sure how he felt about his own words. "There's no system to figure out. You simply play the odds."

"You know, the cat could be right," Ratticus agreed. "Beyond this room may be one like it with four doors, and one beyond that with five. How long can one's luck hold out? The mind is always searching for something other than luck to see it through—a rational system to make sense of. It will see patterns where none exist, and by accepting that pattern and using it to open the logical door, it will ultimately prove false. This vault uses our very minds against us." Ratticus tapped at the side of his head. "Here is the lock that cannot be picked. This is why nothing has ever been lost from the Dwarven vaults."

"Except for the *Codex*," Max said.

"Yes, except that," Ratticus agreed. "It seems history is in our favor, at least."

"I get what you're saying," Sarah said to the thief, "but how can any of us pick a door without our minds locking into some kind of subliminal pattern?"

"I like doors," Moki spoke up. "They're neat." All eyes turned to the small fire kitten.

"You have one choose who doesn't see patterns . . . in anything," Loki said, staring at Moki.

"Have we decided, then?" Ratticus said, looking around at the group. "Do we put our fate into Moki's paws?"

"Sounds good to me," Dirk was the first to say. "That kind of plan is just crazy enough to work." He smiled. "I've always wanted to say that."

"What do you think?" Loki asked his orange-and-white companion. "Do you want to pick the doors we go through?" Moki's face brightened into a wide grin.

"Could I? That would be fun!"

Max was just relieved that *he* didn't have to do the choosing. He looked at Sarah, waiting for her approval. She nodded.

"This is just so counterintuitive," she said. "But in a way, it makes total sense."

Ratticus smiled at the fire kitten. He motioned toward the three doors and said, "Which door shall we open, then, my small feline friend?"

Moki didn't even hesitate. "That one!" he exclaimed, pointing to the one in the middle. The fire kitten looked around the group happily.

"Then that one it is," Ratticus announced. He moved to the door, wrapping his fingers around the handle. "I just want to say, it was a pleasure playing this campaign with you. I hope we respawn near each other if we choose incorrectly."

"*We* don't respawn," Max said.

"Wow," Ratticus said, shaking his head. "Then you *are* brave." And with that he pulled the door open.

᎓ᴏᴏ

The dwarf high mage had dismissed her guards and ordered Jiilk's main gate opened. This was something that technically only the king could order, but none of the guards would dare to cross the high mage. They pulled on the massive gears, listening to the ancient mechanism rumble as the impossibly heavy stone doors slowly opened.

"Close them behind me and say nothing," she commanded as she walked past. The dwarf guards were happy to obey her on both counts.

Outside the city, lingering fires burned, scattered throughout haphazard tents that amounted to a small city near the capital walls. A few structures had even been built—mostly inns and stables, constructed at the base of the great mountain and providing services to travelers making their way in and out of Jiilk. It was a haven for crime, but the high mage didn't think anyone was foolish enough to try their luck with her. But then again, there were always fools with more bravado than brains, and so she watched carefully as she moved down the wide road leading to the coastal cliffs and Hammer's Hilt Bridge beyond.

Her thoughts drifted to the impossibility of the day's events. The *Codex of Infinite Knowability* had been found!

And more incredibly, a living descendant of the author carried it with him. A boy, really, untrained and out of his element. And if her instincts were correct, from the Techrus as well. Rezormoor Dreadbringer had always assumed the lost *Codex* had been hidden there. And it did make sense; the Techrus was largely devoid of magic and the path there was long and arduous. One had to travel to the strange city that sat between the realms—the Mesoshire—or through other magical means that only the monks of the Holy Order of Attenuation controlled. As far as she knew, only dragons had the power to travel to the Techrus directly, but they were left in their human forms and their magic was greatly diminished. Unicorns were powerful and could, in theory, carry some of their magic with them. But they had never managed the journey themselves, and the monks seemed especially wary of unleashing the creatures on the humans who lived there.

It was an hour or so before dawn by the time the high mage made it to the coastline. Thoran butted up against the Crystal Sea as a series of high cliffs that eventually fell as one journeyed south. Traveling the long road to Mephis was the typical route to the sea. But the high mage had no time for that. She knew she must travel to Rezormoor Dreadbringer and bring him news of the *Codex*'s return at once. To do so would certainly further her reputation among the other seven high mages. And for a mage, reputation was everything.

She stood on the cliff and listened as the waves crashed against the rock far below. It had always been a surprise to her tutors at the Tower that she had taken such an interest in the water—it was not the kind of thing dwarfs were usually concerned with. No mage had ever spent time mastering polymorphic spells—that was something typically reserved for only the most talented wizards. But the high mage had done just that, stealing into the library and conducting her own studies while the rest of the Tower slept.

Now her power was such that she could have easily stepped up to the rank of sorcerer. And that was the path that led to becoming regent of the Tower itself. She put that ambition aside, however. For now, she would keep her skills a secret. Timing was everything—as were relationships. And she was about to become a trusted ally to Rezormoor Dreadbringer.

The high mage raised her hands and spoke words in a language known by very few. Symbols began to trace themselves across her skin, glowing gold in the purple hue of the near-dawn sky. They continued to grow, finally climbing up her neck and across her face.

Then she stepped into shadow.

What came through the other side was nothing like the mage who had entered. It was enormous, and it unrolled massive tentacles across the ground and over the cliff's edge. The great creature pulled itself over the cliff, its powerful tentacles stretching, grabbing, and holding fast.

Below, a fisherman had been rowing his boat silently along the smooth surface of the water. He stopped and rubbed his eyes at the sight of the great black shadow that moved down the cliff. There were days, he decided, that one turned around and went back to bed—and this was one of them. He had managed to get his boat going in the other direction when the creature slid into the water and descended beneath the surface.

CHAPTER SEVENTEEN

FINDERS CREEPERS

MAX OPENED HIS EYES. HE WAS STILL ALIVE.

He looked at Moki, who was grinning happily. "That was fun, can we do it again?" the fire kitten asked.

The rest of the group let out a sigh of relief. "There was only a thirty-three-percent chance of guessing the right door," Sarah said, thinking it over. "But the odds of guessing the first *and* second door in a row are, like, seventeen percent if you round up."

"Never tell me the odds!" Dirk exclaimed. "Seriously, math confuses me."

"You may want to recalculate that," Ratticus announced as he looked past the open door.

The next room had four doors, with the addition of another face carved into the floor. The group walked in and stared blankly at the four choices in front of them.

"How many more of these can there be?" Loki complained.

"What are the odds of guessing all the right doors in a row?" Max asked Sarah. Dirk put his hands over his ears as Sarah cocked her head and worked it out.

"Around four percent," she said. "But that doesn't matter because we've already picked the first two correctly. Past choices have no bearing on future odds—not when you're talking about something as random as picking a door or flipping a coin. So for us, it's still a one-in-four chance."

"Three chances to die and one to live," Loki said.

"A lock with only a tiny chance of opening it," Ratticus said, "no matter how skilled you are. That's why thieves avoid probability locks."

"Okay," Max said, thinking it over. "Just how many more rooms like this do you think there are?"

The group all looked at one another—there was no way to tell.

"So lets say there are four doors here and five doors in the next room," Max said to Sarah. "What are the odds we guess those right?"

Dirk put his hands to his ears again.

Sarah did her mental calculations.

"If there's just one more room to go, that would be a one-in-four chance and a one-in-five chance. Which is, like, a five percent chance overall," Sarah said glumly.

"And if there's another room with *six* doors beyond that?" Loki asked Sarah.

"Less than a one percent chance to guess it right," Sarah answered, the weight of it evident in her voice.

"Nobody can do that," Max moaned.

"You know, it's not too late to turn around," Loki suggested. "We can still go back to our quarters and none will be the wiser." But something in Max wouldn't let him leave. He had to get the *Codex* back.

"Moki, did you want to guess another door?" Max finally asked.

"Can I? Oh yes!" Moki said happily.

"Then I think everyone else should go back," Max said. "Moki and I will go the rest of the way from here."

"Max, no—" Sarah started.

"No, I mean it," Max insisted. "You can wait for me outside if you want. And if something happens, well, you can just go with Conall and you'll be safe. And eventually you can go to that Mesoshire city Dwight always talks about and find your way home."

"Dude, no way!" Dirk exclaimed, walking back to his friend's side.

"I'm not leaving you either," Sarah offered, doing her best to smile. "We're in this together."

"It's my fault we're all here," Max said. "So it's my decision. And I'm not going farther until you guys are safe."

They argued awhile longer, but it became quickly apparent that Max wasn't going to budge. He wasn't the same boy who'd mistakenly cast a spell that day in the Dragon's Den, Sarah realized. More and more he was turning into someone else—a leader. And if that was the case, Sarah and Dirk were going to have to listen to him. With time running short, Sarah, Dirk, and Loki finally agreed.

"Ratticus," Max asked, "I'd like you to stay if you could. Do you need to stay close to Dirk to keep . . . working?"

The thief shrugged. "Parties get separated sometimes. Maybe if the others remain outside the entrance."

Dirk gave Ratticus a man hug. "You've always been one of my favorite characters," he said, actually sounding a little choked up. "Except for the time that wizard turned you into a zombie and you destroyed that peaceful village. But that wasn't your fault."

"Thank you, master," Ratticus answered. "I'm sure our adventures will continue."

Sarah gave Max a hug as well. "Trust Moki. You'll be fine."

"Thanks," he said awkwardly. Dirk patted him on the shoulder.

"You can totally solo this, dude," he said. Max nodded and watched them turn and leave. He counted to a hundred to make sure they were safe before turning and addressing Moki. "Okay, I guess. Are you ready?"

"Yep," Moki said, pointing to the first door. "That one."

Ratticus walked over to it and put his hand on the handle. "You're a good wizard, Max Spencer," he said as he tugged it open.

They passed through three more rooms, each with one more door than the last. Moki never wavered, and Max decided he'd have to rethink his whole position on the dogs-versus-cats debate.

The last room was not like the others, however. It was huge, and it reminded Max of the time he visited a professional football stadium. But instead of seats, this room had rows and rows of shelves that climbed up the walls, packed with an assortment of items. Max could see everything from suits of golden armor, lockboxes, and chests, to a good-sized ship in the far corner. It was such an overwhelming sight that Max failed to notice the small green creature working at a desk just inside.

"Don't just stand there, shut the door," it announced. It was small, maybe half Max's size, and wore thick glasses and a whistle around its neck. Stacked all around it were volumes of dusty books and baskets of paper tags. It peered over its glasses at Max as Ratticus closed the door behind them. "So . . . ?"

"So?" Max repeated, not understanding.

"Your paperwork?" the creature said impatiently.

"Oh boy, you're a gnome!" Moki announced from his spot in Max's backpack.

The gnome slammed his book shut and ran out from behind his desk. "You brought a *fire kitten* in here? Are you crazy?"

"Oh, sorry about that," Max apologized. "He's very well-trained."

"This is a flammable area," the gnome continued. "You'll have to take that thing out of here."

"Sure," Max said. "But I need my book first."

The gnome eyed Ratticus. "That's a sneaky-looking fellow over there."

Ratticus nodded but remained quiet.

"Moki, why don't you hunker down and keep out of sight," Max suggested. Moki nodded and disappeared inside the backpack. "There, he can't cause any trouble now," Max said to the gnome.

"This is all highly unusual," the gnome replied.

"We're guests of the king, if that helps any," Max offered.

"The king, huh?" the gnome replied. "Fine, just give me your paperwork and we'll get this over with."

"Paperwork?" Max asked.

"We don't require paperwork," Ratticus announced. "We are on the king's errand, here to provide an . . . *inspection* of a particular item."

"This ain't no museum," the gnome grunted.

"Of course it isn't," Ratticus said. "But this item must be authenticated. It's a somewhat sensitive matter."

"Uh-huh," the gnome replied. "And just what *item* are we talking about?"

"A book," Max answered. "Locked inside a black chest."

"You're mistaken," the gnome said. "*That* particular item is not here."

"But this is the Dwarven vault," Ratticus replied.

"This?" the gnome said with a laugh. "You think *this* is the vault?"

Max and Ratticus looked around the immensely packed room.

"Granted, we keep a few things tossed about, mostly as a courtesy to certain royal families and wealthy patrons and such," the gnome continued. "But this is just the staging area where items are logged and then sent below."

"So there's more of those door rooms?" Max asked, not liking the sound of that.

"Duh," the gnome said. "The final room to the vault has forty-eight doors. There is no better place to keep something than behind a forty-eight-stage probability lock."

Ratticus turned to Max. "And now we know the reason for the reputation of the Dwarven vaults."

Forty-eight, Max thought to himself. That was impossible—beyond impossible. Even Moki couldn't be right *that* many times in a row. There was no way he was going to get the *Codex* back, and his heart sank at the thought.

"And now I'll have my friend escort you two out of here before you get into real trouble," the gnome said. He pulled a whistle from under his tunic and gave it a blow. Max immediately heard the sound of heavy footsteps.

"Whatever's coming is big," Ratticus said, glancing over at Max. "I will do my best to dispatch it for you." And with that Ratticus took off at a run, drawing a long thin blade he wore beneath his cloak.

"Ha! I knew you were trouble!" the gnome exclaimed as Ratticus veered around a tall shelf. Max was frozen, not knowing if he should run after Dirk's character or not. In the online games, he totally would, but this wasn't an online game. The sounds of a struggle came from behind an enormous shelf. It didn't last long.

Ratticus returned, walking around the corner and toward Max at an easy pace. But he was see-through, like a ghost. The thief approached Max and smiled, tipping his head. "Well, that didn't go as planned. I suggest you *not* draw a weapon on the approaching brute."

The gnome jumped back behind his desk at the sight of the thief. But Ratticus was quickly fading. "It was an honor serving with you in this campaign, Max Spencer.

Tell my master thank you for the adventure. But mourn me not, for I will respawn with only a small penalty to my experience points—and perhaps some wear and tear to my equipment." And with that Ratticus disappeared.

"Huh," the gnome said as he slowly rose from behind his desk. "Never seen that before."

Before Max could reply, Ratticus's assailant rounded the corner and approached. The man was massive, loaded with muscle, and tall. Tall enough, in fact, that he would have towered over the big knight Sir Maron. Max didn't even think about drawing Glenn and putting up a fight.

"Get these two out of here, you big oaf," the gnome commanded. "And try not to mess it up like everything else you do around here."

"Yes, sir," the giant said with a sigh.

"Does your little pea brain remember where the exits are?" the gnome said as he opened the large book again and began flipping through the pages.

"Yes," the giant announced glumly. Suddenly Moki poked his head out of the backpack. The fire kitten saw the giant and smiled.

"Tiny!" Moki shouted.

The giant's sad demeanor broke at once, and he smiled one of the biggest smiles Max had ever seen. "Moki, my friend!"

The gnome looked up from his book, annoyed. "Oh, I see . . . worked here less than a week and now you think you can have visitors? You're going to get written up for this." But Tiny had had enough. He reached out and tapped the gnome on the skull with his finger. The gnome began to sway on his feet.

"Come to think of it," the gnome said, "I think I'll go nighty-night now." The little green creature fell over and began snoring.

"Mean and rotten to the core, that one is," Tiny said. "And thinks just because I'm big I'm stupid."

"How'd you get here?" Moki asked.

"Turns out the guild had been working on a bigger teleportation room, and invited me back to test it. I wanted to go to Schil, but I ended up here instead. So I got a job stacking things on shelves for the dwarfs." The small giant shrugged. "It wouldn't have been a bad job except for my jerk of a boss."

"Oh, this is my friend Max," Moki said. Tiny leaned down and shook Max's hand.

"Glad to meet you. Any friend of Moki's is a friend of mine."

"Thanks," Max said, glad his hand hadn't been crushed. "You haven't seen a black case around here, have you?" Max asked. "It's got something of mine inside of it."

"Black case," Tiny repeated, thinking it over. "Sure have."

"You have?" Max asked, surprised.

"Yeah. Just finished processing it and was getting ready to send it to the vaults. But it's yours?"

"Inside there's a book and it's mine," Max answered. "But the king took it from me. It wasn't really his fault, because the dwarfs were supposed to guard it a long time ago. But I really need to get it back."

Tiny considered it for a moment and then said in his deep voice, "Follow me." He led Max and Moki through a virtual maze of shelves until they came to the black chest. Max ran to it and tried to open the lock, but it was shut tight.

"Oh, sorry about your friend," Tiny said. "I had to defend myself."

"It's okay," Max said as he continued to tug at the lock. "He respawns and stuff."

"I bet respawning is fun," Moki added.

Max kept tugging at the lock on the chest. "I can't open it."

"Here," Tiny offered. He grabbed hold of the lock and pulled. Huge muscles rippled across Tiny's arms as the lock groaned in protest and then finally snapped in two.

Max made his way to the chest, pausing at the sight of the *Codex of Infinite Knowability* inside. He took a breath and reached for it, hoping it wouldn't shock him. It didn't, and he quickly secured the book in the leather satchel that he wore at his side.

"I think we should get out of here," Max announced.

Tiny looked at the broken lock. "Wizards will come to teleport the chest into the vaults," he said. "I can misplace the chest, but they'll find it before long. Maybe buy you a day before they come after you—and they will."

Max nodded. "Thank you, Tiny."

"Are you coming with us?" Moki asked. "I'm sure it will be okay with the others."

Tiny grinned, rubbing his chin. "That's a kind offer, Moki, but I'd still like to make my way to Schil. Nice and warm in the winter, and plenty of ways to make a living."

"We'll come and visit you then," Moki said.

"That would be nice. And I hope you have success, Max Spencer," Tiny said to Max. After saying their good-byes, Max and Moki backtracked through the door rooms and found the others waiting for them. Max explained what had happened, and they all agreed they needed to make a run for it.

Back at their guest rooms, they debated what to do about Dwight. Despite the risk, they decided they owed it to their friend to let him know what was going on. They stood around the dwarf's bed, their gear packed and ready to go.

"Dwight," Sarah said, tapping him on the shoulder as his eyes fluttered open. "Dwight, wake up."

"What's going on?" Dwight said, squinting against a massive headache.

"Dwight, we got the *Codex* back," Max said. "And now we're leaving."

Dwight looked confused. "What do you mean you got it back?"

"Yeah, man," Dirk answered. "Max here went down into the vaults and got it back."

"That's impossible," Dwight grumbled, turning over on his side. "I'm obviously dreaming."

Max carefully withdrew the *Codex* from his side and held it in front of Dwight. Dwight blinked several times and then sat up. "I don't believe it," he finally said.

Max shrugged and put the *Codex* away. "So we're going, and you can come with us if you want," he said.

"Go with you?" Dwight replied. "Do you know what they'll think of me if I go with you? They'll think I was behind it all—that on the night they celebrated the return of their honor we were robbing them blind. No, I can't go with you."

"Then we have to go on without you," Max said.

Dwight nodded. "I know, Max. You go and do what you need to. But you have to know that that king will come after you—and probably with everything he's got. You'll need to make for Mor Luin as fast as you can; the king might not risk crossing the border with an army in tow."

"I'm sure Conall can help us there," Sarah said.

"Then do it," Dwight said, returning to his pillow. "This is where we say good-bye."

Max hesitated as they stood around Dwight's bed. They had been together for so long, leaving him seemed wrong. He'd always imagined the four of them returning to Madison: Dwight going back to running the Dragon's Den game shop, and he, Dirk, and Sarah returning to Parkside Middle School. As long as they were together, it seemed possible. It was a hard thing to let go of.

"Come on, Max," Sarah urged. "Dwight's home now. Let's finish what we started so we can go home too."

Max nodded, casting a final glance at the dwarf. For a second it almost looked like a single tear was running down Dwight's nose—but that was impossible.

They made their way from the chamber and through the city. Dawn was breaking outside, and they were the first through the gate. They found Conall and Sir Maron camped near the stables, and before long they were all saddled up and heading out.

"We were resupplied, but you never returned," Sir Maron announced as they made their way down the main road, turning north toward Mor Luin when the path forked.

"We had a slight delay," Max said.

"And picked up a couple of stragglers," Prince Conall said, eyeing Loki and Moki. They had grown comfortable riding in Max's backpack.

"Just fellow travelers," Loki replied.

"Good for keeping tents warm, at least," the big knight offered.

"That's us, two portable space heaters at your service."

Max went on to explain all that had happened and how it was very likely that an enraged dwarf king was coming after them. They considered this for a while before Conall spoke up. "Mor Luin is at least two days' ride," the prince said. "And another two or three days until we reach the first fortified city that can offer us any protection."

"Then we will have to push hard," Sir Maron said grimly. "You've only been in Jiilk less than a day and you've managed to anger an entire nation. Having gotten to know you, I'm surprised it took that long."

Conall chuckled at that and drove his large war-horse forward. Max didn't think it was very funny.

"Gone?!" the dwarf king raged. Dwight had been summoned to the throne later that afternoon, and he did his best not to let the lack of sky and fresh air betray just how panicked he was feeling. "And where is my high mage?"

"Also missing," one of the king's attendants said. The dwarf was bald and wore a long white beard braided into a large knot. "She left word that with the book's return she needed to speak with the Tower's regent at once."

"Mages," the king spat. "Always up to no good. Is it possible *she* took it?"

"I don't think so," the attendant continued. "The chest was found absent the magical book—she wouldn't be able to touch it. And besides, it's the disappearance of the humans that is most suspect."

"Yes, what of that, Dwight?" the king said, glaring down at him.

"You saw them for yourself," Dwight said, clearing his throat. "How could they pass into the vaults?"

"The one, this Max Spencer, who is the heir of Maximilian Sporazo," the king replied. "Who knows what magic he has? But I tell you this, I will not suffer that the dwarfs lose the book twice!" The king jumped from the throne. "Call the army! Assemble my troops! Send scouts into the tent city and find witnesses— someone will have seen what direction they took!"

"My liege," the attendant said with a bow, "we are at peace with Aaredt and Mor Luin, and have been for hundreds of years. How do you think they will react if we raise our armies so close to their borders?"

"This is a matter of *honor!*" the king shouted, grabbing the attendant by his robe. "Wars have been fought for less. I will have the book returned to us and see that the thieves spend the rest of their lives rotting in our deepest mine." The king let go and began shouting more orders. "Bring me my armor! Bring me my generals! I expect to be on the move before day's end!" He then turned to Dwight, pointing a finger at him. "And we'll chip away at the truth until we have it in hand, you can be sure of that."

In the chaos of the activity surrounding the king, a lone dwarf peeled off, swiftly making his way from the royal palace to the small Wizard's Tower on the outskirts of the city. Once inside, the dwarf stood before the human he had come to an understanding with, and dropped a bag of coins into the wizard's hand. "Dispatch a pyro pigeon to Mor Luin. Tell the king that the dwarfs have raised an army and may soon be at the border."

"Trying to start a war, are we?" the man replied, weighing the gold in his hand. It had been a profitable relationship between himself and his associate at the Wizard's Tower in Ledluin, capital of Mor Luin. A few sensitive messages were sent back and forth, and the wizard's pockets got heavier in the process.

"Just send the message," the dwarf said. The human shrugged.

"You're in luck—the high mage is gone. I'll send it right away." The dwarf nodded and turned, hurrying to return to the palace. Things were about to get very messy across the Seven Kingdoms.

CHAPTER EIGHTEEN

KINGS AND THEIR PAWNS

BY NIGHTFALL SIR MARON HAD STUDIED THE HORIZON BEHIND THEM, taking note of a faint orange hue in the distance. "The dwarf army is on the move," he said. "And in large enough numbers that their fires can be seen from here." Any thought of resting for the night vanished at the news and the group pressed on. Dirk recounted more of the specifics involving the probability locks and the arrival of Ratticus. Sir Maron snorted a few times as if the whole thing were completely unbelievable.

"And so with an army at their backs, a magical unicorn on their trail, and the Tower ahead of them, the band of adventurers continue on their quest to reset the *Codex of Infinite Knowability* and defeat Rezormoor Dreadbringer," Dirk concluded.

"And save the dragons," Puff added.

"Oh yeah, and keep their promise to Obsikar the dragon king and save the dragons," Dirk said. "This is no longer just a quest. We are now on an *epic* quest."

"And what waits for you at the end of this epic quest?" Conall asked.

"Fame, fortune, and statues," Dirk said with a smile.

"I just want to go home," Sarah admitted. "I miss my family. I even miss school." Dirk shuddered at the thought.

"School? Oh man, that's the last thing I miss," he said, to nobody's surprise.

"I just miss being normal," Max said. "You know, before I was the kid everyone was after."

"I think you underestimate yourselves," Conall said after thinking it over. "You are already heroes. Not only did you save myself and Sir Maron from the dragon, but you returned with your magical book safely in hand. There is no need to go to the Tower alone. Come to Mor Luin—my father will honor you. Who knows, he might even grant you titles and land. Perhaps even a castle."

"A castle?" Dirk said. "Oh man, I totally want a castle."

Max tried to picture Dirk running around as a castle lord.

"I've already told you what I'm doing," Max said in a tone that made it clear he didn't want to talk about it anymore. They rode in silence as they continued north, and Max practiced running through the fifteen Prime Spells in his head. He was determined that he'd be ready to use them when the time came.

They pressed themselves hard, riding the rest of the following day and finally making camp that night. Sir Maron climbed a small embankment and scanned the horizon. The rest were gathered around the fire and looking forward to a cooked meal.

"I suppose we should get started," Dirk said to Conall with a sigh. The prince blinked several times before responding.

"Get started?"

"Yeah," Dirk said. "As a prince, you've been taught how to use a sword your whole life. Probably had master instructors and all that."

"Yes."

"Thought so. And now you're journeying with a bunch of other heroes who need to learn just enough sword-fighting so they don't get themselves killed."

"I'm not following," Conall admitted.

"Whenever you get a group together like this, the tough sword guy always teaches the nice nonsword people a few tricks—usually to a music montage while dinner's cooking."

Conall turned to Sarah. "I really have no idea what he's talking about."

"It's not that we're expected to be, like, experts or anything," Dirk said. "We just have to know enough to survive is all. This is commonsense epic quest logic."

Sarah shrugged. "It's not the worst idea I've ever heard." Conall ran his fingers through his long curly hair, flipping it back.

"Some exercise would be a nice change of pace," he said, standing and offering Sarah his hand. "You can use my sword—I'd be happy to show you the basics."

Sarah smiled and accepted Conall's offer. Dirk got up as well, brushing himself off. "Hey, I did say *us*, you know."

"Yes, you did," Conall said, motioning him to join them.

"Are you sure teaching Dirk to swing a sword is a good idea?" Loki asked.

"It just might save a life," Conall answered. "And by that I mean one of *us*. You don't want to be near an amateur in a sword fight, even if they're on your side."

"Hey!" Dirk protested.

"And what about you, Max?" Conall asked. "Would you like to join us?"

"Don't worry about him," Dirk jumped in. "He's a magic user. He doesn't need to fight with a sword. Maybe a dagger, but they only do, like, four damage."

"You've obviously never seen a mage," Puff said as he got up and shifted to a new spot beside the fire. He had to be careful that small embers didn't get picked up by the night air and dropped in his fluff.

"Yeah, I'm fine," Max finally answered. He watched as Sarah and Dirk began practicing with Conall. Moki ran off to get a closer look as well.

"It's really getting colder," Max said to Puff and Loki. "I think we're running out of time."

"Just ignore the prince and keep making for the Tower," Loki said. "That's what's important."

Sir Maron suddenly appeared, and Max wondered how the big knight managed to move so quietly. "The dwarfs are gaining on us," he said, sounding none too pleased about it. "These Dwarven ponies of yours are too slow."

"But faster than walking," Puff added. He, for one, liked riding in the small supply wagon.

"Maybe," the big knight said. "I'll take the first watch. After supper, put the fire out—and there'll be no more fires from here on out. A tracking party may be on our heels."

Max retired to his tent early, Puff curled up near his head and Moki at his feet. The little fire kitten really was like a portable furnace, and the tent was soon warm. Sheer exhaustion allowed him to sleep, even though he dreamed of monstrous shadows that danced around his tent in the moonlight.

They continued for several more days, sleeping only a few hours at night and making for the borders of Mor Luin as quickly as possible. Without cooking fires, they suffered through hardened rations and felt generally miserable. They were greeted with early-morning frost as they packed their things and began each day's push, breaking free of the mountains and following the road into more rolling hills and grasslands. It was midday when she found them.

The girl stood in the middle of the road, holding a wand. A wizard stood next to her, wrapped in heavy robes and a tall, floppy hat. There was something odd about the way they were just standing there, and something familiar as well.

Suddenly Max recognized them. Although the last time he'd seen Princess the Unicorn in person she was a metallic monster and Magar was a robotic floating head. But the way she stared at them was familiar—it was hard to forget being looked at like an appetizer.

"I suggest you make way," Sir Maron said coldly, as they came to a stop. Princess ignored him, looking the group over.

"Which one of you is Max Spencer?" she asked.

Sarah, Dirk, Puff, Loki, and Moki all turned to look at Max before they realized maybe it wasn't the best of ideas. Princess smiled. "I see," she continued. "Not exactly what I was expecting for the heir of Maximilian Sporazo."

"We've met before," Dirk said, sitting up in his saddle. "You don't remember because technically it hasn't happened yet. But we did, and Max here kicked your butt."

"He did, did he?" Princess asked, raising an eyebrow.

"One of the Prime Spells is capable of such a thing," Magar said. "As far as the time travel bit," he added, hurrying to clarify. That one of the Prime Spells could defeat Princess was also a distinct possibility, but not something the wizard would vocalize.

"Oh, hi again!" Moki waved. Loki grabbed his companion by the scruff of his neck and pulled him down into the backpack.

"Well, imagine that," Princess said. "That's what I get for letting things live, I suppose.

"So," Princess said, returning her attention to Max. "You are a caster of Prime Spells, are you?"

"Like Futurity?" Max blurted out before he could take it back. He'd been going over the Prime Spells so often in his head that the word seemed to jump off his tongue of its own accord.

"Well, that's certainly not a name many know," Magar said.

"Hmm. So it appears our little friend *has* been reading from the *Codex*," Princess remarked. "Does this make him dangerous or just dumb?"

"You are familiar to me," Sir Maron said, leaning forward in his saddle and looking Princess over. "You are named Princess, and you're wanted for crimes in Mor Luin. There's a bounty on your head."

Princess gave a proper curtsy and then pointed to a shepherd's crook lying in the grass nearby. "I suppose you'll want to add that to my list of offenses," she said with a grin. "I never could resist shepherd's pie."

Sir Maron kicked his mount forward, drawing his sword and charging at the two figures. Princess merely flicked her wand, however, and the horse rose up on its hind legs, neighing loudly as it fought to free itself from ground that had grown soft like quicksand. She moved her wand again and Sir Maron was flung from his saddle, flying twenty feet in the air before landing with a hard crash and rolling to a stop. Princess brought her wand around again and the earth hardened enough for the horse to pull itself free. "I've nothing against the horse," Princess said as it cantered off to where Sir Maron had fallen, "but that is the last favor you should expect from me. Come at me again and I'll kill you were you stand."

Prince Conall slid off his horse and hurried over to where Sir Maron lay. "You'll pay for that," he threatened as he turned to attend to his friend. Princess shrugged.

"I'm to deliver Max Spencer and the *Codex* to the

Tower," she said, addressing the group. "You can't stop me, of course. I'm a unicorn—the most powerful creature in all the Magrus. So give him up and you can leave with your pitiful lives intact."

"Don't you know what the Tower is doing?" Puff exclaimed from his spot on the small wagon. "They're killing the dragons!"

A strange rumbling began beneath Max's feet. He wondered if Princess was about to launch another spell. But instead, she turned and addressed the fluff dragon. "And here we add a fluff dragon to this motley assortment of travelers. Why should I care what happens to the dragons? They are far too full of themselves."

"Because if the dragons disappear, the world will fill with ice," Puff shouted back to her. "You should know that."

"And why should that concern me?" Princess laughed.

Magar looked at the ground with a puzzled look. He was feeling the vibration too, but Princess either didn't notice or didn't care.

"I won't be here to see it," Princess continued. "*I'll* be in the Techrus, eating humans. And all for this boy and his ancient book."

Max could definitely feel the vibrations getting stronger.

"Of course, I don't envy you," Princess continued, obviously liking the sound of her own voice. "Who can say what Rezormoor Dreadbringer and the Maelshadow will do to the boy? I can't imagine it's going to be pleasant."

The ponies shuffled as the vibrations grew stronger. Max began to hear something as well. Something that was large and moving in their direction.

"But for me," Princess said, pointing her wand at herself. "A better deal has never been struck. So where were we? Oh yes, surrender the boy and the *Codex of Infinite Knowability* or die; it's up to you. Either way, I'll get what I want."

Max thought about trying to use the *Codex*, but he knew it was futile. He also knew that Princess was right—there was no way they were going to be able to stop her. And he wasn't about to let his friends get killed. At least Prince Conall was there to take them to safety. No matter what happened to him, his friends would be safe.

"I—" Max began to say, but then something caught his eye. It was a banner rising over the hill in the distance. With it, the rhythmic vibration increased severalfold.

Princess whirled, taken by surprise. She cursed her human ears—they weren't half as good as her unicorn ears. Ahead, the banner rose with others, followed by a long procession of knights riding on horseback.

"My father's army!" Conall announced. He pulled the shaken Sir Maron to his feet.

"Mor Luin cavalry, to be sure," Sir Maron agreed, wincing in pain as he spoke. He'd likely broken a rib or two.

"No!" Princess shouted, turning and raising her wand. But Magar stepped in front of her with his hands raised.

"Too many," he warned softly. "And they'll be supported by mages."

Princess stamped her foot in frustration as the Mor Luin army approached. They numbered in the thousands, riding six astride in armor that glistened in the sun.

"We've made it past the border, then," Conall said, smiling. "We're home!"

"That's debatable," a familiar voice bellowed behind them. They turned to see the dwarf king marching at the head of his own army. A seemingly endless line of dwarf soldiers stretched out behind him, the earth shaking as the two armies approached.

"Where did *they* come from?" Dirk said, swiveling back and forth in his saddle.

"More to the point," Loki added, "how do we get out from being in the middle?"

Princess swung around again and slowly lowered her wand.

The dwarf king addressed Max. "We have found our thief and his band of troublemakers. I thought an army a bit much to catch so few, but now I see it was a fortuitous decision."

"He is no thief," Prince Conall replied on Max's behalf. Three knights rode past Princess, the leader gleaming in gold-and-silver armor.

The dwarf king moved forward with two guards of his own as his army came to a halt. Each group of three rode to face the other before coming a stop, with Max and his friends between them.

"Curious, this," the dwarf king said, addressing the lead knight. "Mor Luin marches an army into Thoran."

The gold-and-silver knight removed his helmet, revealing a man with a hard face and gray hair cut short and near the same color as his eyes. "By my reckoning, it's the Dwarven Nation that brings their army into Mor

Luin," the man replied. He turned to regard Conall. "I'm glad to see you are well, son." Conall bowed.

"Father, it's been a strange journey. But it's good to see you."

Princess watched, curious how Max and the *Codex* were mixed up in all of this. She'd had thoughts of making a run for it, but as many as forty mages had moved forward through the ranks of the Mor Luin army, many eyeing her warily.

"We have only come for the book, and we will be on our way," the dwarf king announced. "It has always been our duty to keep it safe—a duty from which we have not been discharged. It's a matter of honor, which is something Mor Luin understands better than most."

"This boy saved my life," Conall said to his father. "I've offered him sanctuary. Moreover, he is the last descendant of Maximilian Sporazo and carries with him the legendary *Codex of Infinite Knowability*." A great murmur broke through the ranks of both armies at the mention of the *Codex*.

"Which, as I've said, has been our charge to protect," the dwarf king insisted.

The Mor Luin king motioned to Princess. "And how

is this one involved in all of this?" he asked. "She's a criminal and wanted for numerous crimes."

"I am doing the Tower's business!" Princess exclaimed. "I've been charged with returning the boy and the book to their rightful place in Aardyre." The Mor Luin king chuckled as he turned to Max.

"Well, you are certainly of interest to many in high places," the king said. "My son, the king of the dwarfs, the Tower—"

"And Obsikar the dragon king," Dirk added. "We're, like, buds."

"And dragon kings as well," the king continued. "And now two armies face each other, each justified in their respective claims. This is how wars begin, young man. So what do *you* have to say?"

Max had had a hard time speaking in an assembly once because the entire school was looking at him. Now there were thousands of eyes watching him, and he could almost feel the weight of it. He cleared his throat and took a breath. "I don't want there to be a war because of me," he said. "But I have to finish what I've started, and I need the *Codex* to do that."

"It will return with us," the dwarf king said firmly.

"And I have offered him sanctuary," Conall argued. "Mor Luin will rise to his defense if you try to take it."

The dwarf king spat. "Then it will be war."

"No!" Sarah shouted. She jumped off her pony and stood between the two kings. "Who was it that charged you with the *Codex*'s protection?" Sarah asked the dwarf.

"The World Sunderer himself. Maximilian Sporazo contracted with my ancestors centuries ago."

"And with his death, who does the book belong to now?" she continued. "And don't say the Tower, because if he'd wanted the Tower to have it, he wouldn't have hidden it from them, would he?"

Princess opened her mouth to speak but then thought better of it. The circle of mages and knights were slowly closing in on her, watching.

The dwarf king scratched at his beard. "Aye, it makes sense that it wasn't Sporazo's intention to let the Tower have it."

"Then who?" Sarah pressed. "And the answer to that question is found in the *Codex* itself."

"What do you mean?" the Mor Luin king asked, leaning forward in his stirrups.

"The reason Max is so important to everyone is because

he's the only one who can read it," Sarah answered. "And it's not because he studied at some Wizard's Tower. It's because the book is a part of him—it's in his blood. That's how the book was designed. And *that's* how you know who was meant to have it."

The dwarf king considered Sarah's words. "I saw him handle the book when he placed it in the chest," he said. "No other can even touch it, let alone read from it."

Sarah pressed on. "I've seen Max read from it many times. Before we came here I saw him use it to cast magical spells. And believe me, I was the biggest skeptic there was. I didn't even believe in magic. But I'm telling you, he did it, and I saw it with my own eyes."

"There is no deception in her," Conall said, rising to Sarah's defense. "We can take her at her word."

"So what?" the dwarf king continued. "Maybe he is the rightful owner. But it doesn't change the fact that it disappeared while under our watch."

"You've already made up for that," Sarah said. "You found it and returned it. That chapter of your history is closed."

The dwarf king grunted as he considered Sarah's

words. "Even so, it does not change the fact that it was taken a second time."

"But this is different," Sarah said. "It wasn't stolen; it was returned to its rightful owner. And we can put an end to it right now." She walked over to Max and had him lean down so she could whisper in his ear. When she pulled away he stared at her with a strange look.

"That's it?" he asked.

"That's it," she answered. Max turned to the dwarf king and cleared his throat.

"King, you have been steadfast in doing your duty. But now, as the last descendant of Maximilian Sporazo and the chosen keeper of the *Codex*, I thank you for your diligence and release you from your charge." He looked at Sarah, who nodded that he'd done it right. The dwarf king scratched at his beard.

"Yep, that will do," he announced. "Do you hear that?" he shouted to his troops. "Our honor is intact! Our mission is done!" A great cheer rose up from the ranks and the king bowed.

"Time for me to turn around and go home," the dwarf said to the Mor Luin king. "And if you'd be so kind, please remove your armies from our land."

The Mor Luin king bowed his head. "We shall be on our way even so, now that we have ridden to our borders and all is well."

"Ha!" the dwarf king replied, and he nodded to Max as he turned and rode back to his army.

Max let out a breath and turned to Sarah. "I'm really glad the smartest person I've ever met is also my friend," he said.

Sarah smiled. "And I'm glad the greatest wizard I've ever met is mine."

"Well done," the Mor Luin king said to Sarah as he tipped his head.

"She is impressive, isn't she?" Conall added. *That* made Sarah blush. Max couldn't understand how she could judo-flip dwarfs and back down an army without so much as breaking a sweat, only to have prince wonder-hair make her blush with a compliment. Girls made no sense, he decided.

"Now we'll take charge of the unicorn and escort you to the borders of Kuste, if that is what you desire," the Mor Luin king said. Max watched as Princess was forced to surrender, the mages taking the horn that served as her wand, and the knights placing her and Magar in chains.

Suddenly the words of Bellstro came back to Max: *You'll need friends—old and new.*

"What's going to happen to her?" Max asked the king. He had a strange feeling about Princess.

"For her crimes she'll likely be executed."

"Dude, do you realize if Princess goes down now you've pretty much guaranteed the messed-up future we saw isn't going to happen?" Dirk said. "No Robo-Princess, no frobbit hunts, no all of humanity being wiped out, none of it. It's like we just saved the world—again!"

But Max couldn't get Bellstro's words out of his head. Nor could he escape the feeling that was growing inside of him. "What if I need a favor?" Max asked Conall. "You know, for saving your life and all that."

"Yeah, the life debt," Dirk added. "You always got to make good on the life debt."

Prince Conall ignored Dirk. "I would do everything I could to see it happen, of course."

"Then I don't want you to hurt Princess," Max continued. Princess turned at the mention of her name, and the group of guards and mages surrounding her paused. "I want you to forgive her and Magar for what they've done."

"Amnesty?" the king said. "You would ask this for *her*?"

"Max, what are you doing?" Sarah asked.

"Yeah, dude," Dirk added, "you're supposed to ask for a castle or magic sword or something."

"I'm just tired of feeling like I'm always the pawn in somebody else's game," Max said, looking at Princess. "And I kind of think maybe I'm not the only one. I think if we offered her the chance, she would help us."

"It is not her nature," the king declared. "She is a creature of evil and driven by her appetites."

"But, I don't know," Max struggled to say, "maybe she doesn't *have* to be."

"Father, if this is what Max wants, I owe him my life," Conall said, although he didn't sound like he enjoyed saying it.

Max slid off his pony and walked over to Princess. It was strange just walking up to her after their last meeting in a roaring stadium. She had been a metallic monster then, and Max could only hope he wasn't making a terrible mistake.

"You and I really did fight once," he said to her. "The magic in the *Codex* was just too strong and you lost. I know it's kind of hard to believe—I have a hard time believing it, and I was there. But the thing I remember is that you were really angry. Like you were just miserable on the inside, no matter how powerful you'd become. You spent all those years trying to be something that maybe you never were. I think you don't have to become that if you don't want to. And if not, you could totally help us now and do something . . . good."

Princess stared at Max, his words sending her head spinning. She'd always been evil, but nobody had challenged her to actually be *happy*. And what if he was telling the truth? He'd seen what she'd become. There was no reason in the world the human should help her, and yet he was. He had won, but then instead of claiming victory he had reached out to save her. She'd never had anybody do that before. And as she considered it, she felt something new take root inside of her.

"You are not at all what I expected, Max Spencer," Princess said. "Why do I have the feeling you've just beaten me for a second time?"

"I don't want to beat you," Max replied. "I want you to help us defeat Rezormoor Dreadbringer and save this world. Both of you."

"Yes," Princess said, thinking it over. "I believe Magar and I could help with that."

The Mor Luin king sighed and waved his hand. "Then I pardon them of their crimes and they're free to go." The king then turned his gray eyes on Max. "But when the unicorn turns on you, don't forget you were warned."

"What the snuff!" Dirk exclaimed, running up to Max as Princess and Magar were unchained. "You don't let the bad guys get away! Now you've messed everything up—plus I doubt we'll get any experience points."

"It's my call," Max said, and that was the end of that.

The army turned north and Max and his friends joined the caravan of knights, squires, mages, and supplies. They rode for a long time in silence, each to their own thoughts.

Later that night Loki excused himself from their cooking fire. He snuck through the various tents looking for a wagon he'd caught sight of earlier. It wasn't a wagon that carried supplies or armaments, but something more important: pyro pigeons. It took the fire kitten a while to find it, dodging soldiers and horses along the way, but to his delight he found it unguarded and hitched away from the main camp. Nobody wanted a wagon full of pyro pigeons accidentally exploding nearby.

He moved through the shadows, climbing the wooden spoked wheel and up to the cage that held the birds. He whispered to the nearest in flametongue, the language spoken by those born of fire.

"I have a message for you to deliver," he said, opening the cage enough for the pigeon to climb through. The bird listened and then nodded its head. It wore a magical inscription band that captured Loki's message. When he was done, the bird took flight and disappeared into the dark sky above. Loki made his way back to camp and settled in for the night, a strange smile spreading across his face.

CHAPTER NINETEEN

RISE OF THE MONSTERS

THE FOUR STOOD SILENTLY IN THE TEMPLE OF THE MAELSHADOW: THE
dwarf high mage, the Kraken, Rezormoor Dreadbringer,
and the head of the Guild of Toupee Makers. It might
have been a more ominous sight had they not been offered
an assortment of cheese and crackers. Then again, the
toothpicks were black, which was something one didn't
normally see at parties.

The summons had arrived just as the high mage had
slipped from the ocean and made her way to the Tower.
That she found Rezormoor at the door waiting for her
was a surprise. Picking up the creature called the Kraken
along the way was another. Strange things were afoot.

When the Maelshadow arrived, his shapeless form

like a flight of shadows against a dying flame, the four bowed as the temple's acolytes disappeared with their snack trays in hand.

"The unicorn has turned," the Maelshadow announced. "We must now move to capture the *Codex* without her."

"It has already been accomplished," the high mage said. "The *Codex* rests in the Dwarven vaults. I've seen it myself—as I have the one who can read it."

"My agents tell me two armies came together at the Mor Luin border," the guild master added. "Two armies in pursuit of the *Codex*, gone missing from the dwarfs once again."

"I—" the high mage began, unsure what to say. She had seen the book transported to the vaults herself. It was impossible that it could have been taken.

"Tell me of the blood of Sporazo," the Maelshadow said to the high mage. Either the Lord of Shadows already knew the book was missing, or he was hiding his anger well.

"I could scarcely believe it," she replied, "having stood before him. He is but a boy, Techrus born and soft. And he travels with a strange group of associates."

"A mentor?" the Maelshadow asked, his voice deep and cavernous. "Who has taught him?"

"None that I could see," the high mage replied.

"And yet he sought out Bellstro," the Maelshadow added. Rezormoor hadn't heard *that* name for a very long time, but the rumors of the old wizard were plentiful. What might the boy have learned from him? It was a troubling thought.

"They managed to defend themselves from a Shadrus necromancer," the Lord of Shadows added. "Not something easily done."

"I don't know what you're all so afraid of," the Kraken growled. "I know Max Spencer and his friends. They're dorks."

"Well, thank you for that," Rezormoor added, "but anyone who reads from the *Codex of Infinite Knowability* should not be taken lightly."

"And where is this boy now?" the Maelshadow asked. It was the guild master who answered.

"As you know, the Mor Luin lords are blessed with an abundance of hair. Sadly, I have few agents there. Yet I can tell you they are traveling home now, with an army at their back."

"The boy may seek to take refuge in Ledluin," the high mage said. "A logical choice to hole up in the capital. Very well defended."

"Or he may make for the Crystal Sea," Rezormoor added. "From Dun he could take a ship to anywhere in the Seven Kingdoms." The sorcerer paused, a question plaguing him. "But may I ask, how is it that the Lord of Shadows has come to know the unicorn turned?"

"I'm not in the habit of explaining myself," the Maelshadow said. "But the proximity of the Gossamer Gimbal allows me certain insights into the one who carries it."

"I see," the sorcerer replied.

"Mage," the Maelshadow announced, "take your aquatic form and wait outside the port of Dun. If they travel by sea, intercept them and bring them to me." Rezormoor cursed under his breath. *That* was not the deal Rezormoor had struck with the Lord of Shadows, but he decided there was no point bickering about it now. He'd simply have to find the boy first.

"Guild Master," the Maelshadow continued, "put out the word to all your agents, in every city. Find this boy if he travels by land."

"I will do as you command. Our agents will pour like water over shampooed hair." The Kraken rolled his eyes, wanting more than anything to toss the hair freak from the highest window.

The Maelshadow fluttered in annoyance as well, before returning to the topic at hand. "And Rezormoor, keep this Kraken with you in Aardyre. The moment you hear from the guild, send him forth."

"A most judicious strategy," Rezormoor said.

"Fail me and you will all suffer eternal pain," the Maelshadow announced. Rezormoor bowed and left with the others—the *Codex of Infinite Knowability* was drawing closer to him. He could almost feel it. He probably also had time for a shampoo and rinse.

Max spent a fitful night tossing and turning. He dreamed of the Magrus, only it was covered in ice and snow. Against the endless white stood a figure in black armor—armor that radiated power like a living thing. Death swirled about him as black mists rose and mingled with the chilled air. As he moved, the trail of black followed like a smoky shadow. Max looked down at his feet and saw more on the ground than just snow—the plain had been scattered with long frozen bones. Dragon bones, he somehow knew. Then the scene changed and Max was standing at the base of a white tree, its silver leaves playing a magical song despite the cold wind blowing through its branches. The armored man approached and the singing turned to cries as gray veins formed beneath the bark and began to rot. Max turned away, frightened, silver leaves falling around him like giant snowflakes. He sensed the armored man had come to a stop near him, towering over him. Black smoke stretched like probing fingers around his feet.

"All will fall," came a voice echoing through the closed helm. And in a final shudder of leaves the armored man disappeared. For the briefest of moments, Max looked up and saw between the realms. The city of Madison stretched out before him—home! But none there could see the armored man descend toward the sleepy town, or the dark clouds that began to gather overhead.

Max woke with a start and instinctively grabbed for the *Codex*. Moki muttered something and turned over, but Puff blinked, sensing Max was awake. "Are you all right?" the fluff dragon asked.

"I had a dream," Max said, the vividness of it holding fast in his mind.

"A *magical* dream?" Puff asked.

"I think so, yes."

"Ah, I used to dream like that. Before I became this," Puff said, pulling at a lock of fluff.

"It wasn't a good dream. It was horrible."

"A vision of things to come?" Puff guessed.

"How did you know?"

"You lay your head near the *Codex of Infinite Knowability*. Dragons could dream of such things. It's an opportunity to change what will be."

"The world was frozen and all of the dragons were dead," Max said slowly. "And then a man in black armor went to a silver tree and somehow used it to cross into my world."

"The Tree of Attenuation," Puff replied.

"So everything I saw could actually happen?"

"Yes," Puff answered. "Now you know the cost if you fail."

Max sighed. "I never asked for this."

"Heroes rarely do." Puff laid his head back down and closed his eyes. A few minutes later, Max did the same. But sleep did not come.

The next day they arrived in Dun. It was a thriving

port city with a large bay and numerous docks filled with trading vessels loading and unloading their wares. But unlike other port cities, Dun had a more law-abiding reputation, thanks in part to the heavy-handed oversight by the Mor Luin lords.

"This is the fastest route to the Tower," Conall announced as a small contingent broke from the main army camp and led Max and his friends into the city. The king had continued north to Ledluin, wishing Max luck and instructing his son to buy their passage to Aardyre. The king had remained distant with Max following the Princess episode, and Max was somewhat surprised every morning to find that she and Magar hadn't taken off during the night.

"Perhaps the unicorn simply wishes to escort you to the very place you are going anyway," Conall suggested. "You the willing and unknowing captive."

"Ah, if only I were half as devious and conniving as the Mor Luin nobility," Princess responded.

By the time they reached the docks, the smell of salt hung heavy in the air, and Conall sent Sir Maron to secure their passage.

"So what is our plan, exactly?" Sarah asked. "To

just arrive at this Aardyre city and walk to the Wizard's Tower, and then ring the doorbell?" She was being sarcastic, and Max never liked it when Sarah was sarcastic, because it usually meant she was onto something.

"We'll go at night," Dirk said. "We blend in and sneak our way into the Tower."

"Blend in?" Princess asked, looking at the group. "A Tower wizard, a unicorn, two fire kittens, three Techrus-born humans, and a fluff dragon?"

"She does have a point," Sarah said.

Sir Maron returned, pointing at a trireme that was being loaded with barrels. It was tall, with several masts, and had three rows of oars on each side. "The *Murky Merman*," he announced. "Bound for Lanislyr and Aardyre. She'll take us aboard."

"Thank you," Max said. "You really have helped us a lot."

"My pleasure," the prince said with a smile. "And you always have a friend in Mor Luin if you need one."

They said their good-byes and boarded the *Murky Merman*. Loki and Moki had warned Max that they needed to stay in his backpack or else risk getting tossed overboard. The captain, a heavyset man sporting a black beard with a patch of white running up the middle, grunted at them to mind their manners and stay out of the way. It wasn't long before the ship was loaded and set sail.

"I take it we're not booked in first class," Dirk said to the others. They were lined against a long rail, watching as the harbor shrank away. Princess was holding tightly to the railing and looked unhappy.

"Unicorns hate the water," Magar offered in her defense.

"And yet they do like rainbows," Dirk replied, thinking it over. "Very interesting."

Princess scowled at him as a sailor hustled by, pulling at the rigging that helped lift the sails.

"Bad omens today," he announced in a strange accent. "The fishermen have all left. See?" He pointed to the empty bay. "Something has scared the fish away."

"What could do that?" Sarah asked.

"Monsters, of course," the man answered, looking at Sarah like it was the most obvious answer in the world. Sarah had to remember that in the Magrus things worked a bit differently. People took the idea of a monster as a literal truth.

"Probably some hybrid shark thing," Dirk added. "Yeah, sharks are cool."

Puff looked at Dirk. "Has anyone ever had him checked out? You know, in the head?" The others laughed. The crew had given the fluff dragon a few odd looks when he boarded, but they were paid to mind their own business.

By late afternoon, Dun had largely disappeared. The ship then turned north, following the coastline. Everyone but Princess and Magar had gone below to their "room," which turned out to be a small space carved out from the forward storage. Puff left to explore the ship while Max placed the fire kittens near three hammocks stacked in a tight row. He did his best to climb into the lower one, having a hard time with the swaying ship. Dirk scrambled to the top like he'd spent his entire life in the navy.

"Oh, did you want the bottom?" Max asked Sarah once he'd finally gotten in. Sarah laughed—she wasn't about to make Max try and get into the middle one.

"No, I'm fine. I'm not really that tired," she replied.

"Okay. Just let me know if you change your mind." Max closed his eyes and listened to the rhythmic slapping of the oars and the accompanying creaks and groans of the ship. *The wind must have died down and they've gone back to rowing,* Max thought. But soon he drifted to sleep—there was something about the rolling ship that made him awfully tired.

A heavy *thump* rocked the ship. Max sat up with a start and spilled out of the hammock, crashing on the floor below.

"You okay?" Sarah asked, sounding nervous. "Did you hear that?"

"I'm fine," Max answered, getting to his feet. "Yeah, I heard it. How long was I out?"

"Not long."

A second *thump* hit with enough force that the entire ship lurched forward. Max nearly crashed into Sarah as he struggled to remain on his feet. Something very big had come into contact with the ship. Moments later alarm bells began to sound.

Max grabbed his backpack as Dirk swung down from the top hammock.

"Whoa!" he cried out. "Something's hitting the ship!"

"What's going on?" Loki said, poking his head out of the bag.

"We don't know," Sarah answered, the nervous energy of the group filling the small room.

"Probably sharks," Dirk said.

"I like—" Moki began, but Loki pushed his companion back into the backpack and pulled the drawstring closed.

"Just don't leave us down here, okay?" Loki pleaded from inside the backpack.

The third *thump* cracked wood and sent them sprawling. Water began to seep through the floor from the damaged hull as more alarm bells began ringing in earnest.

"Come on, let's get out of here!" Max cried. He flung the backpack over his shoulder and followed Sarah and Dirk out the door.

The sounds of panicked activity grew louder as they made their way to the deck. They could hear the frightened shouts of sailors as they called out orders. One came running past and nearly bowled them over.

"Don't tell the captain you've seen me," the first mate shouted as he descended into the lower parts of the ship. "He'll want to *promote* me!"

Max and his friends reached the deck just in time to see a long tentacle slither back and disappear on the other side.

"Oh, not a shark," Dirk noted. He almost sounded disappointed.

The ship lurched violently to the side as three more tentacles came flying overhead, cracking the main mast in two and collapsing the quarterdeck with an explosion of debris. Max managed to grab hold of some of the rigging, seeing that Sarah had done the same. Dirk, however, slid across the deck before landing in the remains of one of the fallen sails.

A sudden blast of cold air caused Max to look up. Magar was standing over him and firing magical ice at one of the tentacles. The wizard had his hands held out in front of him and was muttering something under his breath. When he struck it, the appendage shot into the air and disappeared back into the sea.

"A cone of cold!" Dirk shouted, having seen the magic spell as well. "Awesome!" Dirk scrambled to his feet as the ship righted itself. He ran back to Max and Sarah.

"He's totally a higher level than you are," Dirk said to Max, as if that was somehow helpful. Max was about to say something when the ship pitched violently in the other direction. They grabbed on to the falling rigging as the monster wrapped itself around the hull and smashed the deck with more giant tentacles. One managed to find

Magar as he was scrambling toward the remains of the main mast. The blow sent him flying over the side of the ship and into the sea below. Max looked down, seeing water streaming past his feet as he felt his balance begin to shift.

"Who'd have guessed rope climbing in gym would pay off?" Dirk shouted, looking far more comfortable hanging in the ropes than Max. Max ignored him and closed his eyes, concentrating on not letting go. The ship continued to roll dangerously on its side, and Max could hear the shouts of sailors falling overboard. His arms began to burn as he felt his fingers slipping.

"Max, hang on!" Sarah shouted. And Max wanted to—he really, really did. But he just wasn't strong enough, and everything was wet and slick. With a gasp, he lost his hold on the rigging and slid down the front of the deck. He could see the ocean over the rail as he fell toward it. Max turned on his stomach, facing Sarah and Dirk, who were watching with horrified expressions as he slipped away from them. His mind leapt to the *Codex* at his side—an instinctive action. He'd once floated himself above a pyramid, and if there was ever a time that called for floating in the air it was now. But again Max felt nothing. Then the deck disappeared beneath his feet and he prepared to hit the water.

But he didn't.

He came to a sudden stop, hanging in his backpack straps. Max craned to look over his shoulder and saw Moki and Loki hanging on to the wooden deck rail, their claws embedded in the wood and the rough canvas of his pack. And as the ship rolled, the other side rose high into the air.

"Hang on!" Loki moaned, struggling to keep himself and Max from falling off the edge.

Max saw the ocean beneath his dangling feet and more of the monstrous creature that was attacking the ship. It was huge, with large eyes and rows of giant, gnashing teeth.

Loki and Moki slipped, their claws leaving trails in the wooden rail.

"You're too heavy!" Loki cried.

"Weee!" Moki exclaimed, the peril of it somehow lost on the fire kitten.

"Don't drop me!" Max screamed. He felt helpless hanging in the backpack straps. A shadow passed over him as a tentacle crashed into the ship while several sailors tumbled off the edge. The fire kittens slipped more, their claws barely holding on to the last bits of the wooden rail. Loki closed his eyes and dug in with all he had. He wasn't trying to be a hero—his entire future was hanging below him, and he couldn't bear losing it. Then, just when he had no more strength left, the ship began to roll in the other direction.

"We're going up!" Max shouted. The monstrous creature and the ocean fell away from him. They were moving fast—maybe *too* fast. The ship slammed back into the water and continued pitching in the opposite direction. Max and the two fire kittens were catapulted over the railing and into the tangle of rigging and broken sails at the ship's center.

"Enough!" came a cry that Max recognized as coming from Princess. He heard a giant *SNAP* as if someone had torn a chunk out of the sky, followed by a flash of light. The growl of a thundercloud rolled over the ship as electricity sent every hair on Max's arm standing on end.

Princess was standing near the foremast, the storm she'd summoned dancing around her, whipping her hair as the sky filled with dark clouds. Lightning crackled and danced in the boiling blackness above.

She raised her wand skyward, and a giant lightning bolt streaked down and crashed into the water. The tentacles shuddered and retreated as the ship rolled back and bounced in the water.

"I thought as much," Princess announced, turning to face Max. He realized he was hanging upside down, and it was hard to see Princess's expression. The ship was rocking back and forth, but the violent pitching had stopped.

"Now to find my hapless wizard—" Princess started to say, but suddenly a tentacle shot out and wrapped itself around her waist. It snapped her backward, and she disappeared over the ship's railing. Max hurried to untangle himself and dropped to the deck (mindful not to land on the fire kittens). He ran over to the side and peered over the rail. There was no sign of the unicorn.

"Princess!" Max yelled. He thought he saw a black shadow moving under the waves, but he wasn't sure. Cries from men in the water rose up, and the crew began rescue efforts. Overhead the wind stopped blowing and the black storm clouds began to lazily drift apart.

"Where's that blasted first mate?" the captain shouted as he descended into the lower decks. "All hands to the pumps! Man overboard!"

Sarah and Dirk joined Max at the rail, looking for signs of Princess. Moki and Loki poked their heads out of the backpack, wet and unhappy looking.

"I don't see her," Sarah said. "Or Magar."

A cargo net was thrown over the side, and the sailors in the water began pulling themselves up. There was no sign of Princess or her wizard.

They had spent the rest of the afternoon pulling men to safety and pumping water out of the ship's hold. The sailors used a special tar to slow the leaks as much as possible, and Max found Puff thoroughly soaked and shivering in the cargo hold.

"The pouty-faced girl saved us," the captain said, finding Max and his friends sometime later.

"Yeah," Max said, not knowing what else to say.

The captain sighed. "Well, my ship's still afloat, the cargo's in the hull, and since the first mate is a slippery one, my commission remains in place. All in all, things could have been worse." He removed his hat. "We must make for Lanislyr while we can. My thanks to your brave friends now given to the sea."

"Do you really think they're lost?" Sarah asked.

"No way," Dirk answered. "Princess and Magar are awesomely talented magic users. And breathing underwater is, like, a third-level spell or something. They'll be fine."

Sarah shook her head. "I wish I could see things the same way you do sometimes," she admitted.

"Yeah, I know," Dirk said. He turned to Max. "And good call saving Princess from the knights. If you hadn't, we'd all been done for. Didn't see that one coming."

"Friends come and go," Glenn said from Max's belt. "But colds hang around for about three days. Makes you think."

The *Murky Merman* managed to hobble its way to Lanislyr. Max and the others remained belowdecks as the cargo was quickly unloaded and the ship made for Aardyre. The goods in the hold had to be delivered on time, and the captain wasn't about to add late penalties to his already mounting expenses.

Late the next evening, they pulled into Aardyre. A sleepy harbormaster met them and assessed the docking fees, noting the damaged state of the vessel with a raised eyebrow. No doubt the tale of the sea monster would begin to spread as the crew dispersed into the various taverns along the waterfront. As preparations to unload the ship began, Max and his friends slipped ashore, saying good-bye to the captain and making their way along the dock. Several guards watched them with bored expressions. Apparently the sight of three humans, two fire kittens, and a fluff dragon wasn't anything worth noting. Before long they passed from the piers into a series of warehouses.

The center of Aardyre loomed in the distance, and Max could see the dark shapes of various structures rising in the moonlit sky. Most distinct was a tall, solitary tower, looking as if it had pierced the moon behind it. Max knew it at once: the Wizard's Tower. It was the home to Rezormoor Dreadbringer and the birthplace of the *Codex of Infinite Knowability*. It was also where his long-lost ancestor had ruled as arch-sorcerer and regent. Seeing it in person sent shivers down Max's spine.

"There it is," Loki said, following Max's gaze. "That is what real power looks like."

"Or evil," Puff added. "I think it is defined by what it does."

"So what now?" Sarah asked the group.

"We sneak in," Dirk answered. "I only wish we had good sneaking music."

Max sighed. "Let's just hope nobody's expecting us."

Not yet, *at least*, Loki thought to himself. *But soon.* "Hey, uh, I'm going to walk from here—stretch my paws out." The fire kitten climbed out of the backpack and landed on the cobblestone. Moki, however, remained on Max's back. After so long on the road with Max, warming his feet and riding in his backpack, the fire kitten had grown fond of the human.

Max felt the *Codex* pressed against his side as he began walking toward the Tower. They worked their way up the street, and as they moved Loki dropped farther and farther back. When the others disappeared around a corner, the fire kitten suddenly bolted.

Loki scrambled through back alleys, hopping over small walls and cutting across residences. He startled a couple of alley cats and was chased by a dog, but the fire kitten was moving at full speed and easily got away. He jumped between balconies and landed in a quiet intersection. From there he had a clear view of the Tower, but more importantly, he could see the light spilling from the room at the very top. That was where the current regent, Rezormoor Dreadbringer, would be waiting.

Loki lit his tail aflame and marveled at his ingenuity.

Against all odds, he'd left the Turul wastes, found the *boy who could read the book*, and accompanied him safely to Aardyre and the Tower's door. Now there was only one thing left to do, and a future of wealth hung in the balance. Loki flung a small fireball high into the air. It was bright and stood out against the dark sky, and it flew perfectly, angling in front of the solitary Tower window. Several dogs began barking in response, and Loki watched his handiwork. It wouldn't be long now. Then he took off again, slipping into the night.

CHAPTER TWENTY

CHEESE IN THE RAT TRAP

FROM THE BALCONY IN THE HIGHEST ROOM IN THE WIZARD'S TOWER, THE zombie duck spotted the small fireball streaking through the night air. It turned and quacked loudly at Rezormoor, who looked up in time to see the ball of flame disappear below the window. He'd received the strange message some days prior from a fire kitten who claimed to have both the *boy who could read the book* and *the book that can be read by said boy who can read said book.* Rezormoor had learned long ago never to dismiss something out of hand just because it seemed implausible. He didn't put enough stock in the message to mention it to the Maelshadow, but just to be safe he'd set his zombie duck watching for the "heavenly ball of fire" mentioned in the pyro pigeon's note.

"Well, imagine that," Rezormoor said. He stood and stretched, his long robes—soft as velvet but strong as steel—moving about his lean frame. His two obsidian daggers, the blades wavy in a way no human blacksmith could forge, hung from the silver belt around his waist. He flung his hair over his shoulders and greeted the zombie duck with a pat on the head. "Time to summon the Kraken," he announced.

Max and his friends moved up the long street called Guild Row, noting a few citizens milling about despite the late hour. A spectacled member of the Guild of Professional Snitches watched Max and his friends through a window, while a long line of people stood outside the Guild of Professional Line Waiters.

"I think we should get off the main road," Puff suggested. Max agreed. They veered through several side streets until they had to squeeze single file between two rows of buildings. Once they were through, Max suddenly stopped, and Sarah nearly ran into him.

"Max?" Sarah asked, sensing something was wrong.

The Kraken was perched on a low overhanging roof, looking down with crimson eyes. His skin, rippling with muscles, took on the same red tint, and it made him even more frightening as he sat perfectly still in the moonlight.

"I can't believe you dorks actually made it this far," the Kraken said as he jumped from the roof and landed on the ground in front of them.

"Who are you?" Sarah asked, fighting against every instinct in her body that screamed to turn around and run.

"Don't remember me, huh?" the Kraken taunted. "I mean, it wasn't that long ago you did your kung fu thing to me in front of the whole wrestling team. Luckiest move I've ever seen, especially for a girl."

"Oh, no way!" Dirk exclaimed, pointing at the Kraken. "No way! You're Ricky Reynolds!"

"What?" Sarah gasped. "How's that possible?"

The Kraken smiled, shrugging his massive shoulders. "You tell me; you're the brainiac. In fact, you tell me how *any* of this can be possible. Because I'm pretty sure if there was, like, this whole different world filled with stupid magic and dorky creatures, somebody would have mentioned it. But I guess it doesn't matter, does it? Because here we are anyway."

"Ricky, what's going on?" Max said carefully.

"Yeah, man, and did you know that you're orange?"

Dirk asked. "Not that there's anything wrong with that, you know, if that's what you're into."

The Kraken grunted. "I left with that stupid unicorn and her wizard. The whole town blamed me when you guys disappeared. The cops said I had a motive, and it didn't matter that I passed a lie detector test. So that's why you're going to pay for what you've done."

"Guys," Glenn spoke up, "maybe you should settle this in the oldest, most barbaric way possible: with lawyers."

"Don't need no lawyer," the Kraken said. "Got me a sorcerer."

"Rezormoor Dreadbringer," Max said, understanding at once.

"So you know him, huh?" the Kraken replied. "That's good, 'cause he knows you, too. And he's really interested in meeting you, Spencer."

Max considered the monstrous creature that had been Ricky Reynolds back home. This wasn't how things were supposed to happen. He was supposed to sneak into the Tower, reset the *Codex*, and use its magic to defeat Dreadbringer. Surprise had been his only advantage, and now that was gone.

"You don't have to do this, you know," Sarah said, staring at the Kraken. "Look, I'm really sorry about everything that's happened. Believe me, I didn't want any of this either. And I'm really sorry about what's happened to you, personally. It wasn't fair for the town to judge you like that. And I'm sorry I embarrassed you in front of your friends. But right now you have a choice. You don't have to be a monster just because the world thinks you already are, even if you look the part."

"Oh, but I *want* to," the Kraken answered with a smile. He turned to Max. "So here's the deal, Spencer. I have to take you back alive and breathing, but the others? Not so much. So I'll ask you nicely, just once. If you don't surrender and come with me—and really, I kind of hope that you don't—I'll teach you a little about revenge right here and now."

"No," Max said at once, holding up his hands. "Don't hurt them. I surrender." Moki emerged from Max's backpack, his paws in the air. Sarah and Dirk raised their hands as well.

The Kraken smiled. "Well, shucks. I guess the five of you get to keep breathing. But you never know, things can change, right?"

Five? Max thought. He swung his head around and saw for the first time that Loki had disappeared. Maybe he'd managed to get away? Maybe he'd be able to help them. The Kraken, however, took note of Max.

"Looking for your kitty friend?" he said with a chuckle. "Man, you really are dumb, aren't you?"

The door squeaked closed, clanging shut with a metallic sound that bounced off the stone walls of the Tower dungeon. Max had been separated from the others and placed in a different cell. Everything but the clothes on their backs had been taken, and that included the *Codex of Infinite Knowability.*

"I don't know why they can't oil the hinges," Dirk said, sliding to the ground as he sat against a far wall. The cell they were in had extra bars and a mesh screen designed for smaller-than-human captives. "I mean, it's not like jailers are so busy that they don't have time for a little hinge maintenance."

"I've been to two dungeons now," Moki said happily.

Puff grunted and began pacing back and forth in the small cell. "We're never getting out of here. No prisoner *ever* gets out of the Tower."

"Maybe guards like being able to hear the cell doors open," Sarah said, thinking about Dirk's comment. "You know, maybe it's part of the security system."

"Nope," Dirk said definitively. "It's like a baby that cries all the time—pretty soon you just tune it out and you don't even know it's there. If you're a guard and hear nothing but squeaky doors all the time, it's not too long before you don't hear them at all."

"I don't think people tune out babies," Max suggested from the cell across from theirs.

"And how would you know if you had?" Dirk asked. "You wouldn't, would you?"

Sarah buried her head in her hands. "I'm not sure I'm going to be able to last very long in here."

"Don't worry," Max said. "I think as long as I do what they ask, they're not going to hurt you guys."

"Yeah, it's called leverage," Dirk added.

"No, it's . . . oh, you're actually right," Sarah admitted. It always caught her off guard when Dirk was right about something.

"What about that potion you drank?" Max said. "That Ergodic Elixir. I know you thought it was gone, but maybe you can make something magical happen again."

"I've been wishing I had wings for the last three days," Dirk said. He turned his head back to look over his shoulders. "Nope, still nothing."

"It sure seemed like Ricky was waiting for us," Sarah said. She put her hand on Moki's head and scratched the fire kitten under his ear. "I think we've been betrayed, and I think it was Loki."

"Loki's been a bad kitty," Moki agreed.

They heard the latch of the dungeon door open as Rezormoor Dreadbringer stepped through. He held the Gossamer Gimbal in his hand, following it as the arrow pointed directly to Max. The sorcerer walked to the iron bars and lifted the compass so Max could see the arrow hovering in the air. "Well, it seems we have our man—or should I say *boy*?"

Max stared at the sorcerer who'd been hunting him. Power flowed off him in waves that made Max's ears ring. His eyes drifted to the daggers hanging from the sorcerer's belt. As a sorcerer, Rezormoor had mastered both the wizard and mage disciplines, and that meant he'd be as dangerous with weapons as he was with magic.

"That belonged to Princess," Moki said, having seen Princess use the Gossamer Gimbal before. Rezormoor shut the magical compass and slipped it into his pocket.

"Not exactly," he answered. "In truth, it belongs to the Maelshadow. As a unicorn, Princess merely had enough magic to make it work in the Techrus."

"Yeah, well, thanks for that," Dirk said. "Princess pretty much messed up our entire world and then became this killer robot thingy."

Rezormoor frowned—he was having a hard time following the skinny human.

"And we know what you're doing to the dragons," Puff said angrily. That caught the sorcerer by surprise.

"Impossible," he declared. Certain members of the black market knew what he was doing. The Guild of Toupee Makers as well. But a random fluff dragon? It didn't make sense. "Why do you say that?"

"Because Obsikar told us," Dirk interjected.

Now, *that* was unexpected. Rezormoor had heard tales of the dragon king, as had most in the Seven Kingdoms. "Well, you are very interesting, I'll give you that much."

"Is Princess alive?" Sarah asked. "Is that how you got the compass?"

"Alive . . . yes," Rezormoor replied. There was a sigh of relief from Max and the others. "She's here—both her

290 Platte F. Clark
290 Platte F. Clark

and her turncoat wizard. The high mage was none too happy about it."

"Oh, I get it," Dirk said. "The high mage was that giant octopus thing that attacked us."

"Indeed," Rezormoor answered. "But weakened as she was after her battle with the unicorn, she dared not try again for the ship. You see, she didn't know if Max might be able to use the *Codex* against her. But now I think that's not the case—there's something wrong with it, isn't there?"

"Yeah," Max managed to say. But he wasn't about to go into the details if he didn't have to.

"Well, Max, here's the problem," Rezormoor continued. "If you can't use the *Codex of Infinite Knowability*, you're of no use to me. That's not to say you aren't of use to the Maelshadow. There's something about your blood, and I believe the Lord of Shadows would like to make a withdrawal—probably in a quantity that you wouldn't appreciate. So I suppose you could fix the *Codex* and do as I say, or this is where we say good-bye. And by that I mean I send *you* to the Maelshadow and give your friends to the Kraken."

"No, don't," Max said at once. "I think I can fix it."

"Then by all means let's do so," Rezormoor said with

a smile. He motioned with his hand and the cell door swung open. Max slowly walked out as Dirk and Sarah rose to their feet.

"Don't worry," Max said, turning to Sarah. "I won't let anything happen to you guys. I promise." His voice sounded different. Maybe it was the way it echoed in the dungeon, or perhaps because it never wavered or hinted at self-doubt? Then Sarah understood. The old Max Spencer—afraid, conflicted, lacking confidence—was gone. What she heard were the words spoken by the *boy who could read the book.*

"I believe in you, Max," she said as he walked past. "We all do." The sorcerer led Max down the row of empty cells before disappearing through the heavy door. It was closed and latched behind them.

He was taken up a long set of winding stairs. Rezormoor was light on his feet—probably a benefit of so much stair climbing. They passed the occasional door, and Max was left with the impression that they were taking a back way to wherever it was they were going. They finally made it to the top, and the stairs ended at a small door that glowed by the light of a magical rune carved into its surface.

"A more private entrance to my quarters," Rezormoor

confirmed. He waved his hand in front of the door and pushed it open. "Fewer students to bother with along the way. We are a university, among other things." Max swallowed and followed the sorcerer into the topmost chamber of the Wizard's Tower. The first thing that struck him was that it looked *familiar*, and then Max remembered the vivid memories he'd had back at the Dragon's Den when he'd first activated the *Codex*. He'd been to this very room and stood on the balcony that overlooked the city.

"Impressive, isn't it?" Rezormoor said, noticing Max staring out the open door that led to the balcony. "Tell me, does the Techrus have such cities?"

"We do," Max said, guarding each word he spoke. Who knew what an offhanded comment might set into motion. "More or less."

Rezormoor moved past his large chair and Max saw the zombie duck waiting there. He could see ribs exposed between dirty yellow feathers and a skull with more holes than you'd expect on something that blinked and looked at you. "Don't get too close to my pet," Rezormoor warned, bending down and patting the duck's sandpaper-like skin. "I suspect he looks at you like takeout." Max decided the thing he liked least about the Magrus was the way everything wanted to eat him.

Rezormoor walked to a black stand that looked like a large piece of volcanic rock set upright in the middle of the floor. Above it, floating in the air, was the *Codex of Infinite Knowability*. Max carefully approached, keeping his eye on the zombie duck all the while.

Rezormoor's hand floated near the ancient book, but he stopped before touching it. Small bits of blue lightning danced across the *Codex*'s surface in anticipation. "Beginnings rarely become the endings they intended," the sorcerer announced. "Take the *Codex*, for example. It started off as the project of an average student here at the Tower. The apprentice had wanted a self-writing encyclopedia that dutifully cataloged all the various elements of life in the Magrus. Quite clever, really, but the book took on a life of its own. The student, of course, was Maximilian Sporazo. Then the accident changed everything." Max remembered the vision he'd seen of the pregnant woman screaming—not because she was in labor, but because she'd been burned by dragon fire. He shivered at the memory; the woman had been Maximilian Sporazo's young wife. The child, his son.

"And in his madness, Sporazo made the *Codex* much more than its humble beginnings," Rezormoor continued, withdrawing his hand.

"So why kill the dragons?" Max asked. "What does that have to do with the *Codex*?"

"Everything," Rezormoor answered. "Have you heard of the serpent's escutcheon? A scale so powerful that neither magic nor blade can penetrate it?" Max thought back to the fight he'd witnessed between Conall and the dragon. The magical lance had shattered against the dragon's breast, and Puff had told him about the serpent's escutcheon on the ride to Jiilk.

"Now imagine a man wearing an entire suit of armor constructed from such scales," Rezormoor continued. "That man would be invincible. Consider a tower fortified from top to bottom with even more. Such a tower would be indestructible. Now this invincible man in his indestructible tower can raise an army, and the Seven Kingdoms will fall and a new empire will rise from the ashes. All of the three realms will bend to this man's will. And it begins, piece by piece, with the single scale that covers a dragon's heart. That is why I must hunt them all."

"But you need the *Codex* for something too," Max said.

"Indeed. Do you think a blacksmith's hammer could bend the serpent's escutcheon? Do you think there's a forge hot enough to temper it? Only the *Codex* has the power to do this." Suddenly Max's dream about the man in black armor came roaring to his mind. If Rezormoor Dreadbringer succeeded in his plan, he would destroy everything that mattered.

"That's why you need me," Max said. "To read the *Codex* and use its magic for you."

"Yes."

"And the fluff dragons?" Max continued.

"Ah, that. Controlling the fluff trade will raise the gold to fund my army. War is an expensive endeavor, as it happens, and the *Codex* will ensure that fluff dragons survive when all the real dragons are gone. And there are other benefits," he added, flinging his long black hair behind his head.

Rezormoor drew his dagger and nonchalantly used it to pick at the dirt under his fingernail. "There really is no need to think of me as a tyrant, Max. If we work together, we can accomplish much. At the very least I can certainly save the lives of you and your friends." He slipped the blade back into his belt and waited for Max to respond.

"What about the Maelshadow?" Max asked. He thought back to the Shadrus necromancer that had attacked them in the forest.

"So you know of the Lord of the Shadows?"

"A wizard told me."

"Bellstro? That would make sense," Rezormoor continued. Max was surprised Rezormoor had put it together so quickly. The sorcerer was smart, Max realized. He'd have to be very careful. "You are correct, of course. The Maelshadow will do things far worse than kill you. But if we work together, Max, we can defeat him. If you refuse to help me . . ."

Rezormoor left the words hanging in the air. "You'll turn me over to the Maelshadow?" Max replied.

The sorcerer smiled but shook his head. "After what I've just told you? No, Max. You and your friends will never leave the Tower alive. So now you must make your choice."

Max looked at the *Codex* as it hovered in the air. He knew what would happen if Rezormoor succeeded. But he didn't think the sorcerer was bluffing when he threatened to kill them either. It was an impossible situation, but Max knew he had to try something.

"Go ahead, retrieve the *Codex* and let us begin our work together," Rezormoor coaxed.

Max swallowed and reached for the book. The lightning danced around the cover and snapped at him the instant he touched it.

"Ouch!" he exclaimed as he jumped back, holding his finger and dancing around in pain.

"Well, that's somewhat less than what I'd hoped for," the sorcerer said, watching him.

"It does that sometimes," Max replied. Despite the stinging in his finger, he reached for the *Codex* again. But this time he managed to grab it. "See?"

Relief showed on Rezormoor's face. "I was a little worried all of this had been for nothing."

"Yeah, me too," Max admitted. He thought back to what Bellstro had told him. *You must take it to the Wizard's Tower—to the very room where it was created.* So here he was, doing just that. Max was standing in the regent's personal quarters, with the *Codex* in hand. Max looked around. He was missing something . . . but what?

"Is there a problem?"

"Uh, no," Max lied.

"So it's working?" Rezormoor asked.

"Er, not yet."

"Not yet?"

"Is this the room where my ancestor added the Prime Spells to the *Codex*?" Max asked.

"Yes. His desk was nearly where you are now." Max took a step to see if anything changed, but the *Codex* remained broken. He stepped again. Then again.

"What are you doing?"

"Just, you know, stretching," Max said. He figured he'd pretty much stepped everywhere the desk might have been, but the *Codex* remained unchanged.

"You don't say," Rezormoor said, growing impatient. "So . . . ?"

Max needed to come up with something. Rezormoor wasn't stupid and Max couldn't keep dancing around the room. The sorcerer needed to believe it was working, but Max also needed time to work things out. He had to come up with something that would accomplish both.

"Mr. Spencer, I'm afraid you're stalling," Rezormoor said, reaching for his dagger.

Then it hit him. Rezormoor had wizard smarts, but

he didn't know how things worked on the Techrus. He'd asked Max about the cities there, in fact. That meant he was a novice when it came to technology, and *that* was something Max might be able to work to his advantage.

"Yep, there it is," Max said, forcing himself to look relieved. Rezormoor hesitated, leaving his dagger in its sheath.

"There what is?"

"It's restarting," Max said. "The system has to reboot."

Rezormoor looked confused. "What does that mean?"

"It's just how it works," Max said. "Basically the *Codex* has to start up again. You know, turn back on."

"And how long does *that* take?"

"Oh, not too long," Max said, trying to figure out how much time he could stall for. "Like . . . a day?"

"A *day*?" Rezormoor exclaimed, his hands balling up into fists so tight Max could hear the leather gloves cracking. Max shrugged, however, keeping his cool.

"Yeah, you know, this thing has a really old magical operating system, and it's going to be slow rebooting itself."

"Rebooting?"

"What, you don't know about rebooting?"

Rezormoor stared at Max before addressing him again. "Fine. Just put it back for now."

Max stepped up to the stand and replaced the book, watching the *Codex* hover in place.

"I'll summon you tomorrow," Rezormoor said, unable to hide the irritation in his voice, "and I do expect the *Codex* to be restored. Do you understand?"

"Yeah, totally," Max replied, hoping he wasn't as sweaty looking as he felt.

"The zombie duck will escort you back to your cell," the sorcerer commanded. "I wouldn't make any sudden moves or deviate from the path if I were you."

Max nodded as the zombie duck came waddling up to him. Rezormoor waved his hand again and the back door swung open. "And by the way, if I find you've tried to deceive me, it will not end pleasantly for you or those you care about."

Max nodded and followed the zombie duck out of the regent's chambers. He felt very much like he'd just dodged a bullet. The problem with bullets, however, was that there was usually more than one coming your way.

CHAPTER TWENTY-ONE

AT LEAST IT'S A PLAN

"WHAT DO YOU THINK THE BATHROOMS ARE LIKE IN A WIZARD'S TOWER?" Dirk asked. "I can't imagine they have plumbing, so maybe there's just a hole. Or maybe some kind of magic spell? Yeah, like a teleportation spell. But then where does it teleport to? That's the real question."

"Dirk!" Sarah exclaimed. Suddenly the door opened and Max was led down the row of cells, a solitary guard and the zombie duck in tow.

"Wow, I hope that's not lunch," Dirk said, eyeing the duck. They stopped in front of the cage door and the guard unlocked it, shoving Max inside with the others.

A final *gwuak* was the only sound as the zombie duck issued some kind of warning before it and the guard left them alone.

"Max, what happened?" Sarah asked. She gave him a quick hug. Max blinked a few times, trying to regain his thoughts.

"I saw the *Codex*," he reported. "But it's still not working. I mean, it was there in the right spot, but it didn't reset or anything like it was supposed to. I'm totally confused—it should have reset."

Dirk scratched at his chin as he thought it over. "Maybe Bellstro was mistaken."

"No, I don't think so. We're missing something." Max went on to recount the conversation he'd had with Rezormoor.

"So he really thinks the *Codex* is rebooting? Man, that's awesome," Dirk said with a laugh.

Max nodded. "Yeah, up until tomorrow when he finds out nothing happened. He won't fall for anything like that again."

"And we're stuck in this cell in the meantime," Sarah added.

Puff was still in shock over what he'd heard. "I can't believe one man's ambition is so big that he's willing to wipe us all out to achieve it."

"That's why we have to stop him," Dirk said. "Epically."

Sarah turned to Max. "What was it Bellstro said again?"

Max thought back to the old wizard. "Basically that we had to take the *Codex* back to the Tower—to the spot it was created."

"The spot it was created," Sarah repeated, thinking it over. Max was glad Sarah's brain was on the case since his kept insisting he run to the corner and throw up.

"That's it!" she exclaimed. "Rezormoor said Sporazo first created the *Codex* when he was a student. That it was like a living encyclopedia."

"Yeah," Max agreed. "So?"

"So if he was a student, he wasn't the regent of the Tower yet," Sarah continued. "So he wasn't living in a room at the top."

"Rezormoor said the Tower was like a university," Max said.

"And where do university students live?" Sarah asked.

"With their parents, if they're lucky," Dirk guessed.

Max smiled despite himself. "No, they live in a dorm."

"The Tower has many such rooms," Puff added. "Students live and study here."

"So it could be Sporazo's old dorm room we're looking for," Sarah said. "Or maybe a library or something. But wherever it is, it will be someplace a student has easy access to."

It made total sense, Max thought. But knowing where to look was a long way from being able to do something about it. "Somehow we've got to get out of here and find it."

"Yeah," Dirk agreed. "Too bad Ratticus isn't around, he could pick that lock easy."

Sarah and Max paused, waiting for the off chance that Dirk's spoken wish might result in the thief materializing again. He didn't.

"Even if we *could* get out of here," Puff said, "we'd have to sneak all the way to Rezormoor's chamber, steal the *Codex*, move unnoticed through the various rooms and libraries until we happen to find the one place where the book was created, then after we fix it go back and use it to defeat Rezormoor."

"Almost," Sarah corrected the fluff dragon. "We also need to rescue Princess and Magar."

"Oh, and hope she's not mad at us for the whole being-dragged-under-the-ocean-and-fighting-a-giant-octopus thing," Dirk added.

"Okay, so we rescue them and then go fight Rezormoor," Max said.

"And the Kraken," Dirk added.

"And possibly the dwarf high mage," Sarah said.

"And the monster duck," Puff finished.

Max slumped down. "All after we escape from a dungeon."

The group remained quiet for several minutes as they each pondered the impossibility of what they needed to do.

"I like escaping," Moki said. The fire kitten looked up at the group cheerfully. "It's fun."

"Uh, Moki," Sarah said carefully, "you wouldn't know how to escape from a cell like this, would you?"

Moki looked around the cell before settling his gaze on the lock. "I've been to two dungeons, and we escaped from the first one," he announced. "Do you think I could try this one too? I'd really like to try, if somebody can lift me?"

Sarah looked from the lock back to Moki. "You mean up to the lock?"

"Yeah, that would be great," Moki said.

Sarah gently picked Moki up and lifted him to the lock. The fire kitten giggled. "Wrong way; you'll have to turn me around."

"Oh," Sarah said, turning the fire kitten so his backside faced the lock. Max stood up and backed away a little, unsure what was going to happen.

"Who knew our fire kitten was actually a character class?" Dirk said. "Cool."

Moki smiled and inserted his tail into the mechanism. Suddenly a blue flame ignited inside the lock—so hot and bright that the others were forced to look away from it.

"Won't be long now," Moki said. "Melting things is fun."

"If Moki gets us out of here, I'm officially switching from being a dog person to being a cat person," Dirk said.

"Me too," Puff agreed.

"I guess that's it, then," Max said. "We're actually going to rescue Princess and Magar and fight all the bad guys in the Tower."

"Max, you pulled me out of middle school to go on this adventure with you—I've lost, like, a whole year that

I'm going to have to make up," Sarah said. "The least you can do is save the world again."

"And you know what?" Dirk asked as the lock began to glow red. "With all the stuff that we've gone through, I bet you're like a level-six wizard now. That means you can probably fight skeletons all by yourself. Skeletons, man, just think about it."

Moki made quick work of the cell lock, its innards melting into a slurry of iron goo. The door pushed open, squeaking on its hinges. They froze, waiting for the sound to alert the guards. After a few tense moments, they relaxed.

"Like a baby crying," Dirk said. Sarah was going to say something but decided it wasn't worth the effort. They made their way down the row of cells to the heavy door.

"What's on the other side?" Sarah asked Max.

"A guard sitting at a desk."

The Tower took its security seriously. The guards were all large brutes contracted from the Fighters' Guild, and wore layers of boiled leather armor with black cowls and the Tower's insignia on their chests. Each guard also carried a finely edged sword. Not that there was any lack of spell casters running around, but keeping hired swords on hand was a long-standing Tower tradition.

"He looked tough," Max continued. "But he should have his back to us. At least that was the way he was facing when I was taken through."

"We'll just have to rush him," Dirk said. "Gangster style."

"No, we're not doing anything *gangster* style," Sarah said, not even knowing what it was. "Just leave it to me."

Max held Moki to the lock and the fire kitten inserted his tail inside.

"Forget a skeleton key," Dirk said. "They should call it a kitty key."

Moki smiled. "Am I doing good?"

"You're doing great," Puff answered. "Really great."

Soon the lock started to glow and Moki withdrew his tail. "It's all melty inside now," he announced.

Sarah put her finger up to her mouth and slowly pushed the door open. Just as Max had said, the guard sat at a desk ahead of them. His arms were folded and his head was down. Max set Moki on Puff's back and watched intently, his heart racing.

Sarah crept up to the guard. It seemed like it took

forever for her to cross the distance, but the guard never moved. When she made it, she expertly wrapped her arm beneath his chin, crossing her other arm behind his neck and then pushing forward with a grunt. The guard sprang to his feet, but Sarah anticipated the action and jumped on his back. She squeezed with all her might, taking hold of her bicep with her hand and wrapping her legs around the guard's waist. The brute scrambled to get to his sword, Sarah riding him like he was a bucking bull.

Max and Dirk sprang into action, running over and grabbing the big man's wrist, doing their best to stop him from getting to his blade. Dirk also stomped on the guard's foot for good measure (something he later said was gangster style). The guard was strong, and despite Max and Dirk hanging on his arm, he managed to get to his sword and begin drawing it out. But Sarah's chokehold was tight, and eventually the man's brain decided it had had enough of going without oxygen and called it a day.

The big guard dropped to his knees.

Dirk and Max scrambled out of the way as the guard fell forward with a *thud*, Sarah riding him all the way down with her arms, like two boa constrictors, cinching ever tighter around his neck. "Hurry, grab something to tie him up!" she exclaimed. Since they were in a dungeon, there was no shortage of shackles, locks, and chains. Sarah released her hold and helped Max and Dirk secure the guard.

"Do we really need all this stuff?" Max asked as they clamped a set of shackles closed. "In the movies, people pretty much stay knocked out forever."

"Yeah," Dirk added, noticing the guard beginning to blink. "You hit a guy on the head and you don't have to worry about them anymore."

"If you actually hit someone hard enough they were unconscious for *hours*, you probably killed them," Sarah said as she pulled the chains tight around the guard's feet.

They stood and admired their handiwork. The guard was nearly covered from head to foot.

"Well, I don't think he's going anywhere," Puff said.

"Just remember the stuff you see on TV isn't realistic," Sarah told Dirk.

"She's right, you know," the guard said, joining in on the conversation. "People think a bang on the head's all part of the job. But a concussion's no laughing matter.

You might want to educate yourself about such things before you go knocking people about."

"See?" Sarah said.

"And thank you for not squeezing me till I was dead," the guard added, looking up at Sarah. "It's a pleasure working with a professional." He turned to Dirk, however, and scowled. "Unlike Mr. Foot Stomper over there. Don't you know how easily you can break a toe? I could lose my job, having to hobble around because you went and broke a toe when there was no call for it."

"Aren't we going to stuff rags in his mouth or something?" Max asked. "You know, so he doesn't yell."

"Stuff dirty rags in my mouth?" the guard repeated, sounding shocked. "I don't know what's going on with you two, but I don't think I like it."

"So you're *not* going to yell?" Dirk asked.

"Oh right, because that would be a *really* good idea seeing how I'm all tied up and defenseless. I'll just yell out as loud as I can so you can come back and conk me on the head and do me in for good. I'm not an idiot, you know. I'm perfectly able to wait around for someone in the Tower to eventually show up."

"Uh, I guess you do have a point," Max said.

"Come on, we've got to get going," Sarah urged.

"Wait, we need to check that box over there," Dirk said, pointing to a strong box nearby.

"We do?" Puff asked.

"We have to be able to get our stuff back," Dirk said. "Every dungeon has a nearby room where all your stuff is kept."

Sarah looked at the box. "More game logic?"

"Exactly," Dirk announced. He walked over and opened the box. His resulting smile said everything.

Moments later they had had their gear back, including Glenn. Max slid the dagger back into his belt.

"Storming the castle, are we?" Glenn asked.

"More or less," Max replied.

"Then remember, a castle made from sand will always fall into the sea," Glenn replied. "Or you can just knock it over. You know, because it's just sand."

"Good to have you back," Sarah said, a little too sarcastically for Glenn's liking.

They moved to the other side of the small room, where two doors stood, one with a heavy bar thrown across it.

"The torture chamber's past that barred door and

down some stairs to your right," the guard said. "The other door sends you up into the Tower. You can keep going up all the way to the top, or veer off at any of the side doors to get at the Tower's interior."

"You're a very helpful guard," Max said. The guard managed to shrug.

"The first week, they make you memorize the whole place," he said. "Don't get asked for directions, really, so kind of a waste of time. Well, until now. I guess it goes to show you never know when something you learned might come in handy."

Sarah lifted the bar off the door and carefully opened it. "I think we'll find Princess down here," she said. It opened into a dingy cellar with various torture racks scattered about. In the center was a square cell covered in fluff.

"Is that what I look like?" Puff asked.

"Nah," Dirk lied.

Max found a large key ring hanging on the wall and grabbed it. He moved over to the cage and unlocked the exterior door. Inside, Princess was chained to the floor in her unicorn form. Magar was scrunched up in the corner with his head buried in his hands. He looked up as they entered.

"Wow!" Sarah exclaimed, seeing Princess standing there as a living, breathing unicorn. The others stopped and looked at Sarah.

"What?" she said a little defensively. "I can like unicorns."

They stepped inside and looked around. The cell's interior was covered in layers of hard scales tied firmly to the bars.

"Oh, hey," Dirk said to Princess, a sudden gleam in his eye. "You have to totally say, 'Aren't you a little short for a wizard?'"

"What?" Princess asked, tilting her head to the side. It was strange hearing her talk as a unicorn; she had a bit more of a neighing sound than the usual human voice.

"You know, because you're a *princess*, and you're trapped in a *cell*. And Max is here to rescue you . . ."

Max sighed. "Ignore him—it's a *Star Wars* reference."

"Star wars?" Magar asked.

"Why is the cell covered like this?" Sarah asked.

"Dragon scale," Princess replied. "But can we stop yapping and get us out of here?" Max used the key he'd found to unlock Princess and Magar while Moki watched from Puff's back. Once free of the cage, Princess transformed into her human form—her horn now a wand in her hand.

"The serpent's escutcheon presented a most formidable prison," Magar said after thanking them. "It kept us from using any magic to free ourselves."

"I transformed before they could take my wand, at least," Princess added. "Not that they were happy about it."

"It's what this is all about," Max said to the group. "Rezormoor is killing the dragons to build a suit of armor." He explained what he had learned.

"It could actually work," Princess admitted. "We can't let that happen."

"And that's just what he's told me," Max said. "Who knows what else he has planned."

"Rezormoor's not the kind of man to put all his eggs in one basket," Princess said, nodding.

"What are you talking about?" Dirk chimed in. "Of course you put all your eggs in one basket. Do you know how long it would take to carry eggs one egg at a time?"

Sarah sighed. "Really, Dirk? Is that important right now?"

"I'm just saying," he continued. "You show me a person who comes up with a saying like that and I'll show you the crappiest egg gatherer who ever lived."

"I find it strangely discouraging that he might be right," Magar admitted.

"Yeah," Max agreed. "Welcome to Dirk's world."

Princess tapped her wand in her free hand. "So does anyone have a plan, or are we making it up as we go?"

"A little of both," Puff said.

"Come on," Max said, leading them back to the door. "I'll explain on the way."

CHAPTER TWENTY-TWO

MAX AND HIS WANDERING EYE

THEY STOOD IN FRONT OF THE RUNE-COVERED DOOR AS PRINCESS TAPPED her finger on her wand and pondered what to try next. On the other side lay Rezormoor's chamber and the *Codex of Infinite Knowability*. Princess had assumed she could use her magic to break the seal that held the door shut. But so far she'd been wrong.

"We could always go around and try getting in through the main door," Max suggested, keeping his voice down. He remembered seeing two large doors when he was inside the room.

"I wouldn't recommend it," Magar said. "Once the general alarm is raised, the entire Tower will converge on us. There are powerful mages guarding Rezormoor's main entrance—not that Princess couldn't handle them, but it wouldn't be quick or easy."

"So in other words, this is our only way in," Dirk said.

"And it's a very tricky lock," Princess grumbled. "The door's held by a magical rune. It's sealed tight."

"Except for down here," Moki said. They peered down at the fire kitten as he swished his tail under the door.

Princess and Magar shared a look. "There is *that* spell," Magar said.

"I couldn't do it myself," Princess said. "I can't touch the *Codex*."

"But Max could," Magar replied.

"If he can control it," Princess said.

Max swallowed. "Control it?"

"I can make it so you can reach under the door," Princess told him. "But it takes some ability on your part to make it work."

"Guys, Max is totally a magic user," Dirk said. "He's got *ability*."

"I've cast spells before," Max said, hoping he wasn't about to get himself into a really bad situation.

"Then we may have no other choice," Princess

announced. She turned to Max. "I think I have a way for you to be able to reach the *Codex*. But it's a very difficult spell to control."

"Normally a student starts very slowly," Magar added. "A fingertip, then a finger. Then two fingers, and only for a short distance."

"Because there's a chance it can't be undone," Princess said. "If you let it get away from you, it could become permanent."

Max didn't like the sound of that. But he didn't hesitate. "I can do it," he said. Princess nodded. She directed him to lie on the floor and stretch his hand out so his fingers pressed beneath the door. Princess then touched his hand with her wand and a strange electric shock shot through his arm.

"Now walk it through," Princess said. "Slowly and carefully. Don't lose control of it—don't let it get away from you."

Max began to inch his hand forward, and impossibly it began to flatten and stretch like it was made of rubber.

"Neat!" Moki announced from Puff's back.

Max strained as his hand tingled violently. It tugged against him as if it wanted to disconnect from the rest of his body, but he managed to walk it under the door.

"That's good," Princess said, her face on the floor as she did her best to peer under the door. But Max was struggling to maintain control. His fingers wobbled like they were made of Jell-O, and he could feel the bones in his hand softening.

"Not too much!" Princess warned. She saw waves moving along Max's hand and arm as it lost more of its form. "Max, don't lose control of it."

Max strained against the storm of pins and needles that had become his hand and arm. He focused, fighting against the pull that threatened to let everything come apart. *Like rubber,* he thought to himself. *Not too soft, not too hard.* The waves along his arm ceased, and he felt his flesh grow harder.

"Yes, that's it, Max. That's it," Princess encouraged him. Max could feel the stone beneath his fingers, although the tingling sensation made it hard to guide his movements. He kept going, and before long he'd lost sight of where his hand was moving.

"I can't see what I'm doing now," Max complained.

"You should be able to tap your fingertips and sense what's around you," Magar said. "It's all part of the spell."

Max tried tapping his fingers, but he couldn't get any read on what was going on. He didn't like how this was going—the storm of pins and needles threated to rise up again.

"Don't lose focus," Princess said. "You just need to get used to it."

Max walked his hand farther inside. He tried to remember what the room had looked like—the large fireplace and tall chair, the stone stand, the zombie duck, the . . . zombie duck!

Max suddenly stopped, his heart pounding in his chest. His hand must have traveled ten or fifteen feet by now, and the only thing he could think about was the horrible zombie duck sleeping at the foot of the chair. He pressed his face against the door and tried to see something—but there was only the long pink ribbon that was his arm.

"There's a zombie duck in there," Max said. Sweat had broken out on his forehead and chills ran up and down his spine.

"You can't sense it with your fingers?" Magar asked.

"No!" Max whispered as loudly as he dared. "I could be inches from it—I could be right on top of it, for all I know." The tingling sensation ran up and down Max's arm, and he had the strange feeling that the zombie duck was very near. "What happens if it bites me?" he asked, both desperately wanting to know and not wanting to know.

"Dude, it's a zombie. I think we all know what that means," Dirk said, trying to be helpful.

"Dirk!" Sarah scolded him.

"He's right, Max," Puff said sternly. "You must not let it bite you."

Princess and Magar shared another glance.

"Are you thinking what I am?" Magar asked.

Princess nodded. "I think we have to try."

"Try?" Max said, fighting to keep his arm under control. "Try what?"

"I'm going to help you see what's going on in there," Princess said. "Now stay with me. You know how your hand is feeling weird right now?"

"Yeah?"

"Well, this is going to feel significantly weirder than that," she said.

"Wait, what?" Max asked. But Princess tapped her wand on Max's head and suddenly his left eye closed.

"What's happening?" Max asked, suddenly very nervous.

"I'm sending your eye to your fingertip," Princess announced as casually as if she were explaining that macaroni and cheese contained cheese. And then Max could feel it—his eyeball had up and left the one place that his eyeball was supposed to be and had begun traveling beneath his skin and down to his outstretched arm. It was the same rubbery, tingling sensation as before, but because it was his eye it felt a thousand times worse. An endless barrage of fireworks exploded in his head and he nearly lost control of his arm. After what seemed like an excruciatingly long time, Max's eye suddenly popped into place at the end of his middle finger. His other fingers raised like the legs of an insect around it. Suddenly his vision was filled with two perspectives, and it gave him an instant headache.

"Close your right eye so you don't get confused," Magar recommended. Max did so and the world came into focus. The fireworks and pain in his head fell away, and for all intents and purposes he was now a strange one-eyed hand bug that was staring into the sleeping face of the zombie duck.

Max forgot all about the implications of having an eye on the end of his finger and backed his hand up at once.

Now that he could see, he felt more control over his hand as well.

"Is it working?" Sarah asked. Max concentrated on backing his hand up before answering.

"Yeah, I think I'm getting the hang of it."

"I've never heard of this kind of magic before," Dirk said. "It's kind of gross."

"We'll add it to the list of things you've never heard of, okay?" Princess replied. She turned her attention back to Max. "Now go and find the *Codex*."

"Okay, sure," Max said. He drove his one-eyed hand critter across a rug and over to the black base he'd seen before. He managed to bend his arm at a ninety-degree angle and begin walking up the side of the rock surface. It was colder than he'd expected, which seemed a strange thing to worry about, given his current arm/hand/eye situation.

Max continued climbing, reaching the top of the stand and seeing the *Codex* floating in the air. He realized the pins and needles had largely gone and he was feeling more confident in his control. He concentrated on his fingers, stretching them even farther. Eventually they extended long enough that they wrapped themselves around the *Codex* like rubber bands.

"I've got it," Max announced.

"Keep going, Max," Puff encouraged him. "You can do it."

Max nodded and continued to focus. He began to retract his arm, keeping his entire arm suspended in the air.

"You learn quickly," Princess said, her own eye pressed against the floor and peering under the door. "You're a Sporazo, no doubt."

Max watched from the strange perspective of his middle finger, navigating the *Codex* around the chair and the sleeping zombie duck. He felt like he was in complete control by the time he approached the door. They heard the book hit with a soft *thud* as Max's fingers unraveled.

"Can you, like, fix my eye now?" he asked.

Princess moved the wand over Max and the spell reversed itself until his left eyelid fluttered open and he breathed a huge sigh of relief.

"Talk about a wandering eye," Dirk said. Max would have slugged him had he been able. Instead, he turned to face Princess.

"Now what?" he asked as an unwelcome thought hit him. "The *Codex* is too big to slide under the door."

Sarah groaned. "You mean he did all that for nothing?"

"Max, just how thick is the *Codex of Infinite Knowability*?" Magar asked. "How many pages does it contain?" Max had a feeling he was being asked a trick question.

"It doesn't work that way," he finally answered. "I suppose it can be as thick or thin as it wants." He knew the pages changed all the time.

"Then make it the size you want," Magar urged him.

"Maybe you forgot it isn't exactly working at the moment," Max said.

"But it's *here*," Magar persisted, "in the Tower where it was created. It's close to where it wants to be, Max. It can do this, I think. If you guide it."

Max nodded and turned his attention to the book. He reached out with his mind, expecting the vast expanse of nothing he'd felt so many times before. Instead, there was something there. It was a small spark of *something*—like a lone lighthouse in the midst of a raging sea. Max focused on it and willed the *Codex* to be thinner.

"Well?" Magar asked.

Max let out a breath as he pulled the ancient book under the door.

"You did it!" Puff exclaimed as loudly as he dared.

Max watched as his arm returned to its original size, and the *Codex* suddenly expanded with pages.

"That was neat!" Moki said. "Can you do it again?"

Max stood and slipped the *Codex* into the satchel at his side. "Let's find where this was written," he said.

"And, dude," Dirk added as they began making their way back down the stairs, "remember the long line of vending machines outside the school cafeteria? You've given me an awesome idea."

Max smiled. Here he was risking zombification to snatch the greatest spell book ever written, and his best friend was formulating a plan to nab candy bars.

They descended a few levels before they felt they could talk in anything louder than hushed tones. "Magar?" Max asked. "You spent years here in the Tower. Where would Maximilian Sporazo have first written the *Codex*? Not when he added the Prime Spells, but as a student?"

"That kind of project sounds like a fourth-year student's," Magar answered. "Fourth-years are on the fourth floor. Makes it easy that way."

They climbed down until Magar directed them to stop. "We're here," he announced. "But I'm afraid Princess and I can't go with you."

"Nervous, huh?" Dirk said, putting his arm on Magar's shoulder. "It happens to everyone. I used to get that way before I became an experienced adventurer." Princess swatted Dirk's hand away.

"We're not nervous, you idiot," she said. "We'll be recognized. Too many here know who we are."

"So what do we do?" Max asked.

"Just find Sporazo's original room," Magar said. "It's late, so the place should be quiet."

"So you're saying we just go from door to door with the most powerful spell book in existence and hope nobody notices that either?"

Magar shrugged. "I'm sorry, I don't have all the answers for you, Max. You'll just have to get in there and figure it out."

Max nodded and turned to Puff. "You and Moki better wait here as well. We don't need to stand out any more than we do."

"Whatever you think is best," Puff said.

"I like waiting," Moki added. "Can I count in my head until you come back?"

"Sure," Max said. Moki nodded happily.

They opened the door and Max, Sarah, and Dirk

slipped in. They found themselves in a dimly lit corridor that led to a much larger door. When they reached it, they could hear muffled sounds from the other side.

"What do you think?" Max asked.

"Could be a trap," Dirk suggested.

Sarah shrugged. "I don't think we have a choice but to keep going."

"Okay," Max agreed. "Everyone should be asleep, so I think it's fine." He pulled the door open and stepped through.

The students, it turned out, were definitely not asleep.

The muffled sounds turned out to be some kind of party: various musical instruments were hovering off the ground and playing by themselves, some kind of drink concoction was bubbling through a very complex chemistry lab, and several groups of students were playing a game that reminded Max of dodge ball (except for the levitating fruit and cones of ice shot from wizard staffs). Others were talking, laughing, dancing, or swordfighting with wands. When the door clicked shut the entire party came to a sudden stop and every eye fell on the three kids. Max looked up to see a red ball of light hanging in the air and flashing brightly. Apparently they had triggered some kind of alarm.

"Oh hey, dudes," Dirk said, raising his hand.

The students were all dressed in black robes with striped sleeves, ranging from one to four red stripes. A four-striped student walked up to them.

"What the heck are you doing here?" he challenged, pointing a wand at them. "Kids aren't allowed in the Tower." He was older, with broad shoulders.

"Yeah," a two-striped female added. "You guys are in serious trouble. And why are you dressed like an elf?" She was motioning to Dirk.

Max scrambled for something to say to get them out of their jam. Sarah also tried to come up with a plausible explanation. But it was Dirk who answered first.

"Relax, guys, we're just looking for our dad," he said. Sarah's jaw nearly dropped. "And I think elves happen to be cool."

"Your *dad*?" the older student said, not sure what to think. Obviously that was not what he was expecting to hear.

"Yeah," Dirk continued. "You know, the scary guy upstairs who you'd totally guess *didn't* have any kids, but if he found out you were hassling them he'd zap you into dust . . . ?"

"The arch-mage Zebuker?" another girl asked tentatively, as if even saying his name was risky business.

"Totally," Dirk said. "Good ol' Dad."

The two-striped girl furrowed her brow. "But kids aren't allowed in the Tower. It's the rules."

"Yeah, no duh," Dirk answered. "Not *usually*, but today's different. It's Bring Your Kids to Work Day." The students all looked at one another with blank expressions.

"Wow, you guys didn't read the announcement, did you?" Dirk said.

"Hey, we just finished *finals*," the four-striped student complained. "Nobody around here has time to read announcements."

"Well, I'm just trying to imagine what Zebu . . . *Dad* . . . is going to say when all the other kids show up and they see you guys partying and making a mess of the place. I think he's going to be very, very angry."

"Please don't tell your dad about this," the older student begged, looking truly panicked. He turned to the room. "Everybody, we've got to get this place cleaned up.

Fast!" The students exploded into frantic activity as they began the cleanup process.

"And thanks for the heads-up!" the four-striper called out as he grabbed a drink-stained sofa cushion and flipped it over. Satisfied, he ran off to help the others.

"I can't afford to get into trouble," the two-striped girl said, "so yeah, thanks."

"Sure," Sarah said before Dirk had a chance to say something else and mess it all up. "It's just that Dad sent us down here to see Maximilian Sporazo's old dorm room. I guess we'll just have to tell him you all were too busy cleaning stuff to help."

"Oh wait, no, don't do that," the girl exclaimed. "I'll show you his room—no problem. Everyone knows where it is. And then maybe you can keep this party business just between us?"

Sarah reached out and shook her hand. "Deal."

The student nodded and led the group through the commons area and into one of the main wings. Rows of doors lined each side of the hallway. "This way," she said, taking them about halfway and stopping in front of a door numbered 423. Max reached for the handle, but the girl grabbed his wrist. "Whoa, what are you doing?"

"Going inside," Max answered. He thought that was pretty obvious.

"That's somebody's room," she said. "You can't just walk in."

Suddenly an explosion of blue sparks erupted from the satchel on Max's side. Flames began to burn along the leather straps, and Max yelped, grabbing the *Codex* and throwing the bag away from him. The flames went out as the last of the sparks stopped dancing around the book.

The student's eye went wide.

"That's . . . that's . . . ," she tried to get out. "That's the *Codex of Infinite Knowability!*"

The two-striper reached for a wand tucked into the sash around her waist. She may have been a student of magic, but she'd never met a black belt in judo before. Sarah quickly grabbed her hand and contorted it into a wristlock. The girl was too surprised to even gasp and dropped her wand. Max opened the door and Sarah drove her inside. Dirk snatched the wand and then followed the others into the room, closing the door behind him.

Once inside, the *Codex* practically flew from Max's hands, dragging him across the floor to an old desk where a small candle was burning. As the *Codex* drew near, the candle suddenly filled the room with a brilliant white light.

A sleeping student in a nearby bed waved it off and turned his back, grumbling something before his snoring continued. For Max, the world seemed to pinch together as if the *Codex* were a miniature black hole, devouring light and energy with an unquenchable thirst. Then the same light and energy exploded outward, passing through Max as he struggled to keep hold of the book. His hair danced wildly on his head and a small cyclone of wind erupted in the small space, sending books and papers flying.

Sarah let go of the student. Everyone ducked and covered their heads against the flying objects in the room. Max felt a white-hot light burning through his chest, spreading out through his torso and running down his limbs. The *Codex* danced wildly in his hands, and visions of its pages began flashing before his eyes: people, places, events, and even recipes slammed into his mind. For an instant, everything the Magrus had ever been exploded into his consciousness, and at the brink of it driving him mad, the enormity of it all folded back on itself and was gone.

The room shuddered as the walls and ceiling bowed outward at impossible angles. Then they snapped back and the *Codex* fell to the desk. The wind ceased and the airborne objects dropped to the floor too quickly, as if discovering gravity for the first time.

Most important, Max could feel the *Codex*, his mind drifting easily into it as the sensation of moving through a vast and powerful universe returned to him. But it was different this time—he wasn't set adrift among forces so powerful they threatened to rip him apart. He moved through them as their master.

The student snarled, grabbing a small marble bust and swinging it at Max. Max held his hand out and she froze in place, the statuette held high above her head. Her pupils grew wide, her rage turning to fear. A Prime Spell coursed through Max, requiring only an inkling of energy to stop the attack—a single drop of water in an ocean of power. The student fell to the ground, her body frozen.

"Whoa!" Dirk exclaimed, rising to his feet.

"Max, are you okay?" Sarah asked.

Suddenly a new light filled the room—a swarm of firefly-like emblems that swirled and took on the form of Bellstro.

"Bellstro?" Max asked, recognizing the old wizard.

The wizard looked around and straightened his robes. "Why, yes. It is I," he pronounced.

"What are you doing here?" Max said, slightly confused.

"I'm your *mentor*, of course," Bellstro said. "I'm here to give you helpful tips and insights on your hero's journey."

Sarah blinked several times. "So you're not . . . dead?"

"Er, why get caught up in semantics?" Bellstro replied. "My job is to pop in at convenient breaks in the action and open your mind to new and powerful ways of thinking." Bellstro wiggled his fingers and moved his hands through the air in what he assumed added a mysterious air to his message. He then began searching the pockets on his shimmering, light-enhanced robes. "Let me give you some important information to help you reach the Tower. Hold on, I've got it all written down."

"Um . . . ," Max started.

"We're already at the Tower," Dirk said.

"Oh, you are?" Bellstro looked surprised and stopped searching pockets. He thought it over for a second or two. "Okay, no problem. I can jump to the next part." He cleared his throat and stood tall, raising his hand. "Max, listen as I give you a powerful clue for resetting the *Codex of Infinite Knowability*."

"Too late," Dirk said. Bellstro deflated a little, dropping his hand.

"Uh, yeah," Max added. "I just reset it. Just a second ago." He held up the *Codex* for Bellstro to see.

"But I didn't tell you to believe in yourself and never lose faith," Bellstro complained. "That's important stuff."

"I think we're all good," Sarah said.

"But maybe you could help us with how to defeat Rezormoor Dreadbringer," Max added.

"You don't just hand out otherworldly mentor advice willy-nilly." Bellstro sulked. "There are forms to fill out and approvals to be had. I don't suppose you could hold off while I get it all worked out on my end?"

"We're kind of on a tight schedule," Max said.

Bellstro nodded. "Oh, of course. I understand."

"Wait, I got it!" Dirk exclaimed. "Why don't you work on some last bit of hidden knowledge we get at the very end of the adventure? Some kind of surprise nobody saw coming."

"I suppose that might work," Bellstro said, his spirits lifting.

"Yeah, totally," Dirk agreed. "Something like 'And did you know Sarah is really your sister?'" Sarah slugged Dirk in the shoulder, and Dirk decided it hurt decidedly more than when Max did it.

"Okay, good. I'll do it," Bellstro said as he began to fade away. "But maybe next time you could stop and think a little before you go rushing off and doing everything on your own."

"Uh, okay," Max said. Bellstro frowned and became a mass of swirling lights, finally flying off through the ceiling.

Just then the sleeping student sat up in his bed and looked around. "Weird. Is this, like, a dream or something?"

"Yep," Dirk answered.

The student nodded and fell back down, pulling a blanket tightly around him. On the floor, the frozen student silently watched.

"Maybe we should go now?" Sarah suggested.

"Yeah, good call," Dirk said.

They followed Sarah out the door and past the diligently cleaning students. Max paused. Whatever was going to happen in the final battle with Rezormoor Dreadbringer, he didn't want to risk hurting anyone else in the Tower. He clutched the *Codex* to his side and rolled through the list of the Prime Spells. He had an idea.

"Uh, attention, everyone," Max yelled. He had to try three more times in order to get the room's attention. "I'm going to tell you guys something that's very important." Sarah and Dirk looked at each other, having no idea what was going on.

"Vacuity!" Max exclaimed. The word rang with a force of its own, and Max felt the power of it as it filled everyone's heads, even slipping under doors and penetrating the ears of those who were asleep.

"Vacuity"—*to empty*, Max thought. He focused on the minds of the students, setting the spell to work. He instinctively knew he had to be careful—if he allowed the spell to unwind too much, every student in the room would forget everything they had ever learned. Max didn't need that, he just needed an empty spot in their heads so he could plant a very powerful suggestion. He created a protective bubble around his friends, both in the hall and in the stairwell. Somehow he'd known how to do that, too.

"You all need to leave the Tower and go into the city immediately," Max commanded. The spell lifted his voice and gave it a strange power. "Nothing else is important right now. Gather your friends and anyone else who doesn't know—leave the Tower and don't come back for an entire day. Do you understand?"

As one, every student in the common room replied that they did.

"Creepy," Dirk said to Sarah.

"Yeah, a little bit," she replied.

Max watched as students began shuffling out. Rows of doors opened along the hallways as more students, dressed in their pajamas, made for the exits. One carried the frozen form of the two-striped student in his arms.

"That's not going to last forever, is it?" Sarah asked, seeing the girl.

Max thought it over. "I don't think so."

While the mass of students left by the two main doors, Max and his friends returned to the stairwell. Princess looked a bit uneasy at their return.

"I felt something," she said to Max. "Such . . . *power.*"

"Yeah," Max replied, "the *Codex* is working again. And I kind of get it now—it makes sense."

They huddled together and formulated their next steps. The plan was fairly straightforward: They'd go back up the stairs, use the *Codex* to smash their way through Rezormoor's locked door, and then subdue the Tower regent before he had time to figure out what was going on. Max felt strong as he clutched the *Codex*, but he also knew he was inexperienced. And with an opponent like Rezormoor Dreadbringer, it might take only one mistake to finish him.

They climbed the stairs, each lost in his or her own thoughts. Except for Moki, who had finished his counting game and was waiting for the next exciting thing to happen. He didn't have to wait long.

They stopped at the top of the stairwell, surprised that the sorcerer's door stood open. A heavy black mist rolled from the room beyond and crawled down the steps and past their feet.

"Please, come in," Rezormoor announced, his voice rising around them.

So much for the element of surprise, Max thought. He clutched the *Codex* tightly and took a breath. There was nothing to do but go in.

CHAPTER TWENTY-THREE

THE TOWERING INFERNO

MAX LED THE OTHERS INSIDE. HE RECOGNIZED THE REGENT'S PERSONAL quarters as before, but it was also another place entirely—a world of shadows that moved as if blown by invisible winds.

As his eyes adjusted, Max could work out others standing there: the Kraken, his orange skin bloodred in the shades of night; the dwarf high mage, her cold eyes hard as steel; and even Loki, his tail aflame and his feline face grinning as he stood next to the zombie duck. In the center stood Rezormoor Dreadbringer, his sorcerer's robes catching the invisible current as the blue stones set within his armored shoulders and belt glowed brightly. He wore his hood over his head so that strands of black hair spilled out, and his eyes were simply two simmering pools of crimson. Strangely, the faint outline of wings spread out from the sorcerer's back, making him look every bit like some dark angel come to wreak havoc on the world.

"The answer to your unspoken question is this," Rezormoor said, his voice echoing as if he was standing in a great cavern instead of a room. "I have gathered the Shadrus and brought it here."

"A dangerous thing to invite the Shadrus into our world," Princess said.

"I did not get where I am because of simple hubris," Rezormoor replied. "I know how powerful the *Codex* is, and I'm not above taking precautions." Rezormoor bent down and reached into the swirling mist at his feet. The Kraken and high mage did likewise, each lifting a single serpent's escutcheon fashioned into a shield. "I am encircled by power," the sorcerer continued.

"Black magic," Magar said sourly. "Drawn from Shadrus."

"Even so," Rezormoor said. "It is a means to an end. Yours, as it were."

Moki pointed to Loki sitting across the room. "You're a bad kitty!"

Loki shrugged. "I'll try to see if I can live with it as I

spend the rest of my life in unimaginable wealth." Moki hissed angrily, and it was the first time any of them had heard the tiny fire kitten do so. It even made Loki look a little nervous.

"Can we just skip to the final battle?" Dirk said, producing the wand he'd taken earlier. "Look, we all know you're going to make your offer to Max that if he does what you want you won't kill us, blah blah blah. And then you'll try to convince him that there's some hidden moral good that justifies everything. So Max will think it over, remember the words of his mentor—who totally blew it, by the way—then turn you down cold. You won't like that, so you'll get all evil and lose your temper, showing your true colors. You might turn into some kind of monster or something, I'm not really sure on that point. But the main thing is we'll have a big fight and we'll totally waste you. So we should just jump to the good part."

The crimson pools in Rezormoor's hood fluttered. "How do you know all that?"

"Duh, I'm a *gamer*. And the thing about being a gamer is, we can cut out all the talk and just get to the fighting. Because we all know Max isn't about to go along with you. I mean, that would totally blow to come all this way and have him be like, 'Oh yeah, I like your style. Let's be buds and go rule the world together.'" Dirk poked his wand at Rezormoor, punctuating each word: "Ain't gonna happen."

Princess turned to Dirk. "Speaking of style, I kind of like yours."

"Cool." Dirk smiled. "Unexpected love interest. I like it."

"That's it!" the Kraken bellowed. "I can't listen to this geek talk anymore!" The monster flung the makeshift shield into a corner, toppling over a large pile of dragon scale. He launched forward, muscles rippling and taloned fingers outstretched. But Max's mind leapt to one of the Prime Spells even faster.

"Irony!" he called out. And this time his voice crashed into the room much as it had done on the day he'd used the same spell to defeat Robo-Princess. In a heartbeat the monster that was the Kraken was no longer, and instead the boy Ricky Reynolds flew past Dirk and landed hard on the floor. He rose, reaching for the talisman that had hung around his neck and was the source of his power. But it was gone. Ricky panicked for a moment, but that quickly turned to rage. He was still the same Ricky Reynolds who

346 Platté F. Clark

was captain of the wrestling team, the kid who struck fear into every student at Parkside Middle School, the bully who'd been humiliated by a girl who'd flipped him in the hallway. He turned to Sarah with clenched fists, but surprisingly, Sarah smiled.

"You're going to get beaten by a girl *again*," she said, "if you're stupid enough to try it."

And then everything happened at once.

Max turned away from Sarah, knowing she could handle herself just fine. The power of the *Codex*'s spell had taken Rezormoor and the high mage aback—it had that effect on people, especially if they were sensitive to magic. But it wasn't likely to happen again. Max heard a growl and caught sight of Moki flying overhead at a wide-eyed Loki. Max figured Loki was in for a whole world of trouble.

Princess drew her wand and sent a lightning bolt ripping through the air at the high mage. But the dwarf had retrieved her own wand and met it with a bright-red bolt of her own. The two struggled, their magic like two intertwined whips fighting for dominance. Magar drew his wand and joined the battle, but as soon as his magic touched that of the other two an explosion of sparks filled the room and Magar was slammed against the wall. He slumped to the floor, his wand rolling from his hand. Max caught sight of the zombie duck as it made a run for Dirk. It moved much faster than a waddling duck had any right to. Dirk tried using the wand to protect himself, but nothing happened. So he yelped and made a run for it, the zombie duck hot on his heels. Puff made a run at something too, but Max couldn't tell what.

Then a force slammed into Max and he tumbled backward, the *Codex* flying out of his hand. Rezormoor stood across the room from him, his palm outstretched past the dragon-scale shield. The smell of old copper pennies filled Max's nose, and he felt something wet drip past his lip. He was bleeding, and the sight of his own blood on the floor was unsettling.

"It's not too late," the sorcerer said as he began to close the distance. Max heard the fire kittens fighting off to his right, and he caught a glimpse of Ricky circling Sarah in his best wrestling stance. The *snap* and *crack* of the battling spell casters filled the room with electric energy. The high mage managed to swing her shield around to deflect Princess's magic, breaking their deadlock. The dwarf spell caster swung her wand around and launched fire balls at Princess.

"Panoply!" Max called out. *Panoply—to cover and protect.* The fireballs never made it to the unicorn but deflected off the invisible shield Max had placed in front of her. Rezormoor paused.

"Impressive," he admitted. "You can use the *Codex* without even touching it."

Princess used the shield to her advantage, taking the necessary time to summon a gust of wind that struck the high mage with the force of a hurricane, wrapping around her shield and sending the dwarf flying backward into the far wall. Anything in the immediate vicinity that wasn't secured was picked up by the blast of wind and sent flying toward the high mage as well. Princess grinned and took off after her, nearly running into Dirk as he jumped over a table to avoid the zombie duck's gnashing teeth. Puff had a dragon-scale shield in his mouth and was dragging it across the room toward Magar.

Max rolled through the list of Prime Spells in his head. "Tutelary!" Max commanded. *Tutelary—to summon protection.* He wasn't exactly sure what was going to happen, but suddenly a knight in shining white armor appeared next to Dirk. The shadows actually withdrew from the being's presence, and it moved to stand between

Dirk and the zombie duck, taking up the fight on Dirk's behalf. If the zombie duck was intimidated by the new arrival, however, it didn't show it.

"Fool!" Rezormoor shouted at Max. The sorcerer muttered something Max couldn't understand, and the shadows on the floor materialized into monstrous claws, grabbing hold of him as he struggled to break free. They were impossibly strong, and Max felt himself begin to slip *down*. With a new sense of horror he realized the floor below him had turned into a thick, dark liquid and he could feel an otherworldly chill begin to crawl up his skin. Evil lurked below the surface, of a kind Max had never felt before.

"You fling the Prime Spells about like a novice learning to light a candle!" Rezormoor roared. "This must end, and you must do as I command!"

Max felt a ringing in his ears and a wave of nausea wash over him. He looked up to see Rezormoor with both hands over his head. The air seemed to grow too thin, and Max could see his breath as a vicious cold slammed into the room. Figures appeared, stepping out of the shadows in perfect unison. On each was a helm of ancient construction, engraved in runes and running much too long to fit a human face. The eyeholes were black, but beneath the helmet's rims, rotting bone and teeth glistened. They wore robes made from a heavy green fabric, flowing over misshapen bodies and dulled by countless centuries of wear. When hands could be seen extending past the long open sleeves, the flesh was black as if mummified, with small plates of steel riveted into the bone to form living gauntlets. Golden snakes, like transparent spirits, slithered around them, traveling up and down the long obsidian staffs clutched at their sides. Max recognized them at once, and the room filled with the icy grip of death.

"Shadrus necromancers," Rezormoor announced. "Devourers of souls. I believe you are acquainted."

Princess swung around, spinning with her wand held out in front of her, bracing for an attack. Max could hear Ricky Reynolds panting somewhere nearby. He turned and caught a brief glimpse of the wrestler lying on the ground while Sarah stood over him, her hands raised like a boxer's.

Elsewhere, Puff had reached Dirk and the two of them raised the dragon scale to protect themselves as best they could. The zombie duck circled the spectral knight, hissing and snapping.

The nauseating power from the Shadrus necromancers nearly overwhelmed Max. He was still struggling against the soft floor when he found the fireball spell. It wasn't a Prime Spell, but it had plenty of power. He called it from the *Codex* and sent it slamming into the middle of the necromancers.

There was a piercing howl as the ball of flame exploded. The heat cut through the room's chill and the shadows pulled back from wherever the magical flame took hold. The fire consumed several skeletons, while others burned and screeched. But many remained untouched—too many, it seemed to Max. Two of them launched themselves at the spectral knight, grabbing the magical being and dragging it to the floor. Dirk tried to use the wand, poking at the air with it. A skeleton advanced on him, summoning a glowing sword and raising it to strike. Dirk dropped the wand and drew his blade. He'd been able to practice some with Conall, and Max desperately hoped it was enough.

A burst of glowing arrows began flying across the room and raining into the Shadrus necromancers. Max turned to see Magar chanting, the magical bolts materializing in front of him before taking flight.

A loud *PPFFFT!* sounded out as Loki flew from one corner of the room to the other. Moki leapt after him in hot pursuit.

The rest of the skeletons rushed into the battle. Max had lost sight of the high mage, but he heard the distinctive *SNAP!* of lightning as a bolt ripped from Princess's wand and struck several of the advancing skeletons, incinerating them on the spot. But there were too many of them. Max slipped farther into the black abyss at his feet when he felt something grab hold of his collar.

"Hang in there!" Puff said through clenched teeth and fabric. Somehow the little fluff dragon had made it back across the room and had come to help Max. Max summoned another fireball and threw it at Rezormoor. The flame exploded around him. But the sorcerer simply walked through it, the flames vanishing as if all the oxygen had been sucked from around his person. It was just a normal spell, and Rezormoor had shrugged it off like dusting sand from his shoulder. Max reached deeper into the *Codex* and found what he was looking for.

"Elementity!" he shouted. *"Elementity"—to affect through fire, earth, water, or air.* The blue ball of flame roared into existence, swallowing the sorcerer and burning like a miniature sun. Several of the skeletons standing nearby ignited and fell to the ground. The dark mist and shadows raced from the fire, clinging to life in the far corners of the room. The ground beneath Max began to solidify, and Puff gave a final pull that broke Max free. The little fluff dragon lost his footing and fell as Max scrambled to his feet.

A shudder filled the room and the ball of flame shrank. Max could see Rezormoor, his hands on either side of the ball, pushing it in on itself. The sorcerer's clothes were smoldering, and both his hood and hair and been burned away. Rezormoor grunted with a final effort and clasped his hands together, extinguishing the blue ball. He stumbled, nearly exhausted by the effort it took to survive the Prime Spell. But the sorcerer raised his head and stared at Max, naked anger on his face. Then he moved, faster than Max would have thought possible, drawing his daggers and flashing across the room. He appeared next to Ricky, knocking the boy to the ground and spinning behind Sarah. She froze, the tips of the black blades pushing against her—one at her throat, and the other at her side.

"Enough!" Rezormoor shouted and the chaos of

the room suddenly froze. Dirk was panting, his thin sword raised against the skeleton necromancer. Magar was lying on the floor, a spectral snake-oozing skeleton standing over him, while Princess had turned into her unicorn form. She had reared, her muscular legs slashing through the air and her horn a dazzling silver against her white mane. A group of Shadrus necromancers had encircled her.

"Use the *Codex*," Rezormoor said to Max. "Make my armor and your friends need not die."

"Max . . . ," Sarah began, but words failed her. She knew Max could never give in to the sorcerer's demands, but she didn't want to die because of it. Her mind raced through her training, but with both knives against her there was no way to could get free.

"Don't hurt her!" Max cried. He could feel the shadows begin to retake the room. The icy chill returned.

"If you help him, we lose," Dirk said, his chest heavy as he caught his breath. But his friend looked flushed and his words sounded hollow. He'd been holding his own against the skeleton, but just barely. And sooner or later it would get the best of him.

Princess dropped to the ground. She glistened with a

sheen of sweat but looked powerful and strong. This was
no unicorn drawn with smiley faces and rainbows. She
was beautiful, magnificent, and *dangerous* in a way that
defied words. Max was grateful she was on his side and
not Rezormoor's.

But in the end there was really no choice. Despite the
visions and the warnings and all they had gone through,
he could not watch Sarah or Dirk die in front of him.
Their lives were his responsibility, and he'd shirked it
before. But not now—he was done with being afraid all
the time. He was done with being used. And with his
resolve, he felt a power begin to grow within him. It
stretched out and connected to the *Codex* like two mag-
nets drawn to each other. The room bristled with energy,
and the Shadrus necromancers began to withdraw from
Max, turning their heads. The air turned electric.

"What are you doing?" Rezormoor demanded. "I'll
kill her!"

"Do so and you will die," Max said. And the way he
said it left no doubt. "I am making your armor, sorcerer."

"Max?" Puff asked from behind him.

Max swam within the ocean of magic that was
the *Codex* and began weaving Prime Spells together.

Something told him that this was very dangerous to do, but he pressed on.

"Gravity," Max said. *Gravity—the power to attract.* His voice resonated with the power of the Prime Spell, and the Shadrus necromancers withdrew farther. The pile of dragon scale lifted from the far corner of the room.

"Let her go and stand there in the center," Max said to Rezormoor. The sorcerer hesitated.

"I will not surrender my leverage as easily as that," he replied.

"I can't do it if you're touching her," Max said. "If you're near anyone, it won't work."

Rezormoor thought it over. "Are you a man of your word, Max? Would you swear to me if I do as you ask?"

"I won't break a promise," Max answered coldly. Rezormoor nodded.

"Then swear to me, on the lives of your friends, that if I do as you ask, you will allow me to don the armor. That I will be able to step into it unharmed."

"Max, don't!" Dirk cried.

"Please, think what you're doing," Puff urged him. But Max pressed on.

"I swear it," he said. Rezormoor smiled and released

Sarah. He sheathed his daggers and walked to the center of the room. "And here I thought I would have to instruct you on what to do," he said. "You are quite an impressive young man."

"If you do this, he will be unstoppable," Princess warned.

"And those who serve him will be rewarded," a voice sounded from the far side of the room. The dwarf high mage stepped forward, bloodied and her armor hanging in tatters. But she lived. "You have made the right choice," she said to Max. "This is the inevitable end."

Max reached out and wrapped the gravity spell around the *Codex*, and it gently glided into his hands. As he touched it, more power surged through him.

"The high mage speaks the truth," Rezormoor said. "All has been done according to my design."

"Think of the dragons," Puff urged. "Think of this entire world lost to darkness. Think of your world falling next. You've simply traded one dark future for another." But if the words were striking home, it didn't show on Max's face. Max continued, finding the next spell. "Unity," he said. *Unity—to unite into one.* The floor shook as the various pieces of dragon scale merged together.

"Unbelievable," the high mage said in awe, "to transform the serpent's escutcheon with a single word."

The scale was a shimmering black on the surface, and soft with fluff on the underside. It had been formed into a perfect square twenty feet wide and floated in the air. The necromancers shrank away.

"Hold!" Rezormoor yelled at them. "You are bound to me! You will serve me until I release you!"

Now Max pictured a suit of armor in his mind. He opened himself to the next Prime Spell, weaving it around the image in his head. Bringing them together in such a way flooded the room with magic. The spells were great ocean tides, tugging at Max and threatening to pull him under. One mental slip, and he'd be consumed by them. He continued to concentrate, drawing from knowledge he had never had, but that he felt nevertheless.

"Panoply," Max said, closing his eyes. *Panoply—to cover and protect.* This time the room shook as if a small earthquake rumbled outside. Bits of stone broke free from the walls and ceiling, and Dirk nearly lost his footing. The high mage gasped, and even Princess stepped backward. The black square wrapped itself around Rezormoor and began to flow like liquid, forming into the intricate armor as if being poured into an invisible mold.

When Max opened his eyes, he saw the man from his nightmare—the solitary figure in black armor that would lay waste to the world.

"Yes." Rezormoor began to laugh. "Yes!" The armor covered him from head to foot as, black tendrils of smoke drifted from the sorcerer. It was exactly as Max had seen in his dream.

"I'm reminded of the fluff dragons," Rezormoor said, stretching his hand and flexing his gauntleted fingers, "to have been adorned nearly as I am now. It's a feeling one can hardly describe. How sad to have it taken away. Sad but profitable. This is the way of the world."

Rezormoor lowered his hand and turned his attention to Max. "Well, you've done this perfectly. Your connection to the *Codex* is remarkable; it's almost as if . . ." He flipped his visor open and stared at Max with a strange expression. "No, it couldn't be."

The high mage dropped to the floor, and the Shadrus skeletons followed her lead. "What do you command of us?" she asked.

"Kill them all," Rezormoor ordered. "When Max dies, the power to defeat me dies with him."

"Good-bye," Puff said at his side. The fluff dragon's voice was laced with a heavy sadness, having lost not just himself but everything in the world as well. And Max supposed he had: his magic, his strength, his family, and now his friends. The very sight of the poor creature left little evidence of his once grand nature. He was a simple fluff dragon now, soft on the outside and hard on the inside.

Fluff dragons, Max thought to himself. *They're the key to everything.* An idea came to life, and Max reached for the *Codex* with his mind.

"Density!" he yelled as the Shadrus skeletons advanced. *Density—to compact or make heavy.* He gathered the Prime Spell and flung it at Rezormoor. Waves of it crashed over the sorcerer, but enough of the Prime Spell penetrated into the dragon scale and took hold. Suddenly the armor became very, very heavy.

It was impossible to say just how much the armor weighed, only that it fell forward and crashed into the floor, sending a spiderweb of cracks spreading across the room. The skeletons halted as Max wove the next spell: "Parity!" he cried. *Parity—to balance and make equivalent.* Max focused on the outside of the armor and willed it to change.

The dragon-scale armor Rezormoor wore was no longer soft on the inside and hard on the outside. The Prime Spell wove through the heavy plate and transformed it so it was hard on the inside, too. And just like with the fluff dragons, the serpent's escutcheon turned the sorcerer's magic back on itself. Rezormoor cried out as whatever spell he was conjuring suddenly disappeared. Max also felt a snapping of magical chains that ran from Rezormoor to the various Shadrus necromancers around the room.

"Your bonds are broken," Max yelled at them. "Flee now or be destroyed." The web of cracks, which grew beyond the floor and began to climb the walls, started to break open. A terrible rumble filled the room as bits of stone dropped from the ceiling. The remaining shadows drained away like dirty water in a tub. The necromancers used their freedom to cast themselves into the last of the shadows and disappear.

The high mage looked up at Max in horror. "Don't kill me," she pleaded.

Max's reply was one word: "Run."

"Max, we've got to get out of here!" Sarah shouted above the growing noise. She reached down and helped

Ricky up from the floor. He blinked, surprised.

"What can I do?" he offered.

"Grab Magar," Sarah said. Ricky moved like the athlete he'd always been and scooped up the unconscious wizard, throwing him over his shoulders.

"No!" Rezormoor shrieked. He sank several inches farther, the floor beginning to bow beneath the armor's weight.

"I promised I'd put you in the armor, and I did," Max said to the sorcerer. "And I promised that I'd defeat you so the dragons would live. And now I've done that, too."

"Impossible!" Rezormoor screeched.

"I know I'm not the strongest or the bravest kid out there. But I do keep my promises."

"Yeah," Dirk said as he ran up to Max's side. He'd found Moki and was holding him in his arms. "Game over, baldy."

"Baldy?" Rezormoor shouted. The armor sank farther into the floor. "BALDY? NOOOOO!" As far as last words went, Dirk thought the sorcerer could have done better than that.

Princess had returned to her human form and grabbed Dirk by the shoulder, spinning him around.

"Come on," she shouted, pushing him toward the door.

"That's my girlfriend," Dirk said as he ran past Max.

"Where's the zombie duck?" Max asked, but Princess gave him a shove and got him moving.

"Don't worry about it," she yelled. Princess scooped up the cowering Loki by the scruff of his neck. They made a run for it with Puff and Sarah on their heels. Max took a last look around the room—there was no sign of the high mage. He turned and ran after his friends.

They flew down the long flight of stairs as the Wizard's Tower shook and began to collapse. They heard the tremendous *BOOM* of Rezormoor falling through the top level, and then the sounds of the next floor rumbling violently as it began to give way. When they made it to the bottom, they joined with Tower guards and others who were fleeing toward the main doors. Sarah grabbed one of the big guards by the shoulder and yelled at him, "There's a guard tied up in the prison! Get him!" The man nodded and turned, making for the basement as fast as he could. Another *BOOM* sounded as the next floor collapsed.

They ran outside, chunks of the Wizard's Tower fall-ing around them. They didn't stop, sprinting through the great stone forest that surrounded the grounds and all the way to the outside wall. Max and the others reached it, panting and out of breath. They turned just in time to see the Wizard's Tower implode, falling in on itself with a rumble that was felt throughout the entire city.

"Now, *that* is how you defeat an evil wizard," Dirk said, grinning ear to ear.

CHAPTER TWENTY-FOUR

A FAMILIAR RIDE

SARAH RECOGNIZED THE WAGON THAT PULLED UP TO THE TOWER GATE immediately. Amid all the confusion, the two-horse carriage driven by Sumyl may have looked out of place, but it felt like a safe harbor in a storm. If there was anywhere Max and his friends felt protected and comfortable, it was there. As they approached, the door swung open and Dwight jumped out. "You're alive!" he shouted. He sounded uncharacteristically happy.

"What in the world are you doing here?" Max asked. He looked up at the elf, who smiled down at him in return.

"You have some very powerful friends, Max Spencer," Sumyl said. "I've been chartered for a special journey . . .

and paid handsomely, if I might add. Enough to purchase a second carriage and driver for my old route. But please, come inside."

"Thanks," Max said. "Let me just make sure everyone's okay."

Sarah stood next to Princess and flagged a city guard. Three of them ran over.

"Are you okay?" the guard asked. All around them, citizens and soldiers were pouring into the Tower grounds to assist any who needed help.

"Yes, thank you," Sarah replied. She motioned to Loki, still hanging from the scruff of his neck in Princess's hand. "This fire kitten was in league with Rezormoor Dreadbringer to not only hunt and kill dragons, but to wage war against this city and the kingdom."

Princess handed him over. "Keep his tail doused in water or he'll be up to no good," she told the guard.

The guard nodded and examined the ragged-looking fire kitten. "Looks like someone got the better of him."

"No more evil for you, mister," Moki said, pointing a claw at his former boss. Loki flinched.

"Please, Officer, take me to jail now," Loki begged. The man shrugged and carried the fire kitten away.

"What about him?" Princess said, motioning toward Ricky.

"He carried me from the Tower," Magar said, stepping forward. There was a nasty welt growing on the side of the wizard's head.

Max walked over with Dirk.

"Hey, Spencer," Ricky said. "And Dirk."

"Ricky 'The Kraken' Reynolds," Dirk said as he leaned against the carriage, striking his coolest pose. "Well, well, well. Back to being a human—or are you?"

"Whatever," Ricky said.

"I think we should talk about it," Max said, addressing Princess. "I don't know what we should do with him just yet."

"Is there anything else, then?" the guard asked.

Sarah cast a look at Ricky and then shook her head. "No, we're fine. Thank you."

The guard nodded and ran off to join the others.

"Thanks for not turning me in," Ricky said.

"We'll see," Sarah announced. "Like Max said, we need to talk about it." She turned to address Sumyl. "Can you keep an eye on him?"

The elf nodded, drawing an elven bow across her lap.

"Why don't you have a seat up here next to me," Sumyl offered. "I don't have to warn you not to run, do I? You know how elves are with bows."

"Uh, not really," Ricky admitted. "But I won't run." He climbed up the carriage and found a spot next to the elf.

"Inside," Dwight said, motioning toward the door. "There's been strange things going on since you left Jiilk."

They climbed aboard the magical carriage to find a figure sitting on the crescent-shaped bench.

"Come on, everyone—take a seat," Dwight directed. They all found a place to sit, Puff plopping down next to Max. The stranger was dressed in black leather and wore a Techrus-style cowboy hat pulled over his face. Max felt the familiar ringing in his ears whenever he was around someone or something that radiated magic. Then he recognized the man who'd sent them back in time from the future. Except he wasn't a man, really. He was a dragon.

"Obsikar," Max said, addressing the dragon king.

"So you know me," Obsikar said. "That's good, as apparently we've met before."

"It's okay," Dwight said, closing the carriage door behind them. "Obsikar and I have had a long while to talk this through. He understands what happened with

Robo-Princess and the deal we made to come back."

"Robo-Princess?" Princess asked, raising an eyebrow. "What a horrible name."

"And we did it," Dirk said proudly. He'd taken a seat next to Princess. "We saved the dragons."

"So it would seem," Obsikar said. "I heard strange whisperings in the mountains—that a band of Techrus humans stepped between Mor Luin knights and a dragon. So I sought this dragon out and was told a rather remarkable story."

Puff sat on the bench with his mouth hanging open before he finally found the courage to speak. "It's all as they've said, my liege. I've been with them for some time. They've always sought to stay true to their promise to save us, even when it put them in peril. They even rescued me from a cruel life with orcs."

Obsikar nodded. "Friends to all dragons, then. I am pleased to hear this."

"Obsikar tracked me down in Jiilk," Dwight said. "I told him everything that happened. After that, he was anxious to find you."

"So you really did travel into the future?" Princess asked. "I had become some kind of living statue there?"

"A robot," Dirk answered. "I'll tell you all about it on our next date."

Princess did a double take. "Date?"

"You were there too," Dirk said to Magar, "but you were just a floating head."

"Oh," Magar said, not liking the sound of that. "I suppose it figures."

Obsikar noted the *Codex of Infinite Knowability* sitting on Max's lap. "So the *Codex* has been returned to the Magrus after all these years."

"Yeah," Max said. "But it wasn't easy."

"And he's, like, the long-lost descendant of the dude who wrote it," Dirk added.

"Not exactly," Obsikar corrected him.

Sarah leaned forward. "Wait, what do you mean by that?"

Obsikar shifted to face Max. "When I said I'd met you before, I wasn't talking about the encounter in the future. I was introduced to you on the day you were born . . . by your father."

"My father?" Max said, confused. His father had divorced his mom when he was little and never came back. "How would my father know you?"

"Because you're not some long-lost relative whose blood contains the slightest remnants of the *Codex*'s author, Max. *You* are the very son of Maximilian Sporazo, born in the Tower by a mother burned by dragon's fire, and taken into the future to live secretly in the Techrus."

"Oh snap!" Dirk said, flinging himself against the back of the seat. "Of course! It all makes sense."

"The *Codex* was taken to the Dwarven vaults for safe-keeping. But when Sporazo disappeared, it went to you on its own."

Sarah looked at Max. "That's what surprised Rezormoor in his chamber. Your connection to the *Codex* was more powerful than he'd anticipated. He must have figured it out."

"Only the son of Maximilian Sporazo could command the *Codex* like you did," Princess added. "You wielded the Prime Spells as if you'd been doing it your entire life."

"Then what about my mom?" Max asked, his head spinning. "Does she know any of this?"

"You were simply adopted," Obsikar said. "No different from any other child in similar circumstances. She does not know who you are, or where you come from."

"So what now?" Max asked. He was glad he was

sitting in the magical carriage, because had he been anywhere else he might have gotten sick.

"What do you want to do?" Obsikar replied. "You
could stay and rebuild the Tower as the son of Maximilian
Sporazo if you desired."

"Or we could go and get a castle from Prince Conall,"
Dirk suggested.

"The kings of the Seven Kingdoms would grovel at
your feet," Princess said. "You could have anything you
wanted."

Max thought about it and then turned to Sarah.
"What do you want, Sarah?" he asked.

Sarah smiled. "I just want to go home, Max. Pretty
much the same as I always have. To rejoin my family, go
back to school, and live a normal life."

Max's decision was easy. "Then we're going home."

Obsikar nodded. "I thought as much. This is why I
have provided the best coach in the Seven Kingdoms to
drive you to the Mesoshire, and from there to take you
home. Consider it my reward, insignificant as it may be,
for saving my family from destruction."

Max took a deep breath. *Home*, he thought to himself.
Finally, we're going home.

Obsikar stood and made his way to the door. "Have a pleasant journey," he said. "Perhaps fate will see you returned to the Magrus someday. If it happens, consider yourself a friend of the dragons, now and forever."

The thought of losing a castle had bummed Dirk out. But hearing he was a dragon friend made him smile. "Cool," he said with a grin.

Obsikar nodded again and stepped through the door. A moment later, the slate in the wall opened and Sumyl peered through. "Do you wish to stay or make for the Tree of Attenuation right away?"

Max looked around. He was surrounded by friends and a magical fridge stocked with food. "What do you say?" he asked.

"Perhaps I could ride with you a ways?" Princess asked. "I think I will return to the Unicorn Nation."

"And if it isn't too much trouble, I have family in Emelen," Magar said. "Maybe I could get a lift too?"

Max nodded, turning to Dwight. "I've had enough of being underground," the dwarf said. "I think I'd like to get back to the Dragon's Den. Maybe do some remodeling. It just so happens I've come across a good supply of silver."

Puff looked up at Max. "I have nowhere to go. Do you think I could travel to the Techrus with you?"

"Why not?" Max said. "We'll just say you're, like, a messed-up sheepdog or something. You can totally live with me."

"I can?"

"Sure," Max continued. "You're the one who gave me the idea to use Rezormoor's armor against him."

"I didn't know that," Puff said.

"If you were never a fluff dragon, I bet Max wouldn't have come up with it," Dirk added. "Dude, maybe you didn't realize it, but you kind of saved the world too."

Puff smiled, and it was the most genuine and joy-filled smile Max had seen in some time.

Moki raised his paw. "Are there fire kittens where you're going?"

"No," Dirk said, "but there are hot dogs." He busted out laughing and the others joined in, unable to help themselves.

"You can come and live with me if you want to," Sarah said to Moki as she wiped tears from her eyes. "We'll just have to have some rules about your tail."

"I think it's unanimous," Max said. "Let's go home."

His eyes drifted back to the small kitchen, where he noticed the "additional fee" sign had been removed.

"I heard about how you all saved the world," Sumyl called back. "Help yourself to my kitchen—I figure it's the least I can do."

Dirk clapped his hands together. "Time to eat, people!"

Magar hurried and turned to Princess. "He means it's time for *everyone to eat.* Not the other thing."

Princess smiled. "Sometimes you're not half-bad for a grumbling indentured wizard."

"You know," Glenn spoke up from Max's belt, "a great adventure is like a glass half-filled with water: You may never know who put it in there and why they didn't finish it. And that can be fairly annoying."

Max put Glenn in a drawer as he made his way to the kitchen.

It was late the following day as they journeyed onward, a range of majestic mountains rising to the north. Max and his friends ate and laughed and slept, and were discussing whether or not they should spend the night at an inn when a mass of swirling lights entered the carriage.

Princess had her wand in her hand in a flash, but Max

put his hand up. "Wait," he called out. "I think I know who this is."

The lights swirled about and gathered into the shape of Bellstro.

"Oh good, I've found you!" the old wizard announced. "You wouldn't believe how much effort it took to uncover a secret to reveal to you, but I did it."

"Is that Bellstro the ancient?" Princess asked.

Dirk nodded. "Yep. Now in postlife mentor form."

"Of course it is," Magar said with a shrug. He'd decided anything and everything was possible with this group.

Bellstro cleared his throat. "Max, you have done well and completed your hero's task. You have gained a reward and now you must return to your home."

"Headed that way now," Sarah said.

Bellstro looked slightly irritated but continued. "Be that as it may, there is still a secret that I must tell you. And once I do, it will change everything!" He strung the last word out and waved his fingers in the air for dramatic affect. "Max, I am going to tell you who your father *really* is."

"The World Sunderer and arch-sorcerer Maximilian

Sporazo," Max said, trying to match Bellstro's dramatic flair.

"Wait, what?" the old wizard said, looking rather upset. "Seriously?"

Dirk nodded. "We totally got that information, like, yesterday. You gotta pick the pace up on this stuff."

"You know what?" Bellstro said. "You guys really stink." And in a flurry of light he disappeared.

Dirk lifted his arm and sniffed. "He might be right."

A lone farmer worked near the road, gathering the last of his hay. He stopped and watched the beautiful carriage drive by—he'd never seen anything like it before. He might have even thought it was elven, especially given the coach's driver, but that would have been impossible. From inside, he heard voices drifting out into the unseasonably warm afternoon.

"When are we going to let Ricky in?" somebody asked.

"Maybe tomorrow," a second voice responded.

"Or the next day," came a third.

Laughter broke out as the coach made its way past the field and around the bend.

Probably a bunch of teenagers up to no good, the farmer thought.

❦

It was night in the city of Aardyre, and what had once been the Wizard's Tower had been reduced to a pile of ruins. Over the days that followed many had come to see what remained, and many more wondered what had had the power to do such a thing. On this night, however, a sole figure moved past the sleepy guards and slipped into the Tower grounds. It walked upright in its hooded cloak, but when it reached the base of the former Tower it dropped to all fours and scampered across the rubble. It stopped and sniffed the air, catching the scent of something. It turned and deftly followed the invisible trail that led to a broken slab of marble. Even under the waning light of the moon, the creature could see the dark drops of blood that clung to its surface.

The creature extended its hand beyond the conceal-ment of the black cloak—a hand taloned and inhuman and born of the Shadrus. It scraped at the remains, collect-ing the dark flakes within a silver vial. Its master would be well pleased—blood from the line of Sporazo had been found! And *that* was the thing the Lord of Shadows coveted most of all.